NOTEWORTHY TRIBUTE

A Novel

by

Mark G. Bradley

and

Josiah D. Bradley

Copyright

Noteworthy Tribute

Praise for Noteworthy Tribute

"A great read. I really enjoyed it." - Carol Ricketts, Alhambra, IL

"I absolutely love the characters of this book and the plot is riveting! This has been the best book I've read this year."
- Dr. Glenda Shepherd, Houston, TX

"*NT* is an exceptionally well written novel that was not only captivating and intriguing to a novice musician, but extremely relatable as a mother of two twenty-somethings."
- Dedra Carey, Miami, FL

"Well written and entertaining, *Noteworthy Tribute* kept my attention and left me anticipating its sequel."
- Rochelle F., 21, Bowie, MD

"Interesting, I want to read more." - Adam McKinley

"I thought it was an easy read and easy to follow. You guys did well with the details and I could visualize each scene."
- Taylor M., twenty-something, Rome, GA

"*Noteworthy Tribute* is a well-crafted storyline and most enjoyable read!" - Teressa I. Leath, author of *And Then Some*

Acknowledgements

The authors wish to acknowledge our family for all of their support. Thank you to Marlene, wife and mother, and Ethan, Matthew, and Daniel, sons and brothers. God blessed us with you.

We thank our editor Christine Townsend-Holmes who provided invaluable assistance which can never be repaid! May your days always be bright sunny and yellow – smile.

We also acknowledge so many of our extended family, friends, fellow students, and co-workers who we forced to read and to reread the many versions of this book. You are wonderful. There are many of you to thank. If we got on your nerves (one isn't doing anything until they get on others' nerves) then you are truly to be thanked.

Dedication

This work is in honor of grandparents Agnes B. "Grandma B" Bradley, Bennie Moore and Roger F. "Pops" and Virginia "Grumma" Holmes. We honor you and pray that you find this a noteworthy tribute.

Noteworthy Tribute

Paperback: ISBN-10: 1514270188 (U.S.)
ISBN-13: 978-1514270189 (EAN)

Overture

<u>SIDE A</u>

Track 01: *High on Progress*

Track 02: *They Might Surprise You*

Track 03: *What's the Move?*

Track 04: *Serenading the Catch*

Track 05: *Dinner with Diana*

Track 06: *Buffering*

Track 07: *Gracing the Food*

Track 08: *In the Company of Angels*

Track 09: *The Open Road*

Track 10: *Heaven's Gate*

Track 11: *The Experiment*

Track 12: *Contending With Horses*

Track 13: *Triad*

SIDE B

Track 14: *Help!*

Track 15: *Girl Talk*

Track 16: *Memories*

Track 17: *Your Services Will Be Required*

Track 18: *Wired For Sound*

Track 19: *Places Friends, Places Please*

Track 20: *Holding Court*

Track 21: *Transcendental*

Track 22: *Discussions with the Past*

Track 23: *The Time for Games Has Past*

Track 24: *So Close and Yet So Far*

Track 25: *Guardians & Hunters*

Track 26: *Still Waters*

Track 27: *Dry Run*

Track 28: *Da Capo al Coda*

Track 29: *Finale*

Outro

OVERTURE

Shadows grew long off Main Street where neighborhoods were sprinkled with Mom and Pop convenience stores. Several stories above street-level, a young girl rests on the inner windowsill of an ivy covered stone apartment building. Solar powered streetlights flickered; traffic signals winked at a passing car. The girl presses her hand to the window to better take in the vibrations from the sounds of life below; the rustling of a passerby and the melody of a songbird. She cocks her head to one side, positioning her ear on the window, as the songbird's chirps grow faint in the distance. A sea hawk launches from a light pole where it once perched, diving for the songbird. Dropping her head, the girl pushes away from the window, the song of the bird no longer audible.

A man in a dark-hooded sweatshirt emerges from a wall of bushes and begins to eye the papers in a newsstand dispenser not far from the street light. Less than a block away, a second young man wearing white, high-top tennis shoes with a green backpack slung over one shoulder stumbles from a parked vehicle.

"You're better than this," calls a voice from inside the car.

The young man slams the passenger door and gestures abruptly with his free hand, flipping off the driver. Clutching his backpack, he walks off as the vehicle slowly pulls away. The man in white shoes makes his way around the corner and up the street toward the newsstand. Joining the dark-hooded man, the two converse, neither of them aware of an older gentleman in a sport blazer, watching them perched between two storefronts across the street. The older man views the two of them through the reflection of a storefront window.

"That the pouch?" asks the man in the dark-hooded sweatshirt, eyes red and darting left and right.

"Last one...there won't be any more of these," offers the other man as he removes the green backpack.

"Look," demands the dark-hooded man, "as long as the stuff is flowing and until the debt is paid, this stuff better keep coming. Now let's have it!"

He again glances left and right, then proceeds to inspect the contents of the green backpack. During his search of the contents, he warily looks up one last time. His eyes fall on the older man across the street with his wrist raised to his mouth.

"Fool, you trying to set me up?" he demands through gritted teeth.

"What are you talking about?" asks the seller while contorting to look left, then right.

"I got too much smarts for you," the dark-hooded man says as he flashes a small .38 caliber pistol from behind his back. "You should've brought some, fool!"

Across the street, the man in the blazer whirls from facing the storefront window. Shots ring out as the man falls, his white high-top tennis shoes reveal their bottoms as his toes point skyward.

The older man in the blazer screams into his wrist, "This is Detective Ellis, 4th and Main - send an ambulance, quick! Send an ambulance!" Detective Ellis rushes to the wounded man. Bending over the blood-stained white shoes, the detective turns to see the shooter fleeing into the distance, pursued by a fourth man with his gun drawn. The fourth man, dashing full-stride, turns only momentarily to squeeze between two fence posts, revealing a golden badge on his belt.

"Get him, Macy," Ellis whispers.

Turning back to the victim, he applies pressure to the wound.

"Oh God!" exclaims Ellis, eyes widening in recognition. "Come on Frankie, hold on."

As Frankie's eyes water and lock with Detective Ellis' he whispers, "Poc...poc..."

"What did you say, son?" asks the detective, urgently leaning his ear to Frankie's mouth.

"Poc...pocket..."

Ellis reaches a bloody hand to pat Frankie's jeans and pulls out a wallet.

"Gram...E...Goes...To..." Frankie's voice trails off, eyes trained on the wallet, tears slipping down his face.

"Oh no... no Frankie!" laments Detective Ellis after finding no pulse. Gingerly opening the leather wallet, he shuffles through the contents and examines the Portland, Oregon driver's license. Detective Ellis recognizes another familiar face smiling through the surface of the plastic rectangle --his Godson, Cory Lynn Faber.

High overhead in the stone apartment building, a grey-haired woman, whose neck and back have been weighed down by time, offers the young girl a white tipped cane. The girl places her ear to the window again but is pulled away by the woman. The two turn from the windowsill as the curtains close abruptly, slapping each other.

SIDE A

Track 01:
High on Progress

"That was the new hit single, 'Snowball', from Underfed Angels! For a chance to win tickets to their summer "Starving Doubts Tour", text the word 'snowball' to ..."

Ken Ellis turned the car off and flipped the keys in his hand while he and Cory Lynn Faber sat in the driveway of the beach house in Sandbridge, Virginia, Ken's home away from home.

"Ever make peace with that band losing their last drummer?" asked Ken.

"Slowly coming around," answered Cory while taking off his seatbelt. "Getting passed this *Starving Doubts* album will let us hear what the new girl, Everett, can do on the snare with a fresh album. The band's first drummer, Lucky, already recorded the latest album with them before he called it quits."

"Wow!" exclaimed Ken. "So the Everett girl has to learn all their old material?"

"Yeah, pretty much," said Cory as he and Ken unloaded groceries from the car, oblivious to the tawny dog running toward them.

"What kind of name is Everett for a girl anyway?" asked Ken.

BEEEEP!

The two almost dropped their bags as a car blew its horn at the running dog, now prancing about them and whining happily. A woman in her mid-sixties, wearing a yellow sun-hat whose brim practically slapped her shoulders, hollered at the car as she crossed the street toward Ken and Cory.

"I'm sorry about Paris. I was on the phone and he got away from me," said Ms. Senor, picking up the dog's leash. "Long-time-no-see, Ken. It's been years. And who is this handsome young man you dragged down here? Are you trying to set me up?"

"You wish, Leslie. No, this is my Godson, Cory. He's staying for the summer," answered Ken, shutting the car trunk as Cory and Ms. Senor shook hands.

"It seems you've brought me one of Heaven's angels, Kenneth," Ms. Senor said with a wink after looking over Cory's blond locks which fell just passed his neck.

"Oh, but you're staying in this old shack?" gasped Ms. Senor in mock horror. Cory couldn't help but stifle a small laugh, which came out more like a cough. Paris, Ms. Senor's dog, a Boxer breed, seemed to smile at the joke as well, tongue lolled at the side of his mouth. Ken smiled wryly at the both of them as they made their way up to the sunroom, groceries in tow.

"Yeah, well it beats that eyesore you call home across the street," Ken fired back jokingly. "All those bright colors, how do you stand it? How does anyone? Thank God the dog is color blind."

"Just say you miss me, Kenneth, and you and Cory can come over anytime," responded Ms. Senor mischievously. "No need to involve the dog. Isn't that right Paris?" At the sound of his name, Paris lunged toward his master. Ms. Senor petted him lovingly and shot Cory a good-natured wink. Cory distracted himself by petting Paris.

"What do you think Paris? Should we leave these two alone?" The Boxer excitedly jumped to lick Cory's outstretched hand. Ms. Senor held the sunroom door open as Ken and Cory walked inside.

"At least you're not a slob like they are, Kenneth," she said pointing at the house next door whose driveway was covered in a miniature mountain of furniture and toys.

"Your mother raised you well," she continued. "Speaking of being alone, have you set a date yet? Superstar isn't going to wait around forever you know."

Ken paused in the middle of setting down one of his bags on the green astro-turf that covered the sunroom floor.

"Superstar? You mean Lucinda? Ms. Senor that was over 5 years ago! Next time you saw me, I was with Barbara." Cory raised his eyebrows, unable to contain the surprise. To release the tension, he silently relieved Ken of his other bag, took the key and went inside.

"Pity, I liked Lucinda I loved the way she waited for you to open doors. She was such a beautiful girl, oh, and that olive skin tone? Just lovely, and she kept you in line," replied Ms. Senor, turning to leave.

Returning to the sunroom, Cory waved to Ms. Senor and the dog as Ken sent her off with a final retort, "Yeah, and shoplifting kept her in line-*ups* after you last saw her. We've been finished ever since."

Ms. Senor waved with her back turned. The wide brim of her yellow hat was all Cory and Ken could see of her head. "Whatever you say, Kenneth, and it was nice meeting you, Cory. I hope you enjoy Sandbridge. If you need anything just holler. Say "bye", Paris."

Shaking his head and turning to go inside, Ken chuckled to himself. "Shame that woman is twice widowed; I guess the men just couldn't keep up with her vitality. She's one of a kind."

Following Ken inside, Cory nodded and smiled. Stopping abruptly he asked, "So what kind of a name is Paris for a dog, Ken?"

By late afternoon a small portion of the groceries was either sizzling on the grill or spread out on the table of the beach house rooftop deck. Ken and Cory relaxed and enjoyed a nice meal of grilled cheeseburgers, shrimp kabobs and potato chips with a few beers to wash it all down.

"Ms. Senor is good people to know," said Ken between bites. "Whatever you need, just ask and she'll be there. She's the model neighbor, and not too nosey." Cory nodded his approval though his attention was on scanning the rooftops and decks aimed toward the beach.

"That was nice, Cory," said Ken, setting down his empty plate. "I kept you out of your inner thoughts long enough to have a laugh with someone new."

Cory continued looking out at the beach. A Navy fighter jet roared across the sky. Cory saw Ken's mouth moving but couldn't make out what he just said.

Ken smiled, "the jets, they are always on maneuver. You'll get used to them."

Taking a swig of his beer, he replied, "Yeah okay. Well anyway, she's nice, Ken...good people just like you said."

"There *are* still some of us left, believe me," said Ken. Cory simply rested his jaw against his fist, arm propped up by the wooden rail. Setting down his beer he exhaled softly, looked at Ken, and nodded while gazing at the jet's contrails.

"I am so tired of chasing people, Uncle Ken," Cory lamented. "When you finally catch up to them, all they do is use you up."

"Like you used the store when you were a kid?" asked Ken.

"Yeah, something just like that. The band back home started off with just Frankie and me. We promised ourselves only *real* musicians." Cory gritted his teeth and shook his head as he tried to stave off the memories that began to enter his mind.

"I know son, I know," offered Ken, leaning forward giving Cory his full attention. The pain surrounding Cory's friend Frankie, and their band made it almost impossible to reach him for the past several months. Perhaps this unfamiliar environment would be good for him and he'd come to grips with his pain.

Ken's eyes joined the direction of Cory's gaze and looked out at the beach sky. He couldn't help but find the positive in all the darkness. "When they played with you and Frankie they *were real* musicians, Cory. You and Frankie paved the way for those guys and your musical dreams became reality. At all the shows you played, the CD signings, the internet...there is no doubt your fans were listening to music created by nothing but authentic musicians."

Cory tightened his grip around the neck of the beer bottle. Ken rose and walked over to his Godson and laid a hand on his shoulder.

"The band might not have created this era's Cobain, Hendrix, Joplin or any of those types. Sometimes you lose your way and bad things happen. You have every right to be angry about what happened to the band. But it's not all your fault. People have to want to be led. You're not the dictating type, Cory. People have to decide what really matters to them and look past the distractions. They have to want to go somewhere they've never been before."

Turning toward the stairs, Ken offered Cory one last piece of advice, hoping something, anything he said that afternoon, might bring peace to his grieving young friend.

"You were a star like the rest of them and you had every opportunity to throw the music away as they did, but you didn't. The journey was your addiction, Cory, evolution is your high."

Cory looked up from the bottle he was strangling. Locking eyes with Ken, he searched for something in his eyes that would let him believe that.

"I'm gonna bring those last cheeseburgers up," said Ken and he descended the stairs.

Cory leaned against the deck railing and looked out over Sandbridge and watched the sky grow pink as the day drew to a close. He was heavy with despair. Jimi Hendrix, Kurt Cobain and Janis Joplin now had more in common with Frankie than anyone. They were all once passionate musicians, who, Cory grimly concluded, died at age 27.

∞

The sun rose high over Norfolk International Airport on the day Ken Ellis was booked to fly back to Portland. He and Cory had enjoyed their time together. The trip to Sandbridge was one of the closest of times Cory had ever had with his Godfather. Back home, Cory's father was always grateful Ken was in their lives during Cory's darkest hour. Some days at the beach house they just talked and lounged about. Other days they took walks on the beach and fished. Last week they ventured out to the strip at Virginia Beach.

Yesterday they had gone movie hopping, joined by Ms. Senor. But now, Portland was calling Ken back home, so he and Cory sat in the airport counting down the time until Ken boarded his plane.

The two rose together, bags planted on either side of them. Ken looked his Godson over and smiled.

"This is it," he said and embraced Cory warmly. Cory returned the hug, holding his Godfather for a few extra seconds.

"You still have people who love you," whispered Ken, holding Cory tightly. "I'm so proud of you."

"I know," Cory whispered back. They released each other. "Thanks Ken... for everything."

Cory extended his hand and Ken shook it firmly nodding in agreement. No matter what, Cory could always count on his Godfather. He waved goodbye and as Ken was about to disappear out of sight, he turned back and called out.

"If you need me, call me!" And with that, Ken was gone.

Once on the plane, sitting next to the window, Ken began to think about the case waiting for him in Portland; the murder of Cory's best friend, Frankie Johnson. Ken rubbed the back of his neck and shook his head.

We're going to nail you to the wall, thought Ken, as if the killer was sitting right next to him. The kid that escaped had devastated two families close to Ken. He had watched Cory and Frankie go through a lot, good times and bad. Cory was one of the brightest young men Ken had ever had the pleasure of knowing. He considered it an honor to watch young men grow up and he had expected great things from Frankie Johnson; everyone had. Ken met angry young men everyday on the police force. Sure, Frankie was rough around the edges and was more *outgoing* than Cory, but he was a good kid. Cory and Frankie were thick as thieves and it tore Ken up inside that Cory had lost someone so close to him. A lot of the parents and adults in the young men's lives expressed sadness and worry over Cory and his fallen comrade.

A little turbulence rocked the plane as it ascended and the young woman sitting next to Ken closed her eyes tightly.

"Don't be scared," Ken assured her. "It's just a little rattling. The plane is tougher than you think." As the ascent evened out, the plane's captain encouraged the passengers over the radio.

The young woman managed a smile and nodded at Ken.

"Thanks," she said.

He nodded back and turned toward his window as Hampton Roads fell further and further out of view. *You're much tougher than you think Godson*, Ken mused. *It's up to you now Cory.*

The drive back to the beach house was a quiet ride for Cory. After having a late lunch, he decided to stretch his legs and made his way to the beach a few houses back. The temperature was a pleasant 78 degrees and the leaves barely danced in a slight breeze. Cory shivered slightly as his bare feet waded through the sand and darkness rose over the beach. With his flip-flops in hand, the sea water pushed and pulled the sand between his toes.

The rhythm of percussion and guitars tugged at his ear. Turning, he caught the staccato spray of laughter and frolicking voices. Then he felt his heart move. The music seemed to whisper his name like the familiar, soothing voice of an old friend.

The song brought his best friend to mind. It was voted Song of the Year back when he and Frankie were in high school. That year several bands vied for the top spots, but this song, *Fumes of Instinct*, was their anthem. Cory would never forget a talk he and Frankie had in the music store about the song, about music for that matter; it was one of the most memorable talks they'd had as they said goodbye to high school.

"Dude, he went through a lot, didn't he?" Cory remembered asking. The singer, Nexus, had endured a lot of bad media attention that year leading up to the friends' graduation.

"Yeah man everybody was pissed, his label... the fans," Frankie offered.

"How does that crap happen, man?" asked Cory. "I mean Nexus is a genius!"

"I don't know bro, nobody's perfect. That's life," Frankie offered. "But that song is flawless man, I wish I'd written it!"

"Step your lyrical game up, bro" Cory teased. Frankie was right, of course. Superstars were still human but it was difficult not to elevate them. There were so few like them.

The smell of BBQ assaulted Cory's nose as he kicked at the surf.

"True, it can all hit you like a wave man; I mean they tore into Nexus!" Cory remembered saying.

"Must have been hard for him to trust anyone, you know?" Frankie had said. "Plus things with his sister didn't help Nex."

"He had a tough decision to make, man. Frankie, I know you had some opinions about it," Cory had said. Frankie supported Nexus's music but family was family and he, like other Nexus fans, just hoped the singer had not acted out of fear.

The star's sister struggled with nose blow, more commonly referred to as a cocaine habit. Her limited success paid for the habit when it was in its infancy. However, over time, she found herself involved with loan sharks to help finance the habit. Debt drove her to Nexus to borrow money. He made a difficult decision to pay the debt, but he didn't trust her to handle the money. He went directly to the shark to pay the money, and sadly, those are the images that the press released.

Frankie's answer spelled it out perfectly, focusing on the big picture.

"Point is his sister is alive, man. That is all that really matters. Maybe he could have helped her differently, maybe not. It's done now. I guess fans need to accept that. She worships Nexus. He's her big brother and she wants to have a career like his, but she's got to put in the work."

Cory recalled being torn about Nexus and the drama with the star's sister as well, leading up to the smash hit *Fumes of Instinct*. That was also the title track of the album. Sad truth was his sister had no instincts and had made a mess of the family image and had put Nexus in a bad situation. Nexus had helped her but he received backlash for his choice and polarized fans.

"It's hard being in the public eye, bro," Cory had admitted.

"Some of these celebs have no support system, man. Simple as that, they don't have friends like we do," Frankie concluded that day. "And you know we haven't been tested, not like that man." It was true. Being a normal adult in the artsy music store tucked away in Portland was nothing compared to living day-to-day in the public eye, and trying to sell millions of records.

"Don't sweat it, Cory, that won't be us." You couldn't spook Frankie. *Of course everyone says that. It could never happen to you, everyone has that attitude. But when Frankie said it, nothing felt truer.* The sand held Cory's feet like shackles as Cory repeated the refrain to himself; *don't sweat it, Cory, that won't be us.* Cory assessed his situation. He was on the beach in a new state. It was a new day and time altogether, and Frankie was gone. Cory began to walk back home, the sand giving way as dry loose grains slid downhill to fill the holes left by his feet. He climbed the little hill between two beach homes, stopping one last time to take in the sounds of the party crashing into the night air above him. They sounded so happy, not a care in the world, everyone together, now in the moment... missing no one. Cory sensed an all too familiar feeling, a crushing against his sternum. Nothing was there of course but somehow emotions managed to manifest physically. The brooding was coming over him again. Despite the bright lamps illuminating the deck above him, Cory's heart was somber. Nothing had gone the way he had hoped.

"No matter what his choice looked like," Frankie's voice echoed in Cory's mind, "Nexus had heart. Dudes give up too easily these days. That move to help his sister might've looked weak to some but, like I said, she's alive. He did what he had to do to take care of her. Not a lot of people sacrifice like that, risking their careers to help family. All I have to say is she better be grateful, bro."

How did he manage to turn like that, Cory wondered. Frankie was talented but sometimes it took him awhile to wrap his head around certain things. Cory remembered he and Frankie at serious odds about the fallout over Nexus, his music and his sister's problems. All the media had something to say about it, from every newspaper, to every news site and blog online. But then Frankie came around. Nothing like what happened with Nexus would ever happen to them, Frankie had said. No one had a friendship like he and Cory, or family like they had. They were fireproof.

"People have to listen to what we have to say man," Frankie would say. "No one's got our sound, man. No one's got us: your hands for music and my head for story. All that crap in the tabloids? That's not gonna be us." Frankie could be so adamant. He believed people quit too much. That was part of the problem he had with the Nexus situation. Nexus had threatened to quit music because his sister and her entourage messed up and made him look bad. They had separate careers but people put Nexus under the microscope and the pressure got to him.

"Girls like that ain't real musicians man. They don't care about the craft. They just want their time in the spotlight," Frankie would rant. "I hate that crap, Cory!"

And Cory had believed him, hook, line and sinker. Frankie was the louder of the two, more rebellious, and the most hopeful. He would make up his mind and you couldn't change it. Making music together was their destiny, practically written in the stars as far as Frankie was concerned. They both had braved so much since they'd met back in middle school. They had survived girls, teen angst and now high school and things were looking up. This was around the time that the two of them started to put a small band together and start their own musical journey.

When they met in middle school, it was initially Frankie's interest in the drums that got Cory really serious about making music. Cory was gifted as a child. He could play anything and even learn by ear; he had raw talent. But Frankie opened up a whole new world to Cory, showing him how applying skills along with talent could make him happy, entertain others and take him far; the fundamentals as it were, and the two were close ever since. Fast forward to their adult lives where they'd made friends with like-minded creators and Portland had found their newest local talent, with Frankie and Cory at the helm leading the charge. Cory had never had a friend more focused and driven than Frankie.

"Brother, you know this reminds me, we still haven't met the Angels," Frankie pointed out cryptically.

"I know man, the other night they were at Trinity House on 5th," whined Cory. Besides falling short of becoming musical legends themselves, they had remarkably failed to see their favorite legends in concert, a group of four guys calling themselves Underfed Angels. Even Nexus took second place compared to Frankie and Cory's favorite quartet.

"Yeah it's a bet. But yeah, it's gonna be right, the way music should be, like those guys: talent plus skill," Frankie would say. "We're a perfect balance Cory, you and me. But you know what? You're the truth Cory. You're better than all of us in the band, and not just because you're a genius or a freak or whatever they label you with. It's because you're a natural. They probably label you that too, don't they? Well you're just a good man honored to play real music. Dang man, there's only one Cory Lynn Faber! And, I think music is happy to have you, heck better for it, even."

Hot tears fell down Cory's face. He didn't know how long he'd been walking. The party on the deck was long behind him but the gentle waves crashing against the shore were still audible. A few cars cruised by him on the road that passed the curious shapes of beach houses. Frankie and Cory's friendship was something pure, something that only came by once in a lifetime, at least that's how it felt to Cory. As big a deal as his friend had made of him, Cory was the one who felt like a mere mortal in Frankie's presence; he was such a force of nature when he was around. Their whole band had been close, very close, for as long as they were together. But in the beginning it was only Frankie and Cory, in the same chord progression, going in the same direction, unified by music. And it pained Cory to think that he and music had lost such unity and that the lights had dimmed on their journey together. Musical prodigies come and go, but there was only one Frankie Johnson.

"And the... Grammy Award... goes to," whispered Cory between sobs. The Grammy Awards was the last item on his and Frankie's list of accomplishments. It was a lifelong dream and an inside joke they had shared. It was something Frankie hadn't forgotten on the day he died. Although it didn't make sense to Ken when he found Frankie dying on the sidewalk, it hit Cory like a ton of bricks when Ken gave him the message. Through everything they'd endured, Frankie hadn't lost the dream, and Cory, in a trance, kept repeating it all the way home.

"And the... Grammy Award... goes to..."

Track 02:
They Might Surprise You

"Yo, watch out kid!"

The miniature wheels at the heels of his shoes propelled the little mo-hawked boy through the mall at what seemed like 100 miles an hour.

Evan Spencer brushed himself off and glared after the boy, "Dang, they still sell those things to kids these days?"

His two friends laughed at him. "It's not like you to be losing your cool like this," laughed Camille LaShea, the prettiest of the three.

"The movie must have really shaken you up, dude," offered Tony Jackson, his other friend.

Evan was a young adult enjoying life in Hampton Roads, Virginia with his mother Diana Spencer. His main interest was music and he was a producer of sorts and a DJ on the side. But having not taken advantage of an opportunity to attend music school, a decision that left a bad taste in his mother's mouth, caused some tension in the house. But truthfully, his mother would have preferred that he drop the music altogether and just attend college. She had enlisted the aid of her brother, Nate, to provide some sort of guidance in Evan's life. There were elements of Nate's past related to music, but these things had not yet been revealed to Evan.

Evan met his girlfriend Camille in middle school. One day while at the bus stop, he caught a glimpse of her through the window as the bus slowly came to a stop. She was seated halfway among the sea of adolescents. While he boarded the bus fidgeting with his security blanket, a golf ball, it leapt from his hands and rolled on the floor in her direction. Camille grabbed it as it rolled near her seat and handed it to him, which was his opportunity. Unbeknownst to Evan, Camille had been watching him for months and had hoped that he'd find the courage to speak to her. The rest is history. The lollipop years found the two always together. Camille's dad kept a close watch on his baby. Although he was concerned at first, tensions eased when he figured out that the young man taking up so much of his daughter's time seemed to have a good mother. Besides, Mr. LaShea's own family concerns were ballooning before him -- balancing work and life as a single parent. Evan and Camille would attend high school together. This ruffled her father's feathers as he had planned on private school. But, her mother's failing health seized his attention and, as often was the case, his baby's desires won out.

Diana, Evan's mother was happy for him; Camille was a promising figure in his life. He daydreamed of her honey melon hued skin and how, in the evening sunlight, her eyes sparkled as her satin black hair framed her face. At five foot two inches, she might be considered average height for a girl. But to Evan, she was 10 feet tall and there was nothing average about her beauty. She seemed to be well-grounded, an untainted addition to his life. After high school she decided on Norfolk State University. With her eyes on International Business, she intended to make the most out of life. The one thing she missed was the closeness of a mother, which was further compounded by the lack of at least one girlfriend. Evan had always been the focus of all her attention, especially considering her mother's situation.

Camille had business aspirations to follow in her mother's footsteps as a buyer in the international marketplace. Unfortunately, this was essentially why their relationship had not developed in the truest sense of 'mother-daughter' bonding. To the contrary, she and her father were really close. Unlike her mother, he was not experiencing the tension of the maternal instinct versus the business world, a balancing act her mother constantly battled with. When 'daddy's little girl' tried to take care of him while her mother was away, he didn't judge her. Camille's father was just pleased to have his daughter, his baby, and she saw it as her role to take care of him.

Evan and Camille had been dating for several years and shared a mutual connection with music. Evan was a budding musician. As of late, he used Camille's vocals on several tracks of an upcoming extended play recording, a small collection of music he and some other musicians had been putting together. They were a struggling band and other jobs and priorities made jam sessions few and far between. But when the motley crew could get together and Camille joined them, they were known to lay a few musical miracles on record.

"Yeah," agreed Evan, whose arm was wrapped snugly around Camille's waist. "I figured Dennis Harley films were too heavy for you, but maybe I was wrong, I think it's affecting you. You wanna sit down bro?"

"You two are positively hilarious," retorted Tony. "You should take this little act out on the road. Don't forget I get 90% of the profits."

Camille blinked. "90% - what?" she asked, looking from Tony to Evan and back to Tony.

"Yeah," said Tony, striking a pose. "For all of the inspiration my life brings to your act, for all the priceless material I'm giving you."

"That's *your* best friend, babe," Camille said to Evan, pointing accusingly at Tony. Evan could only smirk and shake his head in mock shame.

Evan and his friend Tony had been running buddies for many years. They were a shadow of each other. Each was by the other's side during the snotty-nosed elementary years, through the energetic pre-teen years, beyond their teens and now on the edge of manhood. Their differences were now becoming more apparent. Evan was clearly in love with Camille, and he had a definite bend towards music. Tony's passion was basketball and it seemed he entertained a new girlfriend every month.

Just then Tony's cell phone beeped. "Oh, I gotta bounce. Catch you idiots later!"

"Who's texting you? Momma?" laughed Evan.

"Nah, brother," said Tony, pointing at an attractive brunette walking past an electronics store. "I'm just trying to be like you man. My phone beeps whenever candidates for 'Mrs. Tony Jackson' walk by, you feel me? See ya!"

"Tony is a hot mess," laughed Camille as she and Evan found a table at the food court. "And that high top fade is as tall as a regulation hoop. Does he think he's cute?"

"Yeah, I think he does," chuckled Evan in agreement.

"I think I know that girl he was chasing. She don't take no mess," cautioned Camille.

"He'd better D-up then, make sure she don't catch him 'double dribbling'," mused Evan.

Evan, Camille and Tony had known each other since childhood. All of the basketball terminology was fitting in Tony's case as his athleticism had carried him through school, making him a college star.

Evan began updating Camille about his music after returning from getting a light snack for them, setting down a tray of soft drinks and warm jumbo cinnamon pretzels.

"So yeah, that last track we did when you came over a few weeks ago still sucks. Your voice is great, as usual, but it's missing something, I keep playing it back but haven't come up with anything."

"I'm sure you'll figure something out, babe. The secret is probably just waiting for you back in the studio," said Camille encouragingly.

Evan smirked and took a sip of his soda, "Yeah, I'm sure you're right, Cammie. It's just been a while since Ryan or Sam have been able to get together to work on it. It's tough when you can't do this full time, or, at least when they can't."

Camille reached across the table, gently brushing against Evan's dark brown hand. "Babe you have to keep at it and take what you can get. It's like in that movie we just saw. Like Dennis Harley says, 'Don't try to solve the wrong problem'. Look, Ryan and Sam are great but you've got other things going for you, what about the Internet profile? Or your solo gigs?"

When Evan wasn't creating and selling beats online or making tutorials, he survived as a DJ on a steady diet of local college parties, and scoring gigs for his... *band*. He had a chance for a scholarship at a music school last year and his mother really wished he could've taken it, gone to school, and learned a lot and experienced a different environment. All it would have taken was more effort on Evan's part but the whole college boy thing was too overwhelming for him. Registration dates, enrolling fees, FAFSA, tours, admissions…it was a rat race he wanted no part of. And the pressure from his family, especially his mother and his uncle, didn't help. They complained he wasn't goal-oriented. In reality, it was just difficult for them to envision his goals. Simply hunkering down like his mother did, going to college and learning discipline was apparently the only way to make something of himself, according to his uncle. Just because Camille and Tony could do it, thought Evan, it didn't mean he had to.

"Yeah the gigs are okay. In fact they're GREAT… when I have them," Evan said, chewing on his pretzel and shaking his head. "It's no good for business to have one big show then go dry for weeks afterward. I mean my profile online helps a little and I have almost two hundred videos and tutorials that have thousands of views. My account – well it's doing better than some, my cup pretty much runneth over."

A small family sat down at a table nearby and the little girl waved at Camille. She smiled and waved back.

"Uh huh, babe, but," she said turning back to Evan.

"But I'm far from becoming an Internet sensation," Evan concluded. "Hits on videos and selling a few opening or closing theme songs aren't exactly my golden ticket. It's not gonna pay the bills or at least bring in new equipment, you know?"

"Yeah", agreed Camille, leaning back in her chair. "I see what you mean. It's something right? But Evan you're so close. I mean you have to be; you are doing what you love. You're not up all hours of the night doing papers like I'm doing."

Camille enjoyed Spring Break and time with Evan and her friends, but privately dreaded going back on campus. Evan didn't know how good he had it, at least in her eyes.

"Yeah, but you look so hot when you're really into a book," grinned Evan leaning forward "especially when you're wearing those geeky reading glasses. You know you mouth the words when you read?"

"OH MY GOD, YOU SAW THOSE THINGS!" shouted Camille, giggling and throwing a piece of her pretzel at Evan. Sugar lodged in his hair making his braids sparkle.

"Yeah I've seen them. Get a hold of yourself woman!" joked Evan shielding himself from another volley of the tasty treat. "Oh God, chill; I said you looked hot, didn't I?"

The family next to them laughed as Evan jumped out of his seat and started tickling Camille. The two were making quite a scene and needed to put a lid on the PDA – at least that's what the mall cop intended to tell them.

"Uh oh," said the little girl, waving at Camille again.

With the mall and the Hampton Coliseum in their rearview mirror, Evan and Camille laughed so hard on the drive home that Camille almost lost control of the wheel.

"That little girl!" yelled Camille, smiling.

"I know...and that cop! His shirt was so tight I swear he couldn't even carry us out of there if he wanted too," hollered Evan, his hand covering his face, braids flopping everywhere.

"He looked like he'd pull a muscle just breathing!" snorted Camille, tears streaming down her face.

"Oh man, see, I can't take you nowhere, Cammie," laughed Evan.

"Hey," said Camille finally calming down. "I'll make you walk home, babe."

Evan, still reliving the hilarity, felt something hit his foot.

"Oh shoot!" he exclaimed, reaching down on the passenger side for a white golf ball. "I didn't know I dropped this getting out of the car back there," as he gripped the golf ball.

"Forgot your security blanket, babe?" asked Camille teasingly.

"Argh," moaned Evan, looking through his cell phone with one hand, and turning the golf ball in the other. "Not only that, but I forgot to call Uncle Nate back about that fishing trip near Little Island Park.

"Oh... yeah, Little Island," said Camille, with a far off look on her face and forgetting the jab about the golf ball.

"Yeah, dang," Evan said shaking his head. "Uncle Nate left me some messages. But fishing? I know you're trying to reach out Unc, but couldn't we do something we can *both* get into?"

"Ah, I love Uncle Nate, Evan," smiled Camille. "I'm sure you guys will just talk about sports or something the whole time. Or swap manly stories." At the quip about manly stories, Camille lowered her voice down to what most women seemed to think all men sounded like. Evan glanced sideways at her, un-amused.

"Yeah, whatever," he said, dryly. "If any stories will be told it'll be from his life, probably back in the 1800s and be all about how he and his family worked hard, toiled harder and labored the hardest...oh yeah and don't forget the part about work." Evan shook his head again and put his cell phone back in his pocket, annoyed and already lamenting over this latest scheme by his mom and uncle to get him on the so-called straight and narrow.

"It'll be okay, Evan," said Camille taking her hands off the wheel, but Evan withdrew his hand from her touch. Exhaling and pursing her lips, Camille dropped her eyes from the road. She hated it when Evan got like this. When things didn't go his way, he could shut down and it was best to just let him cool off. Even though she wasn't to blame for how Evan felt, she couldn't help feel a little guilty, like she should be able to fix everything.

Just then, a sound on the stereo caught both of their attention. It had been left on from the drive up to the mall but the volume had been low. Camille leaned in to turn up the volume but Evan, fresh out of his mood, beat her to it.

"Ah, yeah," said Evan, brow still furrowed but with the sound of relief in his voice. "This is what I need right here!"

"Definitely," Camille whole-heartedly agreed, increasing the stereo balance to the front of the car.

"The guys and I are gonna nail this beat!" yelled Evan over the stereo, a fusion of Hip/Hop and Rock music blasting.

"I know you will!" Camille screamed back, beaming happily. Her car radio was receiving music from her MP3 player, which lay plugged up in between her and Evan. Artist information emblazoned across the display screen read:

'They Might Surprise You
by
Underfed Angels featuring Tantrums 0f G3nius'

Track 03:
What's the Move?

Later that afternoon, Evan and his friend Sam were eating lunch in Evan's room and catching up on old times. He and Sam met a mutual friend one night when they were all out at a party. Sam DJ'd at the party, while he and Evan talked. He was good at the turntables and kept everybody happy but it wasn't something he did regularly. Sam was decent at it but didn't want to be seen as a disc jockey - something about too much pressure. Their musical conundrums and aspirations were the subject of conversation at that moment as they discussed their experiences with DJing.

"Well, I'm alright, but I like being in the background," Sam had said. "I messed around with it a few times... okay more than a few. A friend showed me some stuff and I was into it for a while but I don't know. How many Filipinos do you know that DJ?"

"Hey, I don't know," Evan said, shaking his head. "I thought you liked it."

Sam tossed some of his trash from lunch in Evan's wastebasket and shrugged. "I do, but people saw me do it and I got carried along for the ride. Making beats is cool enough and sound mixing. I don't know. I want to try some other things."

"I feel you," Evan said, leaning back in his chair, distracted by a patch in his ceiling. Then looking back at Sam, he added, "Same with me, though. I just do the DJ thing because I'm good at it. I mean, I like it, more than you do no offense."

"What offense?" Sam chuckled.

"Well, it is fun. I kind of like that pressure you're talking about," Evan continued. "The party rides on you driving the audience, mixing their favorite tunes, introducing them to new ones, sampling familiar songs and recreating things in a way they haven't heard before."

"Yeah, absolutely. And you kill at it," Sam enthused. "But I just, I don't, Evan. I'm fickle. "

"No, it's fine," said Evan, taking out his white golf ball, tossing it back and forth. "But I don't want to DJ forever. That's why I'm glad we do our thing in my studio, more than just mixing sounds." Evan and his friends didn't just do turntables or beat software, they were very skilled with the more traditional instruments as well. Evan demonstrated tremendous ability on the piano and keyboard in addition to sound mixing. Ryan was quite talented on the guitar and bass, excelling most on the latter, and any musical act would benefit from having him in their roster. Finally, Sam, who had started off on the drums as a teen but had neglected it, was still figuring it out, though he lent a lot of sound mixing and electronic sounds to their little project.

"I just thought it would be cool if I stuck with something, Evan," offered Sam, sounding a little disappointed." The three of them were hard at work on a mix tape of sorts, comprised of a few songs, which Evan's girlfriend graced with her voice periodically. Sam was talented but insecure in his musical abilities. But in Evan's mind, they needed structure and Sam was trying hard. It was Ryan who made it difficult with his crazy work schedule.

"It's just good when we're able to get together, man," Evan assured him. "At least you're trying. I just wish we could figure out that last track man."

"I'm not going anywhere, bro, and my dad's glad I met you guys. I think he imagines himself living through me," Sam admitted. "He played the guitar with his buddies in college but let it go. I think he misses it."

Suddenly Sam sat up straight with a blank look on his face.

"What?" Evan yelled.

"What's up with the 12th of the month?" asked Sam. "Are we still going to D.C. for the Underfed Angels show?"

"Oh yeah, I've got your ticket man," said Evan reaching in his drawer and handing Sam his ticket.

"Can't wait, bro," Sam beamed.

"Yeah, maybe you'll get a little inspiration," Evan encouraged with a smile. "I want to be like them, making music like THAT! That's where I want to be. The beat-making software and turntables are just a means to an end."

"I was getting that from you, Evan," Sam admitted, leaning forward.

"I love Hip/Hop and the club scene, that's fun. Heck, I met you at a party, right?" Evan ventured. "And I've been asked to spin at colleges, too, and people love it so it's fine. But I want to get some guys together man."

"I love that," said Sam, getting excited. "You've got a wide collection of sounds. Electro-House, Hip/Hop, Soul, Rock, R&B and I guess some more."

"Yeah, that's it," Evan interrupted. "I really like a lot of everything and ironing out rhythms and splicing things together, you know?"

"You put in a lot of months on this project before I showed up," said Sam, scooting down to the floor to get more comfortable. "You've got this.... technician, or engineer mindset - style about you. You're not a one-trick pony."

Evan dropped his golf ball, which Sam picked right back up and tossed at him. As the conversation deepened, a little game started up between them as they bounced the ball back and forth, sometimes holding onto it whenever the other one was speaking.

"Take Jerry & Riggs. They have a distinct electronic sound but they incorporate Rock and even Opera into their work sometimes," said Evan, tossing the ball back to Sam.

"I love those cartoon dinosaur heads," Sam smiled as the ball bounced off his hand and rolled aside. "You think they wear those masks everywhere?"

"Beats me," shrugged Evan. "I like what they said about keeping the fan attention on the music as much as possible, it's like those two are mascots for their own music."

"Mascots? Hey sometimes you have to, I mean if you believe in your music," Sam said pointedly as he scooped up the ball and bounced it in Evan's direction.

"And I've always liked camaraderie. Solo acts are great -- but that team effort, a group of those *engineers* you're talking about would be great for me," said Evan, dribbling the golf ball.

"So yeah, the pressure of DJing certainly doesn't bother you. But doing it alone is no good?" Sam inquired, watching Evan bounce the ball.

"I like mixing with someone, sure," Evan admitted, pausing to concentrate on his thought. "Like with you in the studio, or that time with that girl at Soul-Light?" "Yeah, that's cool."

"Yeah she was hot, too. Made it easy for you," Sam teased, beckoning Evan to toss the ball back. Evan re-started the game, swatting aside Sam's comment.

"I'm spoken for buddy but that doesn't stop you. But again, I want to make it bigger. Put together a band, pretty much. Like Underfed Angels or any of these acts." This time, it was Sam's turn to pause mid-throw, the golf ball poised between his fingers as he spoke.

"You're really eclectic, Evan", said Sam. "But you really do manage to make all of those moving parts come together."

"Again, we do the club thing and it's cool," said Evan, tossing his hands in the air. "But I just feel limited. I've got other ideas and I want to move on soon."

"Of course, I hear you," Sam added, bouncing the ball back to Evan. "I'm just processing. I had you figured out. But hearing you tell it, it's all making sense, your project."

"Mix tape or EP or something," sighed Evan. "I want a collection of sounds and songs. Glad Cammie has helped, too. I just like how it's building. It's different. We just have to figure out that last track, but things are going so slow."

"We need to get out to the club," said Sam, clapping his hands together.

"Trying, man," said Evan, wryly. Then, with a raised eyebrow another thought occurred to him. "And my mom wouldn't have a problem with that either."

"She's been on your case again?" Sam inquired, with a knowing glance.

"Yeah, she started up again after what went down at the Player's Club" Evan said, eyes rolling so hard it was almost audible.

"I heard about that. Too bad about that dude that got hit," Sam lamented, shaking his head.

"It's bad, man," Evan grimaced. "I spun with that guy a couple of times. You know he had just signed on to co-produce on a new single?"

"Wait, with who?" paused Sam.

"You know? Little girl back in the spotlight actin' a fool," Evan hinted as the truth dawned on Sam.

"No way? Nexus' little sister?"

Evan nodded, rubbing his golf ball between his hands as Sam shook his head shamefully.

"Dang," said Sam, resting his hands on his knees. "I guess you can't choose family. Your boy was getting his shot!"

Sam winced as his bad choice of words registered. Evan pocketed his white ball and turned to his laptop to check his messages.

"Yeah man, you know I was a little salty when I heard about it? Him getting his chance? It's so hard to collaborate with people. Man, I don't get it. It's great working with you and Ryan and Camille. But sometimes people don't want to share resources and help each other out, you know? Work together to make it."

"Yeah right!" Sam exclaimed, sitting back on Evan's bed and checking his cell phone. "You know there's not enough fame to go around, Evan. You have to make your own way." He was being facetious of course, but the sentiment sounded true enough sometimes.

At first, Sam was too distracted by an update for an app on his phone to notice how quiet Evan had become - until he put his phone down and noticed his friend's face glued to his own cell intently.

"Evan? What are you looking at?" Sam asked, leaning over.

"Change of plans, Sam," said Evan, eyes still focused on the cell phone. "Camille has some issue with her professor."

"Huh?" asked Sam walking over to the desk. "What are you talking about?"

"She was bugging out about this business project." Evan continued reading his girlfriend's text. "Looks like the class has to rearrange some research or something last minute, something with the department heads, I don't know. Anyway, she can't go with us. Her group has a pretty heavily graded project."

"That sucks," Sam said, walking back to the bed to pick up his phone. "Sorry to leave you like this. Maybe we can sell the ticket or something?"

Evan shook his head and leaned back in his chair.

"We were really looking forward to this," he groaned, staring back at the text as if it had changed into good news. Out of nowhere, Evan's bedroom door flew open.

"INTRODUCING..." yelled none other than Tony Jackson, jumping into the middle of the bedroom. Evan and Sam looked on in complete surprise, mixed with fear.

"Dude, did you just break into the house?" asked Sam, wide eyed.

"Naw man, his mom let me in. She just drove up," said Tony nonchalantly as he flopped onto Evan's bed. Evan just shook his head as he collected himself.

"So what's the move, gents?" asked Tony.

Sam walked over to the door pocketing his phone and giving Evan a handshake goodbye.

"Actually, I'm on my way out, Superstar. I'll see y'all later," said Sam, waving to Tony as he walked out of the room.

"Ev, don't forget to send him BACK out, ok?" hollered Sam down the hall. "Your mom doesn't like no *overtime*. She kicks us out if our jam sessions go too late as it is."

"Love you too, Sam," Tony retorted loudly, which got him an even louder rebuke from Evan's mother for yelling in her house.

"So uh, what's going on, man?" whispered Tony childishly.

"Got a question for you," said Evan, turning around slowly and tossing his golf ball at his friend. "When was the last time you were in D.C.?"

Tony's mouth hung open for a second. Catching the ball, he was unsure where his best friend was going with this.

"You wanna go to D.C.? Right now?" Tony inquired. "Are *you* drivin'?"

Track 04:
Serenading the Catch

Nate Spencer wasn't having any luck reaching his nephew. Dang kids today, all about the latest gadgets and phones, then they get them and it's like they forget how to use them. Deciding to hang up and instead call Evan's mother Diana, his younger sister, Nate was surprised to hear a voice on the other end; he hadn't dialed anything yet.

"Nate? Hello?" called Diana's voice through Nate's Bluetooth receiver.

"Hey, Diana? Yeah, I was about to call you. I had my finger on the button and everything", chuckled Nate.

"Well, it must be divine providence! Nate, I just don't know how I should respond to this latest incident."

Halting at a red light, Nate listened as Diana, full of concern, read the byline to an article from *The Virginia Pilot.*

"'*Two local youths arrested at club in drug related incident...*'", she began.

"Oh yeah, I read that too, Dee," said Nate. "It's not looking too good for those boys."

"No, it isn't Nate," she replied.

Apparently police had taken two young men into custody. The police reported that the youths were found in the company of *"known drug distributors"*. The distributors were part of a gang that had gained some notoriety in the community, referring to themselves as the Epps Yard Crew, or Yardees for short. And although there was no evidence of drugs on the boys, their relationship with these *"known distributors"*, these wanna-be thugs, the Yardees, was just cause for the authorities to apprehend them, according to the police.

"Now, just slow down, Dee," Nate offered. It sounded like his sister was about to make yet another giant leap in logic and equate one situation with an entirely different one. He'd heard that tone in her voice before.

"I can't slow down, Nate" she retorted. "And I'm worried Evan won't slow down either. New Year's was too close a call, and then that incident at Camille's school."

"Listen," said Nate, trying to stay calm himself. "Those were months ago. Evan set things right after New Year's. He agreed joy riding was a bad idea. Heck, he even came clean that he only tried the stuff once, he was just... experimenting. He and Tony stopped hanging out with BeBe after that, and they had certainly stopped way before what happened at Norfolk."

Diana sighed on the other end of the phone but seemed to be hearing him out, so Nate continued. Sometimes Diana got worked up over the wrong thing, and this was one of those times. But have no fear, big brother Nate to the rescue.

"I thought it was a real shame. Evan and his band mates worked really hard to be a part of the show at Norfolk. Wrong place, wrong time what with those students trying to make a name for these Epps Yard guys at the party." Nate wasn't really sure about Evan's future in music. Although the Spencer family had toyed with music, this was best left in the past, and nothing that Evan should be dredging up. Maybe life was trying to tell the young man something he just wasn't ready to hear. Sensing he had Diana's full attention, Nate went in for the big save.

"Look, these things take time. Honestly, Evan is becoming his own man and you've got to let him be just that. He's got hopes and dreams just like anybody else. But men need room to accept guidance and still maintain their independence. Nothing like what happened in the papers is going to happen to Evan. Don't get ahead of yourself. Evan would never fall into any gang related stuff."

I swear, thought Nate, *this topic is evidence of what a 'man-thing' is and women just don't seem to get it. Women sometimes don't understand where men are coming from.*

"Maybe I could get the men in my church involved," Diana responded at last. "I think they still have that youth group. They go camping and stuff."

"Sis, Evan is not receiving what they are offering," said Nate. "I mean, don't get me wrong, not that this church stuff isn't good..." Nate felt there was truth to what she was saying about bad company and the close calls Evan had this year. On top of that, he couldn't deny that their own mother had instilled in them a definite sense of church and God. Over the years, Nate realized he had drifted to what he thought was key as far as handling business. Sure, he would go to church for the necessary events in one's maturation, for example, key holidays and what have you. But the command that God and service once had in his life was now less apparent. Even he had to admit that something was inherently lacking, but he just couldn't pinpoint it.

"It's just that the way they bring it", Nate continued struggling somewhat, "It seems so Pollyannaish. Trust me, Evan is no longer Pollyannaish."

"Well Nate, we've got to do something," urged Diana. "I just pray that God sends a solution. We have to keep praying, Nate. Pray that Evan will see God's plan for him."

Believe me, I am, said Nate.

∞

Three days later, Cory Faber passed the time by strolling down Sandpiper Road to Little Island Park. Stars filled the sky and cicadas chirped from their hiding places in the blackness. The walls of the beach house had shrunken in around Cory, prompting his retreat to the street. Ms. Senor was just as Ken had described her. She wasn't a nosey neighbor; she gave him plenty of room, and he appreciated the space. Being connected to her through someone he trusted brought solace. Cory continued to wander past curious shaped vacation homes until he came upon a sign for Little Island Park. Crossing the street, he jogged toward the pier.

Just past the bathhouse, coast guard's office and jungle gyms, Cory found men and women from all over the city sitting together on the dock trying to catch a nibble. From the entrance to the end of the pier, long fishing poles stretched skyward while coolers lined the area underneath the railings. Roosting all around were various waterfowl, especially Laughing Gull, who made quite a racket with their constant heinous chatter that seemed to mock the fishermen. But this didn't bother the locals one bit. Cory leaned against the wooden railing and briefly watched the fishermen. Looking past the fisherman, he fixated on the place where the ocean and the sky converged. Most people pictured freedom when they looked out at the horizon, but all Cory saw was uncertainty. His Godfather once said that the journey was his addiction. But ever since Frankie died, the adventure had become stale. He always thought he and Frankie would realize their lifelong dream together. But now there was only one of them. And for the first time in Cory's life, the future seemed far too big and unpredictable now that Frankie wasn't in it.

"I wonder if this is what cops go through." Cory said to no one in particular as he walked further down the pier. He never thought to ask Ken, who was back in Portland investigating Frankie's murder. The gunman was still in the wind. Cory imagined it was like fishing for the killer except you were looking for him specifically, not like here on the pier where any fish would do for supper.

Cory leaned over the railing, folding his arms tightly in contemplation. The light from one of the lamps shone down on him. He would have shrugged it off if he could. It reminded him of the spotlight so long ago, onstage with Frankie and the band by his side. Like the sheen reflecting off the water's surface, Cory was stuck. The current moved on but his light was frozen.

The warmth from the evening breeze bathed the fishermen who were perched on the pier. Out in the distance were floating cities of refuge, barely visible against the evening tapestry. The list included tankers, military craft and other sea going vessels that transported their wares to the Persian Gulf or the Ivory Coast of Africa. Fishing in Hampton Roads was an activity easily taken up as the main event, especially as summer approached. Almost surrounded by water in some parts, it was a way of life for rich and poor alike. Tonight the pier was home to the scraggly, on the verge of homelessness "fishin' for my next meal" types, and middle-class die-hard sportsmen who were, no doubt, Norfolk Tides fans judging by their blue and black windbreaker jackets. Yes sir, simply throw a rod and tackle box in the car and drive till the tires hit beach.

It was a combination of these same characteristics that brought Nate Spencer out to the pier that night; that, and the chance to renew the connection with his nephew, Evan. They did these things often while Evan was younger. But since the dawning of his teenage years, almost everything and everybody seemed as if they were a distraction to Evan. The distraction that was unexplained, and as far as Evan was concerned, could remain unexplained, was all based on the fact that he'd never known his father.

Periodically, Nate would try to insert himself into Evan's life. It was sort of an informal/formal agreement between him and his sister. Diana had been raising Evan alone for all these years. She sometimes worked from morning to night. Diana was like those ships out in the distance, slowly laboring, but only they were going places and broaching new horizons. Was it too much for a mother to want the same for her son? Nate was searching for ways to circumvent the lack of adult male bonding in Evan's life and to provide guidance. Cliché as it was, Nate felt a little fishing was a way to start the process.

However, it was becoming clear as the night wore on that Uncle Nate was not a natural at this.

"Look, we're here to fish," complained Uncle Nate, finding gaps in Evan's *concert*, so as to elicit some sort of response. He did recall Camille, saying if Evan had any response to this world; it was through his musical abilities. Although shielded from the full effects by the sound of the ocean breeze, which slapped the waves, their fellow fisherman nodded their agreement with the complaint. Cory would have agreed as well, if he wasn't mesmerized by the lamp's reflection, still dancing on the ocean's surface.

"Uncle Nate, we aren't catching anything. Heck, nobody's catching anything!" retorted Evan, matter-of-factly stating the obvious. "And you need to retire that old rod, man, for real" he added, resuming his concert. The "concert" being the dribbling of his golf ball atop the wooden bench he was sitting on while simultaneously tapping its surface with his free hand. The white orb seemed to be the only thing that mattered. Everything else, of course, was an interruption. Was he doing this because of his musical ability, lack of aptitude for the fishing, or a combination of both?

With a sigh, Evan looked skyward, almost imploringly, at the panorama of constellations. Once the full-time escorts of vessels from an era come and gone, now they were guides to this restless young man searching for an escape from the drama that was his life; and its endless questions.

The questions magnified his mother's concerns about his life's direction, or the lack thereof. Uncle Nate had been successful in business and he wanted the same success for Evan and his music, especially if it included his lovely girlfriend, Camille. However, with the looming presence of her over-protective father his relationship with her climbed higher to the top of his list of life's questions. Evan probably never thought the words "wanting only the best for my daughter," could feel so exclusive. His uncle watched him polish the golf ball in circular strokes with his fingers, indicating Evan's battle with his own steadfastness about the decisions staring him down; the ball was his stress-reliever.

Right about now, Cory was wishing he had a stress reliever of his own. All of a sudden, like an involuntary reflex, he chimed in, eyes still glued to the water.

"You have to love this stuff," he exhaled, not far from Evan, who ceased his dribbling, Evan turned in the direction of the voice, as did Nate.

"I've fished dozens of times every summer..." continued Cory, finally looking up from the water. "And I still don't want to be out here too much longer."

"Oh wow, this is rich," said Evan. "We got world class professionals out on the pier, and even they are sick of this."

Could the night get any better, thought Uncle Nate. This tall blonde man, a few years older than Evan, was not making things any easier.

Cory let out a laugh. The melancholy that overshadowed him a few minutes ago was now gone, suddenly replaced with curiosity in these two fishermen. Honestly, introductions and conversations were easy for Cory, especially if music was the focus. But this conversation was tainted with an 'I'll probably never see you again' sentiment. Still, he felt comfortable enough to simply engage these two strangers. Maybe there was something to what Ken was saying about getting away for a while. Propping himself up, back against the railing, Cory turned to Evan.

"Cool sound, or at least the little I noticed," said Cory.

"Oh yeah, and the fish love it," replied Evan sarcastically. "Can't you tell by our haul?"

Cory tried to hide another chuckle. He swore it wasn't quite that funny, yet his shaking body proved otherwise. Unlike most of the others on the pier that were shielded from the wind by their jackets, Cory's intense emotions seemed to have protected him from the sea breeze. Evan noticed Cory's bare right forearm, after he regained composure. It bore the image of a man and a circle on it. The circle was filled with musical symbols.

"Are you some kind of musician or something?" asked Cory, still smiling.

Evan brightened up, abandoning his pole and walking over to engage this stranger.

"By the look of that ink on your arm, I felt I should ask you that too, bro. But yeah, some people say that. I just do what comes naturally for me, you know? What do you think, shouldn't everybody do that?"

"What's your name?" asked Cory.

"Evan, Evan Spencer. And that's my uncle Nate," said Evan, tossing his golf ball from hand to hand.

"I'm Cory. I suppose you'll tell me everybody's got a song to sing or something like that?" asked Cory, folding his arms.

Situations like these were easy for Evan, too. This meeting was intriguing and a big improvement over Uncle Nate's failed fishing trip, even though the intentions were good. Evan was especially sensitive when meeting new people. But when it starts to feel like you're faking care, he's not going to waste that much energy on you. The whole conversation becomes disposable, and what difference would it make anyway? This was all in the back of Evan's mind.

"Well, I think so," answered Evan. "Despite how cheesy it sounds."

"It's fine," laughed Cory again. "Honestly I don't know. I have this pressing dilemma of living in something like a 'I, IV, V' kind of world; where I'm more of a 'I, VI, II' chord progression kind of guy myself."

"So you *are* a musician," laughed Evan. "That's a hard choice between that first and second chord progression. It's kind of like doing what everybody else is doing. Like if everything was pop music versus say, jazz or whatever."

Cory's reply was not far behind, "It's true. Actually, I'd been sort of dating the guitar for a while now. But we've taken a...a break, lately."

"How long did you play?" Evan inquired, more than eager now to connect with a fellow musician.

Cory surveyed the pier and its occupants. Then looking back to Evan and his golf ball, he decided, *what the heck,* and opened up all the more.

"I discovered the guitar at 13 years old," he began. "Trying to impress this girl, and amazingly it didn't work! Her loss though. You know, the guitar is just so compact, ergonomic in design and you're not dependent on outside sources for electricity. It stuck with me; so voila...the instrument of choice!"

The two laughed and discussed more about their musical interests while Uncle Nate and Ole Betsy, his fishing pole and instrument of choice, waited alone enticing the non-existent fish. Nate was surprised at his nephew's openness. Apparently they both liked some of the same musicians. They mentioned one band's tour and angel food or something like that. Then, Evan shared about his latest DJ gig, even going so far as to show Cory a clip from one of his shows on his phone. Cory seemed fascinated, and hinted at working in community outreach and earning a degree from Berklee. Suddenly, Uncle Nate was seeing this meeting, and Cory, in a whole new light.

Nate realized that this was an opportunity to expand horizons. Not content to stay in the background, he offered his thoughts.

"Evan," he interjected. "Have you ever thought about other places and what they have to offer? Or what mark you'll leave on the world? I think you should really experience a little of what is out there and move beyond the limited nightclub life and wanna-be college groupies in Hampton Roads. Music school could do for you what it's done for your friend here, you know, honing your producing talents."

"Oh, here it comes. Man I knew this is what all of this was about. You don't like my friends, or even understand what I do, and you won't let go of the past", barked Evan, with his finger aimed accusingly.

Shot down again. Uncle Nate just couldn't catch a break, even when he was trying to back off. Evan was misconstruing his uncle's encouragement for criticism. Uncle Nate was losing him again. Listening to Evan and Cory connect and hearing how promising and gregarious this new young man was could be the ram in the proverbial bush. The young men and their study group at Diana's church were good guys no doubt about it. But could a connection with people like this Cory guy be the answer? They seemed to be cut from the same cloth. Evan just opened up with this perfect stranger, and Cory wasn't trying to preach. And Evan was just himself – happy and encouraged!

Diana, I think this is what I was trying to say to you, thought Uncle Nate. He was going to try a different approach with Evan, when suddenly everyone's attention turned at the quick-snapping sound of one of the fisherman's pole breaking.

"Darn twisted line! I get the only bite out here and the thing's wrapped around my pole...I'm through!" blasted the fisherman.

Evan couldn't help agreeing with him, wanting to pull it in and call it a night. Snatching his golf ball into his pocket, he grabbed his pole to reel in his line.

"I don't know," Evan said, peering at his uncle, "I was beginning to get bitten myself."

Sensing this was a family issue, Cory turned to leave as well. "I'd better get back to the house," he said. "Nice talking to you Evan and good luck in your endeavors man, really. Based on that link you showed me, music needs men like you to keep the beat alive. And nice meeting you, Mr. Spencer."

"Pleasure... meeting a kindred spirit" said Evan wryly, more for Uncle Nate's benefit than as parting words to Cory. But Cory accepted them anyway and walked back down the pier toward his beach house.

Evan and his uncle began to make their way from the pier shortly thereafter in silence, Evan pulling away from his uncle's pace more and more. Although defeated in the battle, Uncle Nate somehow held out hope that there was a sovereign move afoot, that his epiphany wasn't a fluke. Seeing Evan in his natural environment had shown him something about his nephew's path that Uncle Nate hadn't seen before. Whatever it was, neither he, Diana nor Evan could control it. Cory was evidence of that. Yes, whatever it was, Uncle Nate would just let it be.

Track 05:
Dinner with Diana

The weekend following the trip to Little Island Pier was a pleasant one, and the latter half of it found Diana Spencer waving goodbye to her pastor and his wife as she exited the church parking lot to start the trip home. Passing the hospital where she worked as a full time nurse once again reminded her that where there is a will there is a way. During a rough patch in her early 20s, right before her son Evan was born; Diana thought she'd be stuck in a rut for the rest of her life. She didn't know who she was or where she was going, if anywhere. But family and the few friends she had managed to hold onto brought her through and delivered her straight into her new job as a registered nurse. Finally, she again had hope, and she and Evan were just fine. However, over the years, and this year in particular, their lives and Diana's patience were being put to the test.

It wasn't easy being a single mother. Lately, Evan had been branching out more into music. This was a territory that Diana was all too familiar with, even when factoring in their generational differences, which included music's technological advances of the past 20 years. Sure, she wanted her son to follow his dreams. But the music business had taken too many of those she'd loved and held dear, and she didn't want to lose her only son to the monsters of fame and fortune. That's all the kids wanted nowadays, the glitz and glam but no accountability. The lights and cameras were there when she was Evan's age, and they hadn't faded yet; in fact their allure had gotten brighter. The monstrous machine had eaten up stars both young and old, and had taken away a dear friend of hers when she was younger. She missed him so much and no one could play music and the heart strings like he could.

Diana wasn't going to end up the same way. She didn't have to touch the stovetop to know it was hot; she could see the burning red coils just fine from her vantage point. Instead Diana got herself focused and prospered.

Now, the question was how to save her son from the same pain she narrowly escaped. Hopefully, Nate could shine some new light on things with Evan after this recent escapade at the pier. After all, Nate was her brother and one of her closest friends, and had been there after Evan was born. He was the closest thing to a father for her boy. Though they didn't always see eye to eye, Nate was always the more sensible one. She could count on him.

Yesterday afternoon Nate left her a message saying they needed to talk about Evan; apparently the fishing trip had been a bust. She hadn't seen much of her son this weekend due to their schedules. She was on shift at the hospital and he spent the weekend with his music buddies, Sam and Ryan. But she was determined to have words with her son as soon as he got back today and straighten him up for tonight. Uncle Nate was coming over for dinner.

Pulling into the driveway, Diana noticed the all too familiar grey Impala that belonged to Evan's friend, Sam. Evan and his two friends were together the whole weekend and now her boy had come home.

"Alright mister," said Diana to no one in particular as she climbed out of the car. Once inside, she was greeted by the faint sound of music from the back of the house. She kicked off her flats and strolled through the house, passing photos of her and Evan on the wall. Setting her keys down on the little desk by the steps, she found her way nearing Evan's studio.

"Evan! Evan I'm home!" Diana hollered, approaching the door to Evan's studio.

"Evan?" she hollered again, this time banging on the door causing the sign on a string reading *ON AIR* to fall to the floor. The music stopped and there was some commotion on the other side of the door before it flew open and Evan's head poked out.

"Aw mom, we were recording in here," moaned Evan. "Didn't you see my sign?"

"I'm sorry, honey. It was just louder than usual," said Diana exasperated. "Look, can you tear yourself away for a minute? I need to talk to you."

"Sure thing," said Evan, equally exasperated. "Can I hit *save* first?"

Diana nodded, and waved to Sam and Ryan while Evan walked over to his laptops. Walking into the kitchen to set her purse down, Diana noticed the time on the microwave.

1:30 it read.

"Gonna need to get started soon" she mused, when the light *zing* of the doorbell caught her attention. *Someone's early*, she thought walking to the front door. But instead of her tall, burly brother, Diana was greeted by the petite and cheery Camille LaShea.

"Hello, Miss Spencer," beamed Camille.

"Why, hello there Camille, how are you?" returned Diana as she invited Camille inside.

"Just fine, thanks," Camille replied, following Diana into the kitchen. Almost immediately the ladies began to catch up. They discussed how things were going, how college life at Norfolk State was treating Camille.

Evan had gone from saving the rehearsal he and the guys had just finished, to getting distracted by other music files.

"Hey Ev, you're mom's gonna be on your case again if you leave her hanging out there," warned Ryan. "And Camille's still on the way, right?"

"Oh yeah", said Evan absent-mindedly. "Okay guys, listen to that real quick I'll be right back."

Back in the kitchen, Diana and Camille continued their conversation. Camille talked about the latest song she, Evan and their friends were working on.

"Oh honey I really need to hear you sing," gushed Diana. "You always loved to run around making up songs when you and Evan were in middle school. Maybe you should stay for dinner. Evan's uncle is coming over. You could sing for us."

"That'd be awesome," agreed Camille. "How is Uncle Nate?"

"He's fine. He's been meaning to give Evan some business books he said you had asked him about," answered Diana.

"Hey, babe!" said Evan, almost bounding into the kitchen. "I didn't hear you come in."

"Yeah, I was hoping that you hadn't forgotten about me, and would come in here sooner rather than later, Evan," said Diana, as Camille wrapped her arms around Evan's neck.

"Sorry mom, nature called after I shuffled some things around," said Evan, holding Camille close. "But I told the guys to keep the noise level down."

"Well I just wanted to let you know Uncle Nate is coming over, so I hope you'll be around for dinner," said Diana. "In his message he said he wanted to talk about the pier. Said it didn't go very well and that you left early."

"Wait, what's up with this?" Evan asked annoyed. "Didn't go well?"

Diana folded her arms and had an answer ready.

"When I called him back he said you two had a long talk" she continued. "He was vague, Evan, but I was hoping he wouldn't have to lecture you like I have."

"Mom, we talked about a lot out there," Evan shot back.

"Evan be cool," said Camille with concern as she rubbed Evan's back.

The kitchen was quiet for a moment as both mother and son stood frozen around the little island by the stove. They were both tired from the weekend and didn't need the tension. Finally, Evan calmly broke the silence.

"You said he was vague, mom?" he asked.

"We need to talk this out, honey," Diana said gently. "Your uncle didn't sound upset or anything. He just wanted to have dinner and talk about changes."

Evan nodded, jaw clenched. Camille smiled weakly at Diana and rubbed Evan's shoulder. She didn't want to take sides and instead offered a neutral idea.

"Yeah, dinner sounds nice right?" whispered Camille. "It's not an intervention or anything, just dinner with family."

"Yeah, dinner," said Evan halfheartedly.

The three of them had been so engrossed in their talk that they didn't realize that Sam and Ryan stood outside the kitchen doorway with their band equipment in hand. "Hey guys, sorry" said Ryan. "Evan? Sam and I need to go. He's gonna drop me by my girlfriend's on his way to work, he just got called in."

"Sorry we missed you, Camille," said Sam.

"Yeah, me too. But I need to see my girl," said Ryan. "I just found out I'm gonna be a dad!"

Evan left the kitchen to see his buddies out the door. Afterward he went up to his room to cool off, leaving Camille and Diana to themselves to prepare for dinner.

"Miss Spencer, where does he get this Jekyll/Hyde, sensitive and harsh side to him from?" Camille rolled her eyes.

"Dear, I don't know," admitted Diana genuinely. "His uncle says he's just trying to find himself."

"Well, I hope he finds himself soon. I mean, I thought I knew who he was, or at least who he presented himself to be." Camille flailed her arms, irritated. "Now you're telling me he isn't sure himself. It's crazy and mixed up!"

Upstairs, Evan sat in his room, dribbling his ever-present golf ball at his desk. Playing lightly in the background from his MP3 port was the soundtrack to the latest Dennis Harley film that he, Camille and Tony, had seen at the mall a little while ago.

It had taken a while but he and Uncle Nate had indeed talked on the car ride home after fishing that night and meeting that guy on the pier. Evan couldn't figure out what changed or why they kept going in circles like this. If Uncle Nate couldn't be real with him, then what was he up to? The soundtrack ended and Evan stared into space for a second, when out of the corner of his eye, he caught the sight of his uncle's headlights coming up their driveway. "I'm tired of this endless loop," Evan said to himself, setting down his golf ball. He hesitantly descended the stairs. "Let's finish this once and for all."

Downstairs, Camille put the finishing touches on a chef's salad she constructed from the odds and ends she found in the refrigerator. Meanwhile, Evan's mother was out on the back patio at the grill, where she turned fish as she rained Old Bay, lemon, pepper, paprika, and onions down upon the boat shaped foil containers.

"Camille!" Diana yelled toward the kitchen window. "Bring me some more butter I don't want this Rock Fish to stick." The soft aroma of grilled fish swirled gradually upward as the juices bubbled and snapped. None of this escaped Evan as he made his way down the stairs from his perch of contemplation, readily volunteering his assistance.

"You got fries going?" Evan said, entering the kitchen.

"Babe, potatoes and peeler are sitting in the kitchen calling your name," answered Camille, leaning over to plant a kiss on Evan's cheek.

"Honey, we all know that you make the best fried potatoes," called Diana from the patio.

At that moment Uncle Nate appeared with ice cream, soda, and a large brown box, having followed his nose to the gathering in the back yard.

"Oh Nate, you creep!" joked Diana, half startled by her brother's sudden appearance.

"Easy pickings," laughed Uncle Nate, hugging her and calling to Camille and Evan inside. Nate placed the box on the patio table and handed the ice cream to Camille, directing her to place it in the freezer.

"Crabs!" Diana exclaimed flinging the box open and filling the air with the smell of the hot crustaceans and Old Bay seasoning.

"I told you I'd bring a little surprise, didn't I? Besides, the road to diplomacy is paved with good food," Uncle Nate offered.

"I guess we'll see then, won't we" said Evan under his breath, and he caught a look from his mother.

"Evan why don't you get the cups and we can begin" said Diana, a little too cheerily.

After fighting off the usual neighbor self-invites, the family sat down to share a nice quiet dinner. Midway through, the spotlight shone on Camille.

"How are you handling school, Camille?" asked Nate, sipping from his cup.

"Well, it was a little bit shaky at first," said Camille. "But I've signed up for a tutor and now I'm readjusting my study habits. Apparently, they are the key to doing well. The staff is very good about helping me plan things out. They are really family oriented and make you feel right at home. It is a little tough making new friends, but they have all sorts of activities planned for the new students, like buses going to laser tag, and other things. That can be fun, but then you come back home to the Towers."

"What's that?" asked Diana.

"Oh, that's my dorm," answered Camille, dipping some crabmeat in butter. "The new students get put there. It can be a fate worse than death...but it's working something in us... 'Behold the green and gold!'"

Camille giggled as she said this, which caused Evan to grin with pride. His girlfriend was making the best of her new adventure. He poked her side, knowing she hated that, which made her jump, sending butter flying everywhere. Blushing uncontrollably, she smacked him cutely over the head, after which Evan stole a kiss from her.

"School can be tough, Camille. But I am sure you will follow through with your plans," encouraged Diana.

"Yes," agreed Camille, gingerly rubbing Evan's head where she had smacked him, and Evan going along with the joke.

"My Nanna used to say," continued Camille, "some things are given to you genetically, some behaviors are transmitted socially, and then there are those that you must fight for, but all of it must be in your blood.'"

"Tell it, Camille, tell it!" laughed Uncle Nate, hanging on every word.

"'Something about an eagle and a sparrow she said', wasn't it?" Evan inquired.

"Uh-huh," Camille began to answer while playing with her napkin. "She said both birds are in a fight against everything that would naturally pull them down, despite differences in size or style of flight. Nanna told me to understand my genetic makeup, accept it, and use what I've been given to stay aloft against all that would naturally try and pull me down. College is putting some of that to the test, but that's what I intend to do."

"I know that's right. Your grandmother was a wise woman," insisted Diana, snapping her fingers. "There have been many times when I found that I was on a long descent. When I started off in nursing, from community college mind you, life was like a rollercoaster. It took me a few times around the track, but then I figured out that the downward momentum could be used to carry me to the next experience."

"Actually," inserted Uncle Nate, "I wonder if it takes us all a few turns around the block to figure out what is really going on. For some reason, I don't think the lessons that we learn are solely for ourselves."

"I couldn't agree more," said Camille. "I couldn't agree more... Oh, I got a text from my dad, earlier. He says 'hi' to everyone."

"How is your old man? What's LaShea saying these days?" asked Nate.

"You know Daddy," said Camille, shaking her head. "He's all work and no play."

"Business is important. You have to take care of business first," Diana affirmed.

"Yes, Miss Spencer. But I," started Camille.

"Hold on, little Miss Missy," interrupted Diana, pursing her lips. "Now I've been meaning to spank you all night. That's what I forgot. What's all this Mister and Miss Spencer stuff? We're kin, but not married."

Everyone at the table threw their heads back and laughed.

"Oh, you gonna get it now, Cammie," warned Evan, jokingly.

"I'm sorry Miss Diana," Camille said between giggles.

"Catch your breath now," said Uncle Nate, chuckling.

"But, I worry about him," continued Camille more calmly. "He wants to do so much to make sure that I'm taken care of. And with the bills from Mom's care, he's just juggling so much."

"I know it must be tough," remarked Diana. "Evan, pass that mallet, please."

Camille cocked her head to the side, studying her cup of soda while thinking about her dad.

"I've been bugging him about checking his blood pressure," she said. "And watching his cholesterol, and to keep taking his pills...but sometimes it seems so hard. Like he just runs and runs. And he pushes his staff at work. He says it's like some of them are bent on tearing things down, while others are trying to build."

"He just wants to get things together for you sweetie," surmised Uncle Nate. "It's all about trying to secure a future for others."

Evan just seemed to take all of this in while enjoying his meal. His silence was provoking.

"Evan, have you and Camille begun to plot out any type of future?" his mother asked.

"Well...none other than the one that's already prepared for us," Evan answered, somewhat caught off guard. "We're just taking things a day at a time." Evan looked to Camille for affirmation and was glad to have her nodding back.

"What do you think, Nate?" asked Diana, looking to her brother. "Don't you think being a little more proactive is a good thing?"

"Yeah Unc," said Evan forcefully. "What *do* you think?"

"We all just hope for the best for you," said Uncle Nate calmly. "And that you would be able to channel those energies as early as possible and specifically as possible, toward becoming a real musician. Sometimes you have to live through the thing..."

"It ain't all head knowledge," finished Evan, perking up.

"Just like *we* talked about," acknowledged Uncle Nate.

"I'm sorry, Nate I don't understand," said Diana turning to her brother, a bit disoriented.

Uncle Nate wiped his mouth on a napkin, "Nephew why don't you and Camille go for a walk and enjoy some quality time together. It's nice out." Evan and Camille didn't need to be told twice. Evan heard what he needed to hear. He winked at his uncle and assured them that he and Camille would be back in time for dessert.

After cleaning up the patio, Nate and Diana made themselves comfortable in the living room with a cup of hot tea. Discussions on the patio were just icebreakers. The living room was where the deepest conversations always took place. Here the eyes of family members gazed down at the occupants from the myriad of framed pictures that adorned the little room. A stone sculpture of a prophetic figure with outstretched arms holding tablets of the law sat in the corner, welcoming them to the sanctuary.

"Nate, you said you wanted to talk about Evan," said Diana, still confused as to why Nate sent her son away.

"I remember saying that I wanted to talk – to you, Diana," said Nate sipping his tea.

"So talk, Nate," demanded Diana. "What happened with you and Evan after you left the pier?"

"Diana, you should have seen him," Nate began. "Before he and I left, we met this local, at least I think he was a local, and he and Evan just hit it off. He was a young guy, a little bit older than Evan. They traded stories like they were best friends."

"Okay," said Diana, at last calm and sipping her tea. She didn't venture to say anymore, so Nate continued with his story.

"The guy's name was Cory, I think," Nate continued. "And Evan said the guy went to Berklee and played the guitar. Evan went a step further and said that Cory even taught there once."

"He taught there?" asked Diana amazed.

"Not for very long. Maybe a summer course or special program as a guest I suppose. But nonetheless," offered Nate,

"The young man sounded gifted. Evan was so riled up after meeting this guy; I think he even whipped out his phone to show Cory his website or a video or something."

"Wow" was all Diana could say, setting down her teacup.

"Look, my point is, Evan and I did have a disagreement," said Nate. "But, Diana, he misunderstood what I was trying to tell him on the pier. He thought I was being hypocritical because I encouraged him to get out of his comfort zone."

"But Nate," chuckled Diana. "You have never gone outside of your comfort zone."

"We all have to go at our own pace, I guess," sighed Nate. "But Evan isn't getting any younger. It's true, it's not all head knowledge, and I can't live this life for him. No one can."

"It's just so crazy out there," lamented Diana. "That crazy music industry that Evan wants is full of disappointment and it changes people. We know that better than anyone in our family."

"I know," agreed Nate. "I know it was hard growing up with that legacy in the family. Music could be good to us one day and bad the next. But I just don't think I can lay claim like this anymore. It's not mine to own."

They both took a sip of their tea and let the things Nate said hang in the air for a few minutes. For the first time, Nate was exposing himself. He was going against a belief system that he had held for many years; one that was tried and true. It kept him secure and he had successfully sold it to his sister. Previously, he, Diana, and other's in their family had practically convinced themselves they were the authority on making it in the music industry; but they weren't. They made mistakes. And instead of protecting Evan from the harm they perceived for him by honestly telling him where the landmines lay in the field, they pushed him totally off the field. He was being robbed of the important experiences gained from failure. There were too many voices in his head, too many cooks in the kitchen.

Nate realized the truth. Evan was unhappy. He didn't know where he came from or where he was going. And no one understood him. Or those that did, like that Cory fella, seemed few and far between, or were going on different paths themselves. No one, not anyone like Cory, or in the musical Spencer legacy, was walking alongside Evan.

Evan has grown up in a cowardice community, thought Nate. But he didn't dare utter those words. He didn't know what was in store for Evan, and he was exhausted with pretending like he did. Diana needed to realize this too, but would she hear him?

"I appreciate everything you have done, Nate," said Diana at last. "You've been one of the most – no, *the most* consistent male force in Evan's life."

"And I don't want to lose that, that familiarity, that place you and he have carved out for me," admitted Nate.

"But he is my son," affirmed Diana. "No one loves him like I do."

"That's right," agreed Nate. "So, I won't dilute the situation. I love you Diana. But I think I have been going about things with Evan all wrong. He's not perfect, but he's not trying to be. He wants to be himself. Someone as brilliant as Evan deserves to be himself. Heck everyone's got to be especially with the ones they love… otherwise we may all lose."

Diana sighed and looked around the living room, surveying photos of, Evan's cousins, grandparents, aunts and uncles; some had passed on, some were still alive and well. Diana's cheeks showed the creases of time. Small streams gathered and descended those crevices along her face as memories of Evan growing up and of the family who loved him flashed through her mind. Lastly, her watery eyes rested on the sculpture of the prophet standing sentry, whose eyes pierced as its arms held up the stone tablets.

Nate's eyes fell upon the statue as well. He touched his sister's hand, desperate to comfort and encourage her. "Maybe what we should do isn't carved in stone. Maybe it's gently whispered inside of our hearts."

"I know you miss him," offered Nate. "It's crazy. The man performed miracles... he just did it with music."

"And with my heart," sighed Diana, turning her face to wipe the tears. Nate nodded and rubbed his sister's arm, recalling the man and knowing he was treading into sensitive territory.

"Strings," said Nate. "It sounded like you said that thing you used to say about him. Heart strings..."

"Structure," Diana said, whirling back on him, eyes perfectly dry. "Nate. I was saying structure. Evan needs structure." And with that she collected their dishes and started for the kitchen.

"Diana!" called Nate.

Diana stopped in her tracks, shoulders visibly rising and falling. Inhaling and exhaling through her nose alone, each breath was perfectly audible.

Now standing beside his sister, Nate's business mind kicked into gear. "Imposed structure has a purpose, which I won't argue with. But you lose innovation. When we dictate structure, we choose the path of least resistance. It's the easy way out. And the price we pay is that we lose the creativity necessary to solve the inevitable challenges of life. In the end, I don't think it was ever about being protected from something; but being empowered to face the problems head-on...remember that. I love you, Sis."

"I love you too, Nate," replied Diana, comforted by the kiss her brother planted on the back of her head.

"Tell the kids dinner was great," said Nate, walking to the door. "I hope they enjoy the ice cream. I know Evan still loves Cookie Dough."

A little while after her brother left, Diana found herself back in the living room starring at the statue and his laws of life. Cheery sounds of Evan and Camille came bursting through the front door.

"Hey Mom, Uncle Nate, we're back. Where's the ice cream?" yelled Evan.

Solemnly staring at the statue, Nate's words still rang in Diana's ears.

Track 06:
Buffering

Loading was taking a while. Cory sat tapping his finger, staring at the laptop. There, finally, now it would play. On the screen, three men and two women were lounging around in lawn chairs. In the background stood a shed, intriguing as "the Bat Cave" with double doors flung wide-open to reveal Batman's cycle. Only in this case, it was a red Gold Wing motorcycle. Sitting next to it was a riding lawnmower which could not be mistaken for the Batmobile. More lawn chairs hung from the shed's ceiling. Behind the five loungers was a tomato garden. Farther out onto the lawn was an apple tree that stood several feet from a brick barbecue pit.

But the people weren't gathered to eat. One of the women was actually friends with the three men and sat next to them; together they made up the band, Underfed Angels. The band members sat across from the other woman, who was a journalist by the name of Dharma West. She was chipper and dressed in a cobalt blue dress, with a beautiful blue, grey, black, and white-checkered scarf draping her neck. Though it was sunny in the video, Dharma wore a black suede blazer and black boots.

The four guests sitting before her were dressed more extravagantly.

"Thank you for joining us," said Dharma, looking straight into the camera. "I'm Dharma West, sitting here with the remarkable band, Underfed Angels."

"Starting with lead vocalist Bryan Guest, code name 'Fearless'," continued Dharma smiling as she introduced each band member. Bryan 'Fearless' was dressed in mostly blue denim, with a jacket and cut off shorts, a low cut tank top with stripes, black high tops and a beanie cap to top things off. He smiled at the introduction.

"Skipping the lovely lady in the middle for only a moment," said Dharma chuckling, "We have guitarists and twins the Brothers Resurrecion, Daniel and Jonah." The others were laughing also. Daniel was the oldest, wearing black pants accessorized with chains, and a green graphic tee shirt bearing the face of Jesus and the phrase "Rebel since Birth" at the bottom. Jonah was taller and lankier than his older twin, and stood out by looking the sharpest in the group, sporting a tailored suit and cartoonish fedora.

"You're looking very dapper sir," said Dharma. "And last but not least, the newbie, the beautiful Everett 'Hot Wings' Grier." Her band mates applauded raucously, hooting and hollering. Dharma laughed, holding up papers to her mouth in a poor attempt to stifle them. Everett covered her face bashfully, at the same time showing off the fiery wing tattoos adorning both hands.

"You guys are a playful bunch, aren't you?" asked Dharma.

"You know what they say about all work and no play," answered Bryan Fearless.

"Is that why some of you have nicknames?" inquired Dharma, crossing her leg.

"They only wanted nicknames because our surname is basically *Resurrection!*" the younger twin blurted out.

"Hey man! My friends were already calling me 'Hot Wings' before I joined the band" asserted Everett, having composed herself.

Everett sat there for a few seconds, arms crossed childishly, nose turned up and the sun glinting off her glasses.

The video was buffering again.

Cory shook his head irritably while leaning on his elbow out in the sunroom.

"Well I wanted to say your grandparents have a beautiful home, Bryan," said Dharma, as the video resumed playing again. Cory smiled as the loading bar progressed next to the *Play* button.

"Thanks Dharma," said Bryan beaming proudly. "I have a lot of memories of this place. So glad they agreed to let us talk here."

"Yes. Well, Everett," continued Dharma. "I wanted to start off with something else. But you said something that alluded to your life before joining the band, the nickname? How has it been playing with the guys and filling in after Lewis "Lucky" Ladder left?"

Cory leaned in, watching as Everett shifted in her seat. She sat in the middle and looked really on the spot. But Cory could tell the guys totally supported Everett. Cory clicked the small 'X' on an ad that appeared at the bottom of the video as Daniel Resurrecion rubbed Everett's leg encouragingly.

"I'm actually not nervous about the topic," began Everett. "I'm like this because I'm just so grateful and excited for this opportunity. It's not that it isn't an uncomfortable subject about Lewis leaving. It is. He didn't have to leave the way he did. He, Bryan and the twins are like family. They deserved better...and so did Lewis."

"Ditto!" said the twins.

"Yeah, I hope he realizes that," said Bryan. "It's not about the music but the friendship. It's about love and about family."

"That's very big of you, all things considered," said Dharma, squinting her eyes in contemplation.

"But back to your question," said Everett crossing one bright red pant leg over the other and folding her hands under her thigh. "I loved these guys growing up. Bryan's married to my sister. When we were all kids, I always wanted to be like her and go wherever she went and be friends with all her friends. All I keep thinking is often times you feel as if things could have gone differently. I wanted a chance as a little kid for all kinds of things. Being like my sister was one manifestation of it I guess. And I was angry about things as a teenager. I think I was just so full of doubt and wanted the chance to prove myself. The way things went with Lewis was a bummer. But then I suddenly found myself forced out into the open like I always wanted..."

The video was frozen again.

"Ah, come on!" said Cory through gritted teeth. "Buffering again? Why are you acting up?" Cory hit the 'Refresh' button again and again to no avail and finally just threw his hands in the air.

"Right when the interview was getting good, too," he sighed, taking a drink of his beer.

From across the street, Ms. Senor cracked open her door, smelling some of the ocean breeze, and noticed Cory upset in his sunroom.

"Oh that's right!" she said to herself, and darted back inside.

Several weeks had passed since Cory's walk to Little Island Pier. Lately he'd found himself browsing through his band's music and memorabilia, at least what he could easily access on message boards with a little wi-fi. He read emails from fans back in Portland, comments and photos left on the online fan page and social network sites at the band's disposal. It was like going back in time.

Today, Cory was researching his favorite musical influences, the same as his band mates at one time. He found a recent interview featuring his idols, Underfed Angels. The band was covering the bitter departure of their original drummer when the video site started having problems. He had been sitting in the sunroom for a couple hours now and a few beer bottles sat on the table. Then, in the bottom right corner where the site features video suggestions similar to the current video, Cory saw something that caught his eye: his own face.

"Oh wow, yeah," said Cory, scrolling down and selecting the video thumbnail. "Man that was a great night."

The home video loaded and colorful text appeared on the screen that displayed Cory's name and those of his band mates.

"Introducing... THE KINDRED!" announced an off screen female voice that made Cory chuckle.

"That girl is so crazy," he said, grinning.

There seemed to be a party going on in the background and the video footage was very shaky.

The picture was of Cory sitting in the living room of his Portland home surrounded by friends and family, his band mates... and specifically Frankie.

"I remember that night," muttered Cory as he leaned forward over the table, resting his chin on his folded arms and knocking over a bottle or two. This video was of the last concert The Kindred had performed. Cory and Frankie sat side-by-side laughing. Frankie's arm was wrapped around Cory's neck, while the other three, Avery, Rick and Harrison, horse played, with Harrison sprawled over his friends' legs like they were a human hammock.

"More ale!" hollered Harrison, shooting his hand straight into the air, his clear plastic cup empty.

"Ale?" asked Avery. "That was fruit punch you just had, fool!"

"Crazy," chuckled Cory to himself, trying for another swig of beer only to realize he'd already drained it. Shaking it absentmindedly, he set it down and kept watching the video.

"Get off me, boy!" laughed Rick, shoving Harrison's legs off him. "Laying around like this is like King Arthur's court...there ain't no ale up in here."

The video was a picture of absolute celebration and marked the last time Cory and Frankie played music together. It was the last time they smiled together or even looked like friends, before that fateful day.

The video shook vigorously, panning the room as friends and family smiled. There were cups of punch and plates of food in every hand. A bespectacled older man winked and pointed at the camera.

"Hi dad!" yelled the girl from behind the camera.

"Yeah! That's your brother, Frankie, baby girl," said her dad, grinning and dancing a little jig.

The camera focused back on the rowdy young men on the couch and the voice hollered again.

"Guys," she said. "Guys tell me that wasn't your best performance ever!"

"Hey," said Cory on the video, smiling into the camera. "Frankie, your sister is trying to interview us."

Playfully snatching the camera away from his sister, Frankie held it out and pointed the lens at himself and Cory, the both of them leaning in.

"Folks," said Frankie, "that wasn't our best concert ever... that was our greatest concert ever!"

"Like playing a concert for God!" hooted Cory, brushing his blonde hair out of his face. "We're the greatest and leading the charge, so follow or get out of the way because The Kindred are coming for blood!"

"For real," said Frankie, leaning into view. "Barbara, the Grammy goes to The Kindred this time, every time!"

The footage wobbled some more as Avery, Rick and Harrison's face pass over the camera.

"Just give us all of them!" screams Avery. "Heck we'll take them from our favorites, too!"

"We're accepting Grammys and awards from everyone," Rick chimes in loudly. "From Graven iMage... rO-Ok*...Underfed Angels..."

"We're gonna run everything one day. Barbara you heard it here first," Harrison yells into his cup like a microphone. "One day all the awards will be ours, the charts will be ours and all the fans will be ours!"

"Watch out, we're gonna steal all your fans, too!" yells Frankie popping back into view. "Especially if Cory keeps playing that guitar the way he does. What'd you call that thing? Viola'?"

"You rocker dudes are so wild," laughs Barbara, taking the camera back, all five band mates back in full view on the couch.

"I love this band!" screams Frankie at the top of his lungs right as the video freezes.

Cory didn't budge. He didn't make a sound. He wasn't angry with the website or the buffering and he didn't mind that there was seven minutes of footage of him and his friends left to load. He just stared.

"You look so happy."

Cory turned to look behind him. He hadn't noticed Ms. Senor standing outside the green room, Paris resting on his haunches, tawny fur glowing in the May sun.

Cory stood up and let Ms. Senor inside. She took a seat in one of the white wicker chairs. Cory resumed his seat at the picnic table, absentmindedly petting the excited dog.

"I haven't seen you much," offered Ms. Senor, setting down some mail in her lap.

Cory stopped petting Paris to close his laptop and pick up the fallen bottles.

"Been keeping busy," answered Cory, sitting back up and running his fingers through his unkempt hair.

"Working on that beard, I see," said Ms. Senor, cocking her head thoughtfully to the right. Paris whined at Cory as if he agreed, then laid down on the astro-turf between Cory and his master. Cory hadn't shaved in weeks -- not since his encounter with Evan and Nate Spencer on the pier. To Ms. Senor, he looked tired and thin. Messy hair and bags under his eyes, he was wearing just a white undershirt and jeans but no shoes.

"Yeah," he smirked. "I've been working on the beard, among other things. Chasing down the fire you saw in me in that video."

"Have you found it?" Ms Senor gently asked.

Cory looked down. Uneasy, he swallowed. Paris, picking up on this, whined and inched across the floor toward him. Cory cracked a weak smile at the dog and reached out. Paris's stubby little tail wagged excitedly and he tilted his head as Cory lightly scratched it.

"Some of it," said Cory. "I guess the past managed to extinguish part of it. Something is still missing."

"I think we both know what that is," said Ms. Senor, looking at the laptop. "But friends like that shouldn't stay hidden in a computer. You have to go out and find them."

Cory's eyes widened as he looked up at her.

"What if you lost them and you can't get them back?" he asked, rubbing his hand against his fist. "What if the hardest part is letting go... and starting over?"

As if able to sniff out the specifics, Paris whimpered the more Cory opened up, regardless of how vague he was. "Shhh, Paris," Ms. Senor commanded firmly but gently. Paris craned his head back at his master, then rolled onto his side and exhaled dramatically.

Ms. Senor looked down and picked up the envelope off her lap.

"It's true," admitted Ms. Senor. "But it won't get any better... the hardest part won't soften if you hold on when you shouldn't. That's what my late husband used to say - or something to that effect. If you hold on too tightly for too long, you'll miss when it's time to open up and receive what's new and exciting."

Cory nodded solemnly and sat up straight, taking in a deep breath through his nose.

"Ken told me you lost some special people in your life," admitted Cory.

"Your face told me you did too, Honey, the first day you came here" said Ms. Senor.

Cory nodded and flipped open the laptop thoughtfully.

"I've been writing down my feelings," he said. "I don't know if you've ever done that, Ms. Senor. It's what got Frankie, the band and me started in the first place, way back when. We wanted to be like our favorite bands but all the stuff we came up with in the beginning was terrible, laughable really. We were fakers who hadn't endured anything."

Cory lazily rubbed the worn patch on the 'Spacebar' of his laptop as he spoke.

"It wasn't until Frankie's sister Barbara lost one of her clownfish. Frankie had gotten her this great fish tank and some clownfish for her birthday. She took care of them but the fish started to die. Barbara was so emotional, so sensitive, just like her brother, even though she could buy more. Frankie wrote a song about it for her. He called it *The Clowns of Life*. It was our first hit."

Ms. Senor clapped her hands together at Paris, who bounded up happily and nuzzled her.

"Kind of cheesy, I know," chuckled Cory. "But we figured out that being real about what you felt could make for great music, especially with your friends. Plus, we were good at it... really good. I'm remembering how to do that again. I just need the friends."

"Are all of your friends gone now?" asked Ms. Senor, rubbing Paris behind his ears.

"In varying degrees, yes," answered Cory, looking at the blank laptop screen.

Ms. Senor stopped playing with Paris to fiddle with the envelope in her hand. It was a big white durable envelope for express packages.

"Well, I know it takes a while. My husband – husbands, understood that," said Ms. Senor. "And that's really just fine." She handed Cory the envelope. Somewhat confused, he took it.

"This was intended for someone else I know," she said. "But from the looks of things, I think it was meant for you, Cory, a trip within a trip."

Cory tore open the envelope and a lanyard with some kind of card or pass dropped to the floor. Cory's eyes grew very wide. He looked back at Ms. Senor with a smile.

"It would do you well to be around creative and rowdy people like yourself," winked Ms. Senor, getting up to leave. Cory stood too and hugged her.

"This is sweet," he whispered. "Feels like the past catching up to me."

"It's the past progressing forward with the times," said Ms. Senor, hugging Cory tightly. "Be in the moment."

"Thank you, Ms. Senor," said Cory, releasing her.

"My pleasure, honey," she said, holding his hands. "Since you'll be in his neighborhood, ask the president if he'd help feed those poor guys. Angels can't rock on an empty stomach. His ads say he cares after all."

"She really is something else," Cory said, looking at Paris. The usually playful dog slumped onto his side again, one eye on Ms. Senor and the other covered by his paw.

Track 07:
Gracing the Food

At last, Cory stood facing the 9:30 Club, having survived the drive to Northwest Washington D.C. Somehow it felt longer than the odyssey he and Ken Ellis had taken from Oregon to Virginia earlier in the Spring. Maybe it was because on the drive to the beach house, he didn't know what to expect and didn't expect much anyway. Here on a hot Saturday afternoon in the nation's capital, in line to see his favorite band play, maybe it was natural he'd want to stretch his legs and never drive again. Funny, he almost wondered if this was why he'd left home, to see his favorite band play some great music.

"All VIPs!" yelled the venue contact at the head of the line. "Listen up! Please form a line to your left, right here next to the bus; VIPs only. If you purchased the VIP package have your passes out so we can check you off the list."

Cory pushed himself off the hot brick wall of the 9:30 Club and, along with the other VIPs, formed a line next to what must have been the band's bus. As Cory took his place in line he heard a small commotion behind him. Something lightly bounced on the sidewalk.

"Oh see, put that away," said a very stern and maternal voice, as Cory turned around.

"Sorry," said a young male voice. "I've been listening to their music all month and I want Hot Wings to sign my drum sticks."

Cory laughed, the rabid fans were out tonight for sure, or was rabid too strong a word?

"Is this UA's bus?" inquired the girl in front of Cory.

"Nope, I don't think so. It's too early," answered the girl that was with her. "Tantrums Of G3nius is opening for them, remember?"

"Oh yeah!" her friend said excitedly. "I keep forgetting. All I can think about is seeing the Resurrecion twins."

"I know!" her friend gushed. "Jonah's fedoras are so cute!"

"Oh, when is this gonna start?" whined some guy back in the other line. "We've been out in this heat for over an hour."

"They said get here early, right?" whispered another girl in Cory's VIP line.

"Okay guys in my VIP line," shouted the contact again. "Take out your passes. We're gonna check you in now. After I look you up, you can go right in, VIPs only."

"Right on time let's get this show on the road," Cory said, stepping inside to see his inspiration, Underfed Angels, make music.

Inside, the 9:30 Club housed 1,200 people of all ages. They offered drink and snack bars all around. After purchasing a live concert DVD at the merchandise booth, Cory made his way upstairs to the VIP section. Anyone could view the show from up there; it was after the show that things got exclusive. For now, all could enjoy a bird's eye view of the show. Cory leaned against the railing and surveyed the scene. He hadn't been in this realm in what seemed like forever. Music lovers young and old clamored all over the floor below, the atmosphere was heavy with anticipation.

"What's up D.C.!" boomed a charismatic voice. The crowd hooted and hollered as all attention turned to the stage. The voice belonged to the lead singer of the female trio, Tantrums 0f G3nius, who would open tonight. They met in college and started making music together. Although the numbers zero and three that stylized their name signified when the act formed, back in 2003, but it was also a nod to the ladies' prior stint at college as accounting majors. They were three of the most attractive and brainy young women Cory had ever seen; their beauty matched their talent note for note.

Tantrums 0f G3nius was led by the charismatic firecracker Justice Jonez who took the club on a wild, hour-long ride of a fusion of Hip/Hop, Funk and Rock sounds. The song set ranged from tunes about bad break ups, gossip, political awareness and just good clean fun. The crowd went wild as the girls strutted across the stage and struck dramatic poses.

Drea Novella, usually the quieter songstress in the trio, took the lead on the song that pushed them to the top of the charts when they debuted.

"Come on, clap your hands everybody!" she yelled into the microphone. "Y'all remember our song 'Grad Party'? Come on now; scream if you graduated college this year!" The crowd roared and cheered.

"Yeah, college boy swag!" said one guy close to Cory.

"Alright, alright," said Drea. "Now let me hear you if you graduated high school this year! Come on, let me hear it!" The second wave of cheering was just as loud as the first, only more enthusiastic with hoots and whistles shooting all throughout the entire club.

"Alright, yeah," yelled Cory, pumping his fist encouragingly. No matter how you looked at it, this particular song reminded everyone that one quest had ended and another one waited right around the corner. All of this energy reminded Cory of many of his favorite things from high school, including music; but they were all things that he and Frankie had shared. As bittersweet as the memory was, Cory jumped to the party mix as the lights and nostalgia engulfed him.

Toward the end of their set, Tantrums 0f G3nius slowed things down as Michelle sat center stage. Surrounded by Justice and Drea seated on stools they switched things up by singing a cappella. As a single spotlight highlighted the ladies, the crowd grew silent. The group sang of the importance of taking one's time and of the good and bad times we face in life. Then, piano keys joined the ladies until Michelle was the only one singing, having transitioned to a beautifully operatic voice.

"My God," exclaimed Cory, shaking his head in wonder. "They are so eclectic in their style." Not far from him, Cory heard other fans in the darkness express their wonder as well.

"Her voice is so powerful," said one girl, recording on her phone.

"I swear, that's about my life," some guy blurted.

It was amazing how three girls who had mapped out one path for their life could turn so sharply in different direction and both surprise and unify so many people. In Cory's mind they were still accountants, but in a different form. They absorbed the feelings and energy of the crowd, processed them, and dispersed them back out to the sea of fans. Even though the main attraction hadn't taken the stage yet, Cory knew that the emotional reckoning that Justice, Drea and Michelle performed for them was the inspiration a lot of people needed. He knew for certain their music hadn't been wasted on him.

After the lengthy trip from Portland to Sandbridge with Ken and the talks they shared, the interesting uncle and nephew he met on the pier, the isolation, and the heart-to-heart with Ms. Senor to reevaluate some of his past and creativity, Cory was beginning to sense the dawning of a new season. He felt the small beginnings of a rebirth in his soul.

"Before we say goodbye," said Michelle, "we're going to sing one last song for you guys."

The drummer started things off on the high hat. Soon, the bassist joined him. Finally Justice strutted to the front of the stage, spewing rap lyrics into her microphone, flanked by Drea and Michelle. Over and over again the ladies of Tantrums 0f G3nius continued to challenge the audience to look past the superficial and let go as they closed out the show with a funky beat that included trumpets and a saxophone.

"Come on, be the change you want to see tonight!" asserted Justice. And with that, all three of them leaned back dramatically, ending on a superb harmony while stamping their feet together as the last beat fell.

The crowd went wild as Justice, Drea and Michelle curtsied and strutted off stage, waving and blowing kisses.

"God they are so sexy, dude," stressed one of the many male voices the surrounding Cory.

"See, this is exactly what I needed after the week I had," said an exasperated female voice.

"Divas from start to finish," commented yet another woman in the crowd. "God, I love it!"

Instruments and pieces of equipment clinked and clanged as stagehands rearranged the stage for the main attraction. Cory used the break as an opportunity to visit the bathroom. Returning to the balcony, he checked his smart phone while the stage below was still being put together for Underfed Angels. He'd missed a voicemail from Ken Ellis.

"I'm supposed to be on vacation," Cory joked to himself. *Quit harassing me officer, I'm supposed 2B getting away from it all*, Cory wrote Ken in a text message.

Nobody can harass U if UR career is over ya little diva LOL, read Ken's snarky reply.

Cory's eyebrows rose up and a tight grin formed on his face as he replied back.

Bringing up the past isn't a good idea. I'm still on suicide watch down here, Sir, Cory retorted, going along with the childish joke.

Enuff of that b4 I send a team down there. Been a few weeks, how R U? Ken replied.

In D.C. at a show believe it or not, UR 1 true love Miss Senor hooked me up 2 c ...Underfed Angels! 9:30 Club!!! Cory wrote back, thumbs flying over his keyboard.

0_0

That was the last thing Cory saw on his phone before a big drumbeat rang out from nowhere and everywhere all at once. The crowd screamed out as Cory stretched to see what was happening on the stage. But there was nothing except darkness and the silhouettes of various instruments onstage. "Where the heck are they coming from?" Cory said aloud. The answer came from directly below.

Parading through the crowd on the ground floor was a processional led by someone holding up Christmas lights on poles. Someone else held up lights on the end; drumming in the middle was Everett Hot Wings and the rest of Underfed Angels.

It was quite a sight. A four person drum line bouncing up and down, taking in the cheers as dozens of cellphone and camera lights flashed all over the club. The light show created by the band was simple in form, just two poles on each end with lights on wires suspended from end to end. It was almost dream like. The stage was lit up by a giant white dinner plate and equally oversized spoon, fork and knife that began pulsating bright blue as the band made their way through the crowd. "Oh my God," said Cory, beaming from ear to ear. "These guys really own this food theme!"

And adding to the excitement was the sudden return of the three harmonious female voices delivering energetic vocal runs over the drum beats. Manning their instruments and picking up their microphones, Tantrums 0f G3nius and Underfed Angels took the stage together.

Lights flashed everywhere and the giant size eating utensils glowed like blue fire as Tantrums 0f G3nius and Underfed Angels performed their collaborative masterpiece.

"Admit it, y'all," yelled lead vocalist Bryan Fearless Guest, donning a steampunk aviator hat, goggles gleaming. "There are some people in this world you've been around for so long... you think you really know them. And then out of the blue, they surprise you!"

The room erupted. Everyone was jumping up and down and screaming, including Cory. He hadn't felt this good in a long time. Underfed Angles had been with him for years, from his early teens to this very moment. They were his muse.

Over the next several minutes, things in the club got really funky again. Justice, Drea, Michelle and The Fearless took turns belting out their joint hit *They Might Surprise You*, while the Tantrums Band along with Everett Hot Wings and the Brothers Resurrecion beat and played on their instruments like their lives depended on it. All over the room people clapped, stomped their feet and bobbed their heads. Each time one of the Tantrums ' horns blared, every heart in the room felt as if it had been smashed to pieces and every drop of blood and joy wrung out of them.

Cory noticed that one woman was so overcome she fainted and had to be carried out. He didn't know whether to envy her passion or pity her for missing all the fun. All he knew was he wasn't going to miss a minute of this. This was the first full-length Underfed Angels concert he'd ever been to.

While growing up he'd seen other acts, many in large venues. Some were native to his hometown and others were more recognizable to the public at large. But somehow Cory had never gotten around to seeing his favorite band live. And doing so only got harder when he and Frankie formed The Kindred, although they did manage to see other famous bands in concert as inspiration to seize their music dreams.

Cory had seen performances like this before, but he hadn't been a part of it like he was in person at the 9:30 Club. After they performed their joint hit alongside the dazzling college dropouts, the ladies relinquished the stage to the four superstars.

"Give it up for Tantrums 0f G3nius, everybody!" Bryan cheered. "And thanks for coming out to Washington D.C. to hang out with us, to uh, "eat out" with us. As introductions go, ladies first. On drums we have the lovely Everett 'Hot Wings' Grier, the twins, Daniel on bass, and his little brother Jonah on guitar."

At the mentions of the two brothers all the ladies screamed at the top of their lungs, even Hot Wings. Daniel and Jonah both looked up smiling and waved at the crowd. "And yeah, ya'll don't care about me, right?" grinned Bryan, as a barrage of boos answered his facetious question. "Well, allow me to introduce myself. My mom calls me Bryan. But friends and enemies alike say... that I'm *fearless*." It's like the crowd just kept getting louder. Every time it seemed like they couldn't get any louder that is exactly what they did. And Cory loved every minute of it.

Bryan Fearless gave Cory the best that Underfed Angels had to offer that night. He and the band played every single song on their new *Starving Doubts + Devouring Our Fears* album, as well as hits from their previous records. And while playing certain songs, things got crazy.

When they got to the song *Snowball*, jet streams of white and blue confetti shot from the stage out into the crowd. There was so much that confetti drifted as high as the balcony and reached Cory. A bright light shone from the stage, igniting the whole room as he reached out to catch some floating near him. For the first time Cory was able to see how packed the 9:30 Club really was, how many waving arms and screaming fans had turned out, just like him. It was breathtaking; despite only a little over a thousand people filling the room, to Cory, it felt like millions.

Later in the set the band rocked out to an older hit. When it came time for the drummer's breakdown, Cory wasn't prepared. The next thing he knew, Hot Wings had somehow made her way offstage and to the center of audience. Balanced atop an apparatus of some kind, the spotlight illuminated her form and she hammered away on her single drum. Bobbing up and down to the beat, the surrounding fans cheered and jumped in sync. Then she froze, as did the guys onstage. After a few seconds they blasted the music again. The music froze once more, and an impish grin stretched across Hot Wings' face as everyone, including her, held their breath.

Once again the band resumed the song full force with a drum finale so strong that the drumsticks flew out of her hands. Hot Wings simply slid onto the hands of the crowd and surfed back to the stage.

But it was Bryan Fearless who stole the show. As the concert drew to its inevitable conclusion, Underfed Angels played the last song from the new album. Fearless sang of "just desserts", "heads on silver platters", "dishes best served cold" and a plethora of other topics and ideas, desperately trying to describe the human condition, all while balancing on a circular white object that looked like a dinner plate with Christmas lights strung into it. He wore a long white bib tied around his neck like a dinner napkin while still wearing his aviator hat with goggles that were firmly placed on his face. He sang as the upturned palms of adoring fans ferried the prop all over the floor of the club. Now and then, Bryan would stretch out his arms like an airplane, further dramatizing his stunt of surfing the crowd on a giant dinner plate. As the song drew to a close, Hot Wings rapidly beat on her snare drum while the twins aimed their guitar and bass heads at Bryan still surfing the crowd. The crowd howled with laughter as Bryan faked being shot-up off his plate and fell gently into the arms of his fans that passed him overhead until he was back at the stage. "Thank you, D.C." said Fearless, out of breath. "You throw a heck of a dinner party!" The applause went on forever.

Cory resumed writing a message to Ken on his cell phone. As he did so, he nonchalantly tracked the length of time from when the band exited the stage to now.

Ten minutes of straight clapping. Putting his phone away after sending out one last text, Cory rejoined the mob in cheering and whistling for Underfed Angels.

"FOOD FIGHT!" Fearless yelled from offstage. Cory gawked in the darkness. What was happening? Wait, he wasn't off stage. He was still on stage but yelling without a microphone and wrestling with some equipment.

Suddenly the crowd began to take up a new battle cry.

"FOOD FIGHT! FOOD FIGHT! FOOD FIGHT!" they cheered over and over again.

"Also known as encore," whispered Cory grinning and leaning forward in anticipation. Lights exploded onstage and three human forms jumped in unison. They were back onstage performing one last song and the crowd couldn't be happier. This time, Fearless wore a white plate on his head in place of his previous aviator hat and goggles. Daniel strummed a guitar in the form of a fork while his twin brother Jonah sported a bass in the form of a spoon. But it wasn't until right before the end of the song that Hot Wings skipped over and the three guys fell to their knees and bowed before her and Hot Wings struck a sassy pose.

"How much awesome can we take in one night?" said Cory rubbing his head exhausted from sheer delight. There was so much energy in the room that Hot Wings could cut it with the knives she held up. "Sixteen inch wooden knives as drumsticks," said Cory shaking his head in amazement. "These guys have thought of everything, nothing goes to waste!" Right then, Bryan and the twins lifted their heads; all three were now wearing the plates. Hot Wings commenced to skillfully tap out various complex drumbeats on the edges of each of her band mates' dinner dishes. Cheers and hoots filled the room. Then intense silence as Hot Wings played various beats at different tempos over the plates.

As if things couldn't get more remarkable, Bryan, then Daniel and finally Jonah, all managed to spin on their knees at different times, still in the same spot, as their drummer rapped over their plates, and pull out their vocals, guitar and bass and continue the song. They brought the pace down low, Hot Wings stomping her foot and the whole club joined her.

"Shhh," said Hot Wings, as she and the band played quietly. The audience stomped softly. She was amazing. Just as glasses filled with different amounts of water make distinct sounds when air passes over them, Hot Wings managed to turn out different pitches and cadences based on whose plate she hit, whether on the edge or in the middle.

"Do it, Hot Wings!" urged Cory.

The instrumental began to slowly increase in volume when Bryan yelled out.

"Pass the salt and pepper!" Two small maracas materialized in his hands and he began to shake out beats that accentuated those that belonged to Hot Wings. All the while the Brothers Resurrecion steadily played the guitar and bass, never skipping a beat.

"Turn up the heat!" Bryan yelled. The song got louder and one of the twins began to lightly beat his instrument in between playing the strings.

"Yeah," yelled a voice in the crowd.

"Crank it up!" hollered another.

Everyone was in sync with the music and everyone was feeling the mood. Finally, Fearless gave the signal for the finale.

"No more mild sauce," he yelled intently. "Raise the fire alarm, Everett!"

And she did just that. Strobe lights flashed as her hands moved like lightning striking the plates balanced on their heads. Fearless and the Resurreccion Twins sat still as statues as Hot Wings beat out the finale and shattered each plate, ending with Bryan. The lights went out, and the place exploded with cheers!

Track 08:
In the Company of Angels

"Oh my God! I can die and go to heaven now," said a female voice as the crowd began to disburse. People were milling about on the balcony and on the floor below now that the set was over. Cory agreed with the girl's sentiment. That show was the best he'd been to in quite some time, and an experience he wouldn't soon forget. Frankie would have loved this.

A rowdy group to the left undoubtedly enjoyed it. Cory noticed a group of guys, high-fiving and hollering, when a white object fell to the ground and bounced over to him. It was a golf ball.

"Whoa!" exclaimed one of the men with twists in his hair. "It's you from the pier!" Cory couldn't believe his eyes either. It was the young man who was fishing on Little Island Pier that day.

"Yeah, I was going to say the same thing. Ethan right? No Evan," said Cory correcting himself.

"Wow man, Cory Faber made it after all," said Evan excitedly. "These are my friends Tony, Sam and Ryan."

"Good to meet you guys," said Cory, shaking each of their hands.

"So this is the dude?" asked Tony.

"Uncle Nate and I didn't catch squat that day," explained Evan. "But it was cool to have someone like-minded out there, even though we only met for like a second."

"You made the three hour drive, Cory?" asked Sam. "This band is worth it!"

"It was a surprise from a friend really, and I got VIP tickets," answered Cory. "What about you guys?"

"Oh, we parted with the dough for the VIP tickets too," shared Tony.

The five moved into a line that had formed against the wall. All VIP patrons were treated to pizza on the balcony while Underfed Angels cleaned up for the meet and greet that would shortly follow. Cory and Evan continued to catch up after the plates and cups were cleaned up and the line to meet the band began to form. Bryan, Hot Wings and the Resurrecion brothers walked out in more casual wear, garnering cheers from lucky VIP fans.

"You in a hurry?" asked Cory.

"Nah, not at all man!" answered Evan for his friends.

"Well let's migrate to the back of the line," Cory instructed walking past fans. This way, the five friends could have the band all to themselves, and Cory and Evan could catch up while the line dwindled. As the line moved slowly, the four buddies explained to Cory about helping Ryan move that week. He and his girlfriend were going to have a new baby and he had been offered a new job.

"Yeah, Baby Momma breaking up the band, Cory," joked Sam.

"Shaddup," said Ryan, as Tony nudged him in the ribs.

"It's all love," laughed Tony. "Shoot, peep Hot Wings over there. Ryan might not be the only one smitten with the fever."

"She gives you fever, Tony," said Cory, going along.

"Ha, in the morning," began Evan.

"And fever all through the night," interrupted Tony, throwing his arm around Evan's neck. Even some fans ahead of them laughed in agreement. Hot Wings was one of a kind.

The ladies from Tantrums 0f G3nius couldn't escape evaluation either. But soon the conversation turned from physical beauty to the lyrical and artistic.

"Cory, did you see the movie, *The Good Fight*?" asked Evan.

"No, I can't say that I have," answered Cory contemplatively. "I did hear that song from earlier was in it."

"Yeah, man. I think Dennis Harley is a great filmmaker," said Evan. "And his musical selections and collaborations are on point."

Cory, Evan and the guys talked about other movies and music that they liked all while getting closer and closer to meeting Underfed Angels. But it wasn't long before they were so deep in conversation that they forgot that's what brought them together.

"Yeah, rap doesn't belong in a period piece movie," said Cory.

"I get what they were trying to do," offered Tony.

"Why did that duo change their style?" Ryan asked later.

"Oh yeah, thank God she got her voice back!" exclaimed Sam.

"I noticed his lyrics improving, too," agreed Evan.

"He's in that band that pronounces their name 'Castling'," answered Ryan.

"Did you say *castling*? Please explain my good man," said Tony.

"Yeah RO_Ok looks like it's spelled 'Rook' like in Chess games," said Evan. "It's a play on words. They just stylized it but that's how you read it, it's Castling."

"Yeah sounds nerdy," said Ryan. "Rocky says its portable game, something notation?"

"Who's Rocky?" asked Cory.

"Oh, that's my girlfriend," replied Ryan.

"You're girlfriend's name is Rocky?" Cory questioned with his eyebrows raised.

"Rocky, it's short for Raquel," laughed Ryan.

"See why we're trying to save him?" said Tony. "It's all science, inertia fields and board games with that girl."

"She's fine, Ryan. Cory, don't listen to these clowns," said Evan.

"Yes, yes she is fine!" declared Tony.

On and on they went, laughing and questioning each other on various music topics with Cory and Evan right in the thick of it. It was like they just picked up from where they started that day on the pier. Only now they felt more liberated, courtesy of being in the presence of their favorite music. Even though they had been unaware of each other at the venue, maybe, in a manner of speaking, angels had brought them together again. If there was one angel looking down on this little celebration, it was Frankie. Hot Wings joined the music that Bryan, Daniel, Jonah and Lewis had made together and it meant the world to Cory and Frankie. It was the soundtrack to their lives.

It's like you don't want me to be alone, thought Cory.

He was so deep in thought that Cory jumped when Evan tapped him on the shoulder, bringing him back to reality. He didn't realize he had zoned out.

"Yo Cory, the girls in front of us are almost done," said Evan pointing ahead. The girls that were in front of Cory earlier were posing with the band as the chaperone snapped photos for them. The two girls smiled and said thank you, hugging each member of the band. And then, it was Cory's turn.

Without realizing it, Cory took the lead, shaking each band member's hand. Evan, Tony, Ryan and Sam followed suit. The moment was surreal and Cory didn't want to miss a minute of it. If there was any small talk that was the only thing Cory missed because the next thing he knew, he was talking and couldn't stop.

"Your music defined us for the longest time," he began. "Sure everyone says that, but it's true. Frankie would call me Corny Cory when we were young musicians because nothing I came up with was original; I was the prince of clichés. He laughed at me because he knew that was being as genuine as I could be. We always dreamed of meeting you guys."

For as long as Cory spoke, no one could take their eyes off of him. He just took the microphone, as it were. To Evan, it was like a big weight was being lifted off of Cory's shoulders. The band was a sight themselves. Surely they had heard gratitude like this from millions of fans before. But they were in awe of Cory and hung on his every word. For Cory, 'Underfed Angels' music was frenetic and alive, subtracting and reacting. Frankie once said there are songs for every emotion but Underfed Angels had songs you needed to hear over and over so that you could find the answers you were looking for. Sometimes the emotions had to conform to the truth, even if it was painful. Their music could help you do that, mold and conform the truth you needed in your life.

Sometimes you needed to morph into something new by listening to their music. Other times, listening to the band's music was like a friend or parent dispensing tough love, telling you about yourself, even when you already knew you had messed up. Every now and then you had to take that bitter guilt trip when you listened to their music.

At the same time, their music was uplifting. It gave the feeling that someone was making a stupendous promise of better times. The dreams they dared to imagine in a world like ours summed up Underfed Angels' music. The music was like that: constant and enticing. You loved and hated it because of its essence. Their stories were like the clique in school that everyone wanted to be a part of but knew they were unworthy. Still, you yearned to be counted deserving enough to be granted admittance. Cory managed to express all of this to the band. It was like he was feeding them instead of the other way around, the way the band had intended. After all, it was their *Starving Doubts Tour*.

Suddenly, Cory wasn't talking anymore. No one was; even the chaperone was speechless. Finally, Hot Wings broke the silence. "I think everything you just said is exactly why we made our music, and why it was time for this album to come to light," said Hot Wings, lightly touching Cory's arm. It seemed to Evan that Cory hadn't noticed he was breathing a little heavier than usual, and the young woman's touch calmed him down. Looking over the other band members he decided to chime in.

"I think you're personally a great example of that during this tour," said Evan standing next to Cory. "You stepped up when the others here needed you the most. Things were a little bit dark for the fans, too." Tony, Sam and Ryan all nodded their agreement.

"You have to know when to say enough is enough," Fearless added somberly.

"We have to stop feeding our doubts and fears and attack life head-on when the fears are too weak to do anything about it."

"Not to toot our own horn," said the elder twin, Daniel, "But as people, we have to be that elixir of life, the ambrosia or manna from Heaven, if you will. We didn't write that because of how high we might get on the charts. Those words and sentiments really got us through some hard times."

"Indeed," added the young twin, Jonah. "We put a song like that on the album after we lived it. We knew our fans would sink their teeth into something like that. We have to nurture each other. It still amazes us that even though we don't know you all very well, we can add something real here and there. And you all do the same in your own way, like your friend here."

At that, everyone looked to Cory who smiled weakly, taking it all in with his hands in his pockets.

"This really is what it's all about," said Ryan. The others made space so he could be heard.

"It isn't easy connecting," he continued. "But I can say your music is spot on. More people should fight harder to engage in the relationships that are out there. But opening up and looking out for others can be scary. I'm lucky though. I'm getting married later this summer and I can't believe I get to tell you this. But my fiancé and I, our song is your song *The Flame*. It describes us perfectly and I wanted thank you for writing it."

The guys all looked at Ryan.

"Marriage dude?" asked Tony.

"I was waiting for the right time to tell you guys," answered Ryan proudly.

"Good for you, man," said Sam.

"Oh you're gonna make me cry," squealed Hot Wings. "Did you get the ring?"

To his friends' amazement Ryan pulled out a little black box and showed off a dazzling diamond ring.

"Oh, how sweet," Hot Wings said excitedly. "Do you know how you're gonna propose?"

"Slow down, girl," said Bryan. "Don't interrogate the man."

"I have to make sure he does this right," she asserted.

"You've never been married. How do you know what's right?" asked Fearless.

"I *know*, don't ask questions," said Hot Wings, with her hands placed firmly on her hips.

"Okay, it's time to get her to bed," Fearless joked while gently patting Hot Wings on her head.

"It's about time for all of us to get going," said Evan.

"Would you like us to sign anything before you go?" asked Daniel.

"Or take any photos? Steve doesn't mind," said Jonah, nodding at the chaperone.

"You don't have a drum set you want me to autograph do you?" asked Hot Wings with an eyebrow raised.

"I don't think so," laughed Sam.

"I kept expecting someone to pull one out," she said, taking out a black permanent marker. "I already signed this guy's drumsticks as it is."

The friends each had some merchandise for the band members to sign. When they were done, each one took a picture with the band. Tony was last and managed to get a shot of him kissing Hot Wings' hand. Finally, the friends parted ways with the band but not before they asked Cory a question.

"You grew up with all these guys?" Fearless inquired.

"Feels like it, but no," answered Cory. "I was thinking about my friend Frankie. He couldn't make it."

"Aw, well I'm sure he's here in spirit," added Hot Wings.

Cory couldn't help but smile.

Outside, the five of them walked out to the parking lot feeling refreshed.

"That was deep, Cory," said Tony. "You always like this?"

"Believe me, Tony," said Cory. "I don't know where all of that came from. I hope I didn't come off too strong."

"I don't think so, bro," encouraged Evan. "They really seemed to soak it up. Real ice-breaker and it beats the awkwardness of first meeting them."

"So you're headed back to, where is it, Little Island, Sandbridge, Cory?" asked Ryan.

Suddenly, Cory stopped dead in his tracks.

"No," he said. "Not before making a call first."

"What's up?" Sam asked.

Cory reached into his pocket and pulled out his cell phone. Evan looked concerned and then noticed glass mixed in with the gravel and tire tracks.

"I want to report a stolen vehicle," said Cory to the 9-1-1 Operator.

"Mine."

Track 09:
The Open Road

"LOVE" greeted Cory's eyes as he came up from sleep. Giant white letters L-O-V-E were displayed proudly on the lawn of the Rest Area. The message "Virginia is for Lovers" sat inside the glass filled "O", welcoming them home as well as travelers from near and far.

Exhaling softly, Cory leaned his head back again and shut out the world except for the sounds of the highway behind them and folks getting in and out of cars throughout the parking lot. The concert had really taken a lot out of him. His car had been stolen and here he was on a ride back with Evan, Tony and Sam. After Cory had reported his car stolen and met with the police, Ryan parted ways with them to reunite with Raquel in their little place back by Union Station. Evan absolutely insisted that Cory ride back to Hampton Roads with them. It was already remarkable enough that they had reconnected with each other at the same concert. As far as Evan was concerned, Cory was the perfect replacement for Ryan. Giving Ryan a hard time about moving to D.C. and getting engaged was all in good fun. They were growing up. That's how Sam put it, having known Ryan the longest. Busting each other's chops was how the young men coped. So Cory had to accept the ride. Even if he had worked out rental car arrangements, the silence would have been overwhelming compared to riding with this motley crew. They were a show all to themselves and you couldn't pay to find entertainment like this. But since they hadn't cut a CD for the comedy routine, Cory settled for a few hours' drive with them back to Sandbridge. They would have to go past Virginia Beach to get there, but Tony and Evan assured Cory it was no trouble at all.

"Are we ever going to get back on the road man?" Evan asked Tony sarcastically as the two reentered the X-TERA Tony's uncle had lent him. Tony was at the wheel on his phone answering messages.

"Yeah, yeah my bad. Chill out," retorted Tony. "These women man, jeez. I leave the state for a day and it's like the world's come to an end. They can't live without me. You ever been to Puerto Rico, man?"

Evan looked in the back seat at Sam and Cory. Sam was fast asleep. Cory appeared to be asleep as well, until a smile spread across his face. Evan shook his head and chuckled.

"Uhh... no? Whatever, I guess these two in the back aren't in a rush," said Evan playing with his golf ball. "Go ahead T; touch base with your groupies. Let 'em know you're safe... I over reacted."

"You just mad cause you ain't got one," grinned Tony, despite his friend's sarcasm.

"Sir, I already got a woman, or did you forget about Camille?" said Evan.

"She's not worried sick about you, bro?" asked Tony.

"Dude, you know she had a professor change an assignment that's like half her grade," answered Evan. "I guess you forgot she was gonna come with us?"

"She was just gonna get stolen by Raquel if she'd come anyway man," chuckled Tony, starting the car and merging onto the highway.

Evan laughed and threw his hands up in the air.

"Would you chill with Ryan's girl, man?" he said. "What's with you? You better not be texting her too!"

"Ah, have a heart Evan," said Cory sarcastically, eyes still shut. "You've lost a good man in Ryan; Tony's just using the humor to cope."

"See?" said Tony, poking his thumb back at Cory. "Your boy here gets it and he's not even been initiated into the fold yet. How does he care more than you, Evan? I'm disappointed."

"Shut up, man," smiled Evan, looking out at the passing cars.

"After everything we've been through," continued Tony's lamentation. "Poor Sam hasn't said a word since we left."

"That boy probably could sleep through the end of the world," joked Evan, looking back at Sam.

"Ha, true," agreed Tony.

Sitting up in his seat, Cory checked his phone for messages. Uncle Ken had replied back to his text message saying glad he wasn't hurt in the car theft and for Cory to notify him if anything turned up. Cory half hoped the car wouldn't turn up seeing as it would cost an arm and a leg, and maybe a thigh, to get it back from D.C. to Sandbridge. Sure, he could cover the cost, but still this was an inconvenience to him. But he couldn't let himself get too stressed. He'd just have to make a point to get a rental when he got back home, if he had the energy. Putting his phone away he decided to join in Evan and Tony's conversation.

"Hey, I really appreciate this, guys," he said, leaning forward.

"Oh yeah man, don't worry about it," said Evan.

"No problem at all," agreed Tony. "We couldn't leave you out there stranded in the hood."

"Nice," said Evan, dripping with sarcasm.

"What? I wouldn't wanna be stranded out there myself!" said Tony earnestly. "And you and I both know you wouldn't last out there, Evan."

"Yeah," admitted Evan with a chuckle. "I can't even lie."

"So, you guys grew up together, I take it?" asked Cory.

"Yeah man, known each other for years," answered Tony. "We survived school together and everything."

"Yeah, ran Hampton Roads," said Evan as he pumped his fist.

"No, I ran Hampton Roads," corrected Tony. "I just brought you along for the ride as my apprentice."

"What about you, Cory?" asked Evan.

"Oh, I grew up far away from here," answered Cory. "Portland."

"Oh so you're from the East Coast? You down here for early vacation?" asked Tony.

"Oh no, not Maine, sorry," said Cory shaking his head. "Portland, Oregon."

"Whoa, where's that?" asked Tony and Evan in unison.

"Oregon?" repeated Cory, eyebrow raised.

"Sorry," said Evan. "I get that, it's just no one talks about Oregon. How is it out there?"

"Portland's a nice place," offered Cory. "The temperature stays in the mid to high 70's."

"That must be nice. Bet it's a regular Disneyland," said Tony.

"Well, it could be, but it's cloudy most days out of the year," noted Cory, adjusting himself in his seat.

"Are there a lot of people?" Evan asked.

"Well, I would put the figure somewhere around half-mil," began Cory. "So, it's a decent sized city. There is crime just like anyplace else. But, I might say that considering the back-woodsy reputation, there is probably a little more than there should be."

"Can't be as bad as here, though right?" Evan prompted, ready to compare Virginia Beach.

"Well, there are almost 9,000 violent crimes a year, which is still probably more than Norfolk and Virginia Beach combined," answered Cory shrugging.

Evan dropped his defenses in amazement.

"Deep," Tony chimed in as he merged lanes.

"Take robbery for instance," continued Cory. "There are over 2,000 per year and rapes are approaching 500. Those are relatively significant, I'd say. And that's why it ain't no Disneyland."

"Whoa," said a drowsy voice. "I thought it was tight living in Virginia Beach." Everyone turned to look at Sam as he adjusted in his seat and fell back to sleep.

"Y'all, I almost crashed into that car right there," said Tony wide eyed.

"Jeez, Sam!" exclaimed Evan. "That boy scared the crap out of me."

"Yeah," said Cory, rubbing his chest.

"Anyway," said Evan recomposing himself. "How do you know all of this?"

"Honestly, I guess you could say that Portland law enforcement gave me a crash course," said Cory. "Believe it or not, I think a portion of the crime rate in Portland, which is largely people against people, versus people to property, is because the sun doesn't shine that often there. It's like people's attitudes just simply change when it's cloudy and overcast the majority of the time. I guess they get uptight with each other."

"Like some gloom over the city," Evan slipped in.

"I think so. But all the same, it's the one and only home I've known and I think I've turned out alright." concluded Cory.

"But how is it you got here?" Tony probed.

"That trouble, well it touches everyone, you know," said Cory. "I knew someone...kind of like how you lost Ryan. Only he was not so lucky, since Ryan has a choice to come back."

"Like some of the stuff about growing up that you told the band back there," offered Tony.

"You could say that, yeah," said Cory.

"A girl?" asked Evan, just as serious. "I remember you talking about a girl at Little Island Pier?"

"No, no," said Cory, as he recalled the talk that day. "And I remember that, Evan yeah, but uh ... no he was my best friend. We were like you guys. His name was Frankie."

The car was quiet for a while as the three young men pondered what Cory said. Eventually, Tony turned into a gas station and Cory and Evan realized they were closer than they thought.

"I'm gonna fill her up, gents," Tony announced.

"I'll be back guys," said Sam fully awake now. "I'll go in with Tony and maybe look for the bathroom before we get back."

Cory and Evan remained in the car.

"Sorry about your friend, man" offered Evan, over the whir of the pump dispensing gas into the vehicle. I'm sure he was a good dude."

"The best, though he had his moments," said Cory, lightly smiling. "But his passing has been tougher on his family of course."

"Yeah," said Evan, nodding his agreement. "That's great how you both had the same love for Underfed Angels man. Tony loves music but we have different passions, I guess; he's the basketball star. It's great that I've had the chance to create music with Sam and Ryan. But the way you talked about Frankie back in D.C., even though I didn't know who you were talking about yet... I could tell you too were like, the same; you were bonded by the same thing. And that's special."

"Yeah, I guess I didn't tell you," said Cory as Sam got back in the car. "I had a little band too. We both were in it, Frankie and I."

"No way, dude!" said Evan.

"Yeah, were kind of Indie Rock/Alternative I guess?" offered Cory.

"Okay, on the road again boys," said Tony, jumping back in the car as he started the engine. "Who's starving? I know I am!"

"Wow, you're just full of surprises, Cory," mused Sam.

It would so happen that Evan, in particular, was very hungry – for another musician he and Sam could do music with. Ryan had just moved away as they had finalized the latest song for the EP he, Evan, and Sam had been putting together. Evan felt really good about how the EP was turning out but there was still that one song he was struggling with. Adding to that, he thought that they missed something. He did not know what that something was, but he'd know it when he saw it. Evan worked around these challenges and the EP would have a few songs. But the track hadn't been touched since that day Camille and his Uncle Nate had come for dinner. Evan really wanted to add one more song to the project but the difficult track eluded him. Now, an idea was forming in his mind.

The rest of the trip consisted of the four friends lunching on burgers, fries and stories about their music. As they neared Sandbridge, Cory shared some of the things he and Frankie and the band had done back home in Portland and how they found their sound. Evan listened intently as Cory continued on about learning the guitar, what Berklee did and didn't teach him, and what a great lyricist Frankie had been.

"Frankie was a wellspring of feeling and experience," said Cory at one point. "He really loved telling the story in his song writing. Some don't get that. They just want to string clever words together and get them stuck up in your head with a hook. We loved that too, but Frankie's stuff always seemed to me, and maybe I'm bias, like the stuff in Country music."

"Ah, but only you didn't do Country," Sam chimed in. "But you were probably telling epic stories just the same."

"Yeah," agreed Cory. "We learned how to share stuff with audiences because that's what our favorite musical acts did for us growing up, RO_OK, Underfed Angles and guys like that."

"Rocky explained that name perfectly," said Sam. "It's pronounced of all things, 'Castling'. See, sometimes a band doing clever stuff like that seems pretentious. But I don't know, I kind of like it."

"It's like he was saying," said Evan, nodding at Cory, "There's a story to the name. Every time you see the word 'R', 'O', underscore, 'O', 'K' it gets people talking if someone says 'Rook'. If they say the name wrong they get a crash course in where those guys came from. The band's roots in gaming and Electronic House music really come through, if you think about it. It tells you something about them."

"Yeah, I mean, of course every band name should do that," agreed Cory. "But it's a little heady, that band name origin and all that stuff. But little narratives or unique anecdotes stick in your mind and people like that it gives us something to identify with."

"There you go, dropping that hot knowledge again," Tony enthused. "You should be a writer, Cory."

"You tell him about Operation: Mustangz, Evan," asked Sam.

"Nah, what's that?" asked Cory.

"This was a while ago, but we were in church one time with Evan and his mom," continued Sam. "We were just starting to mess around with some song ideas when the minister said something about footmen."

"Say what?" yelled Tony squinting his eyes.

"I got it, Sam," Evan jumped in. "Yeah, it was about these guys in the bible trying to do God's work. But the prophet, or man of God or whatever, said if the people couldn't keep up with the footmen, then how, could they hope to contend with horses."

"There you go," agreed Sam, looking at Tony.

"Look bro, pay attention in church. I had no idea what you was saying," said Tony, hand raised in defense.

"Anyway," Evan continued. "It's not that impressive of a story, but on the way out of service we saw a guy running after his old Ford Mustang."

"What?" laughed Cory as he looked from Sam to Evan.

"I remember you two telling me about that. Old dude left the stick in neutral and didn't put his emergency brake on," laughed Tony.

"Pretty much," chuckled Evan. "But the next time we got together to play a little music, we got Camille to lay down some simple vocals to a jam inspired by that little sermon. After that we started calling ourselves The Mustangz."

"I always thought that sounded cool, old school and simple," said Tony grinning. "Like those old bands, you know? The jams our parents listened to."

"What did you guys call yourselves, Cory?" asked Sam.

"Kindred," came the answer. "Or, The Kindred? I forget, but yeah."

"Cool," Sam nodded, downing the last of his fries.

"Yeah, I thought so too," Cory agreed.

During the rest of the ride, the fellas referenced bands and compared musical techniques, until finally, Tony turned onto Sandpiper Road and they were sitting in front of Ken Ellis's beach house. Cory said goodbye to Tony and Sam and shook their hands. He and Evan walked up to the side door.

"Thanks again, Evan. You and your friends are good people," said Cory.

"Anytime, man," said Evan. "It was crazy meeting up with you after the concert man. What were the odds?"

"That's what I'm saying, brother," Cory replied.

"Listen man that was a good talk. You, me and Sam, have a lot in common," said Evan. "What do you say to a jam session sometime since you're in the neighborhood?"

"Oh well, Evan," began Cory.

"We're not a full band or anything, yet," interrupted Evan. "Maybe you could at least give a listen to what we're doing, give us some tips. You and Frankie sounded like you'd seen some things playing together."

Cory put his hands in his pockets and thought on his guitar. He hadn't played that thing in so long. Things were looking up, and his attitude was undoubtedly more positive. The concert had been just what he needed. Reconnecting with this young man, Evan, from the pier, was a bonus.

"I've been working on this song," continued Evan. "My girlfriend, Camille, she's great, man, and she's a great singer. She helped out before Ryan had to leave. I'm having trouble with it. Maybe you can help me figure it out, you know? Show me what I'm doing wrong, you know, be a fresh set of ears."

Evan wasn't asking him to sign another contract or demanding a cut of anything. Cory rubbed his head and sighed as he thought to himself. He was just a kid, fresh into the music scene that had a puzzle to solve and had the guts to ask someone else for help.

People didn't ask for help anymore, Cory mused.

"So... everyone's got a song to sing now, Evan?" chuckled, Cory.

BEEP! BEEP!

"Come on Evan," hollered Tony. "Let the guy rest. I gotta get the jeep back to my uncle. Kiss him goodnight and let's go. I won't rat you out to Cammie."

Evan's face was the picture of pure exasperation.

"That guy won't be there," said Evan straight-faced. "If that's what's stopping you, he won't be there. I swear on everything."

"Don't sweat it. I like Tony," Cory assured him.

"But yeah, man, I guess you're right. Everybody's got a song to sing," Evan concluded. "At least do it for my girl. She's got a voice that would make an angel cry."

Evan dug out his phone and pointed to a photo of Camille.

"You're not gonna leave her and us out to dry like that?" pleaded Evan melodramatically. "It's for the art."

Cory shook his head and smiled. "I guess if she's making angels weep then it's worse than I thought?"

"Yeah, man," agreed Evan. "We owe it to the gods to get this song tight! Oh here's my card, text me your number and we'll set it up."

"Deal," said Cory, shaking Evan's hand.

Cory leaned on the mailbox as he waved at the guys who pulled off down the road. He swirled his hand around inside the metal container to check for any forwarded mail when none other than Ms. Senor pulled up in her car beside him.

"Welcome back, handsome," she said, with that same yellow sun hat on her head nearly obscuring the windshield. Paris sat in the passenger seat panting.

"Where's your ride?" she asked.

"Had a little mishap back in D.C. but I'm alright," answered Cory. "Someone was having too much fun at my expense I guess. But I've got it under control."

"Just let me know if you need anything," said Ms. Senor.

"I'm working out getting a rental real soon," said Cory, resting his hand on the roof of the car.

"How was the concert?" she asked, pulling down her brown bug eye sunglasses.

"It was fantastic," exhaled Cory, nodding his head. "I'm grateful, Ms. Senor. Thanks to you, I ran into a buddy of mine there."

"Oh good," Ms. Senor gushed. "You hear that, Paris?"

At the mention of his name, the boxer pressed up against his master as if to get in on the conversation and interject his opinion.

"Yeah," Cory said smiling. "He's got some music trouble so I'm gonna help him out."

"That's great," cooed Ms. Senor. "Sometimes it's good to just step away and look at the problem through a fresh pair of lenses. Remember that teamwork makes the dream work. Listen, I have to run, Honey. I'm glad you had a great time."

"Me too," said Cory. And with that, Ms. Senor was on her merry way down Sandpiper Road.

"Teamwork..." Cory mused, "Makes the dream."

These words were interrupted by the sound of his cellphone ringing.

"Hello?" said Cory. "Oh wow, I must be tired."

It wasn't a call but a voicemail alert set to the same ringtone. His phone had still been on 'vibrate' since the concert. "Thanks to the combined efforts of the police and a tip from the station," the message was saying, "we believe we have found your car in Virginia Beach..."

"What are the odds, man?" said Cory to know one in particular.

Track 10:
Heaven's Gate

Several weeks after the D.C. show, Evan lounged about in his home studio, headphones shaking from the blaring of his music. Eyes shut, arms crossed and head bumping back and forth, the young creator's mind was solely on his business.

The room was previously a garage that had gotten little use since the car was never really parked there. Evan reasoned that since there was no basement, which is totally common for townhouses and homes near the water, this solution minimally gave him his own domain. Of course soundproofing was added to sweeten the pot.

"Let's see here," he mumbled to himself. "If I pan right, I'll get a nice fade.

BZZZ! BZZZ! Evan jumped a little as the sharp tremor in his pocket demanded he attend to the phone call.

"Evan, it's Cory. Whatcha doing man?" said Cory.

"Oh, hey, what's up, Faber? I'm laying down some tracks in my studio, that's all. "Evan reached for the board and turned the volume down. "What are you working on?"

"Absolutely nothing," said Cory.

"Maybe this would be a good time for you to see my studio," said Evan. "How about you check it out?"

"Sounds good, it's been awhile since I've been in a studio," Cory admitted.

"Oh and bring your guitar, Faber," Evan added excitedly. "Sam's at work, but I can introduce you to this song that's dragging its feet, ok?'

"I got it." Dead silence hit the line as Evan heard Cory hang up.

∞

Back inside the Sandbridge beach home, Cory cast a wary eye at his bedroom which contained his guitar. Exhaling, he stood up, picked up the case and carried it to the car. It appeared it was time for him and the guitar to call a truce.

"This should be interesting," he mused, as he drove down the road.

∞

Evan's mind echoed a similar sentiment. *Hmmm, this dude's done studio work before.*

Suddenly his music didn't monopolize his mind. As he drummed his golf ball, he considered this newfound friend. He wasn't drumming for long when his thoughts were interrupted by another series of sharp buzzing from his cell phone.

"Hey, Boo," came the sweet voice of Camille.

"Hi Cammie, what's up?" asked Evan.

"I'm Good, Daddy had to go into work for a while," Camille answered. "He's turning into a real workaholic and it's stressing him and me out... but yeah, whatcha doing?"

"Well, I was sitting here recording," Evan began. "When that guy I told you about, Cory, he called. I invited him over. Figure I'll show him the studio and let him hear that problem song I've been struggling with."

"I think I want to meet him," suggested Camille. "He's desperately different being from Portland. That's pretty far removed from your usual set of homies, and the little that you've said about him sounds interesting. My woman's intuition says he could be good for you."

"You haven't even met him, yet," inserted Evan.

"Exactly: intuition, Honey. I don't need to meet him," Camille laughed, "I'll be right over."

Evan knew Camille was good for him. It was her father who didn't necessarily like the arrangement. It was okay when they were in the lollipop stage. But he wasn't as thrilled as their friendship grew.

"No daughter of mine is going to be hooked up with no young boy who ain't got his head on straight and ain't going nowhere!" he always said. As far as Evan was concerned, this became her father's theme song. When Evan didn't choose to

go straight into college, that's when Mr. LaShea started tightening the reins on their time together. And when Evan found it lucrative to do some DJing and weekend band stuff up at Hampton and clubbing around Virginia Beach, things really got testy. Camille though, was Evan's supporter. Even when Norfolk State required much more of her time, she always found a way to work in some time for him. He could count on Camille.

Cory had been ambling along after returning from the concert with Evan and his friends. Things seemed very peculiar as curious events occurred regarding the concert: random kindness in the VIP tickets themselves, catching up with Evan at the concert, getting his car stolen and returned all in a day, and Evan wanting coaching on his song. It was all just so bizarre, but he didn't know why.

It was a miracle he'd gotten his car back. It had been ditched several miles from Virginia Beach. The police later said something about a possible connection to local thugs representing the Epps Yard crew. Low rent hoodlums nicknamed Yardees that were guppies compared to the sharks in the war on gang violence. But as Cory had learned, it didn't mean they weren't trouble. It was possible their ranks were spreading, but this was just speculation since the incident took place out of state. Cory's car had been the getaway car in a robbery close to the 9:30 Club back in D.C.; it was just a case of right place, wrong time. Thankfully, the car suffered little damage with just the broken window and a lever on the steering wheel. But the rumors of gang connection to his car being stolen had been on Cory's mind lately, causing him to think too deeply about Frankie's life choices. Seedy goings on had surrounded his death, which the police along with Cory's Godfather, Ken, were still investigating. He had answered all the questions he could surroundings Frankie's death back then, but it didn't stop Cory from interrogating himself from time to time. Life, it seemed, had a way of throwing him back in the hot seat whenever it wanted to, especially when similar circumstances re-entered his life.

But Cory, desirous to fight off the negative harpings, decided to think on the positive memories he had of Frankie. He decided to slowly return to music. As strange as it was, Evan's invitation after the concert was a welcome one. And so Cory had called him up to get his mind off of the ghosts of the past for one night.

It was late afternoon when Cory finally arrived. As Evan strode through the kitchen for a snack, he heard the limp *zing* of the broken doorbell followed by the immediate rap of the manual doorknocker. Evan knew it had to be Cory; everyone else knew that the doorbell didn't work. Balancing some milk and a paper towel full of gingersnaps, Evan welcomed Cory. As Cory eased in the door, his cowboy boots caught on the edge of the rug.

"Ah man, don't worry about that," Evan assured him.

Cory's six foot, two-hundred pound frame pounded floor as he walked, his hair tied into a ponytail. With gig bag over his shoulder, he appeared John Waynesque. Plain and simple met hip-hop fashion. Cory's Levi soft cut jeans and T-shirt with a sea lion quoted as saying "Save the baby humans" contrasted Evan's drooping jean shorts, which Camille jokingly referred to as 'men Capri's', simulated diamond studded belt.

At almost six feet, Evan peered at Cory while asking, "Can I get you anything?"

"Sure, I'll take what you're having," said Cory placing his gig bag down on the rug and taking in his surroundings. "Nice place you got here."

Evan fumbled with the bag of gingersnaps in the kitchen, "My Mom works hard but yeah, we do alright."

Evan placed the snacks together on a tray and called for Cory to take his gig bag and to follow him through the laundry hall to the garage.

"Come on in here," said Evan. "I call this door, 'Heaven's Gate.'"

Cory munched and eyed the setting. "Wow this is incredible...trim, line, remote punch in/out, pitch control, auxiliary busses, loop machine... you are the man, Evan, and nice sign out there."

Fumbling with EQ dials while popping in a CD; Evan was interrupted when a text message chimed on his phone.

"Hold on, man," he said. "Camille, my girl is coming by. Let me get the door."

Evan worked his way back through the laundry room and after emerging into the hallway, paused, grabbed the door and swung it open.

"What took you so long?" asked Camille.

"Cory and I were talking," answered Evan.

"I thought I was supposed to be the only thing on your mind," Camille said smiling as she spoke. Evan grabbed her by the hand, pulling her through the house. He led her to his studio, excitedly babbling about his talk with Cory. Camille was pleasantly surprised by his evident optimism toward the upcoming introduction. Arriving in the studio, she thrust out her hand to Cory who had risen from his seat.

"Cory, man," started Evan, "This is my girlfriend Camille - Camille this is Cory."

"Good to meet you, Camille," responded Cory while retaking his seat.

"And you also, Cory," smiled Camille.

"Yeah, I messed up on my way here," Cory said. "I made a right when I should have made a left at Indian River Road. I hate that app. I need a new one. "

"You use Phileas Fogg?" asked Camille.

"Yeah," said Cory, eyebrows raised. "How'd you know?"

"Lucky guess," Camille said. "A girl I know was complaining about that app, says it's *foggy* alright."

"Oh yeah, the Puerto Rican chick, Tony was talking about?" asked Evan grinning.

"Uh, yeah," Camille said rolling her eyes. "Anyway, try Jurneez. Or, I use Sojourner."

"Thanks, ok, I'll go with yours," Cory said with a smile.

As the three young friends snacked and made small talk (Camille helping herself to the few cookies that Evan left), Cory coyly pulled out his guitar, which got Evan's attention.

"Uh, give me a minute," Cory said, taking hold of the tuning peg on his guitar; "Give me an *E*... I need to retune... it's been a long time."

As Cory reacquainted himself with his instrument Camille kicked off her low-top sneakers and ventured a question about where he went to school.

"Well," said Cory, strumming a familiar tune he employed when loosening up to play the guitar. "I remember changing schools when I was just a youngster say third or fourth grade. It was a tight time. I mean I'm young, ya know? So, I get there and I'm trying to see who's gonna be my friend or not. This school was in the city versus my other school."

"He means urban and they were Black, right?" shrugged Evan on the *E* key.

"Well, you said it," was Cory's response. "So... already... I'm not fitting in. There was a little corner store right across the street from the school. I remember like it was yesterday – a little red brick joint, with places to live upstairs. The kids would go to the store every day and buy junk food. Well, some rough necks would just take what they wanted. I didn't want anything to do with them. One time I was in the store and they wanted me to cause a distraction, so that they could pull off the shelves what they wanted. I wouldn't do it and they didn't like that."

"See?" Camille leaned in. "Now that's some stuff."

"There was about three or four of them," continued Cory. "And they decided to jump me outside the store, had me cornered right there on the front steps. I guess I was a coward, didn't know what to do. Suddenly, out of nowhere, a lady across the street starts yelling at them to leave me alone and they did."

"So, it was cool?" Camille reached for snacks.

Evan twisted in his chair with a frown, "Naw, his rep was damaged."

"The lady got me out of that situation," continued Cory. "However, I had been trying to make some friends. Anyway, there were a couple or so, who would walk my way home. I thought we were getting close. Sometime after that, this group was walking home with me, when I realized something was up."

"You mean someone was following you?" Camille asked in between bites.

"No, I saw a few of those dudes who tried to jump me earlier," Cory said while fine-tuning a string. "They were ahead of us, hiding behind a building. So I wanted me and my friends to speed up – I just wanted to get past that building and fast. Well, they said, 'no'. And, just as I suspected, the other dudes were waiting and jumped me. My enemies grew throughout the school years and they were relentless. I learned that I didn't really have friends. Except for one dude, and that was Frankie. He helped me out and dusted me off."

Cory stopped strumming. He had wanted to get away from the ghosts, not rush into a hive of them. Why was everyone so interested in his past as of late? He fidgeted with his guitar to distract himself for a moment from the memory and asked, "How 'bout a musical break? Let's look at that song you were telling me about."

"Yeah, man," agreed Evan thoughtfully. He handed Camille the rest of his cookies.

"It's currently *Untitled*, Faber. Here's what we've got so far," said Evan turning toward the keyboard and computer monitors.

The two musicians took to each other quickly. At least it seemed that way to Camille. Evan led off with the keys creating a musical tapestry of notes. He kept it basic, inserting some midi with strings to lay a foundation but still allowing room to show flares of direction to which the sound could go. Cory interweaved throughout the piece, demonstrating his versatility for not just ad-libbing, but also inspiring Evan to venture into new sounds. The sound of the acoustic guitar added a dimension that expanded Evan's traditional hip-hop palette with a more mature feel; the intersecting of cultures left Evan reeling for more.

For the first time in a long time, Cory felt weightless as he strummed his guitar, gradually approaching that heavenly place again. Frankie had a point: concert for God indeed! This was where Cory belonged.

Shifting to autopilot on the keyboard and allowing the loop to roll for a while, Evan quickly fumbled through his papers and thrust some unfinished lyrics Camille's way. Camille was used to his ways and she began to hum a little as she got the feel of the words paired with the instrumental. After a few bars her melodic voice began to embrace the microphone. Cory lowered his levels a little while turning his head. He raised one-eyebrow in approval. Like fish swimming in a school, the group would flow in unison. The men were bobbing their heads in time; Cory couldn't hold back any more.

"This girl can blow!" he said excitedly, losing himself in the moment.

"Man, you're doing other worldly solos on that guitar," bellowed Evan.

"I'm used to making sure I can do it all," said Cory as they gradually slowed down to a finish.

"I like not having to depend on anyone else for the sound that I need," he concluded, breathing heavily.

"Yeah, you got some versatility," said Evan. "You have a way of like, introducing her lyrics and you got that thing singing with her."

"Yeah, Cory, it's like we had a duet going," sighed Camille.

"Imagine what we could do with some back-up," inserted Evan.

"I dunno. It's cool to me the way it is." Cory re-bagged his guitar. Something just didn't feel right to him, his hands were shaky, and the high was gone.

"No, but really Cory, I could sense a whole lot going on here if we just got some more backup. I have to call Sam." continued Evan. "Wait, are we quitting now?"

"Look, I just think things are solid as is…I'm just saying," Cory rose with his gig-bag.

"This is the puzzle I was telling you about and we were on to something," said Evan perplexed.

"Oh... yeah," Cory said, pausing and looking from Camille to Evan. "Right... okay well, I mean it sounded good. You know it's just these soft hands."

"I'm sorry?" said Camille, angling her eyes at him.

"Yeah, you know Evan. I haven't played in a while." Cory faked a chuckle. "I'm getting my music hands back and they're getting sore. I was too aggressive on that one, I guess."

Evan and Camille exchanged glances.

"I need to get back. My Godfather was gonna call me about the house," Cory lied. "You've got a great voice, Camille. You're right Evan. She almost had me in tears."

A couple of hours had passed as early evening began to approach. With the engine running, Cory checked the antifreeze in his vehicle before pulling out.

Evan leaned over the engine with Cory to assess things.

"You need any help dude?" he asked.

"Naw, man – I got this," said Cory.

Pausing before getting into his car, Cory turned back to Evan; he seemed smaller.

"Look man," he began. "You've got something good in there. Camille's voice is great. I'm just a little rusty. Sorry I couldn't stay longer."

"Hey, that's fine man," assured Evan, resting his hand on the hood. "There's no rush. I mean, I want to finish the song but I didn't expect you to knock it out of the park the first time. Team work, man."

"Yeah," nodded Cory as he got inside his car.

"Take your time," said Evan. "Maybe it was a rush with you getting back in the game? Sorry if I got too excited there. It was just so abrupt how you ended it."

"Thanks... I better get going," said Cory.

"Next time, man," said Evan. And with that, Cory pulled out of the drive way and headed back to Sandbridge.

Evan stood there, hands in his pockets. *That was a little awkward*, he thought...way more interesting than he'd expected.

"He's pretty cool," Camille said, walking up beside him.

"Yeah," agreed Evan, still peering out onto the road. "He's different - definitely keeps you on your toes. You have to be ready for anything. But he's genuine... it's kind of refreshing."

"What was that stuff about his hands?" Camille asked as they walked back to the house.

"Guitarists get welts on their fingertips when they play," Evan informed. "It looks easy but the more you play it, the tougher the calluses get."

"Oh," said Camille, hugging on Evan as he shut the door behind them. "Sounds ... tedious."

"I heard about it once," he said, kissing her on the head. "It's not that bad - necessary roughness to achieve the sound you want."

Track 11:
The Experiment

A few days later Cory found Evan among the fishermen of Little Island Pier, just where he'd asked him to meet.

"Hey Faber," waved Evan, leaning against the railing.

"Hey Evan," Cory greeted him. "Sorry I'm a little late. I was catching up with my neighbor, Ms. Senor, on the way."

The two made small talk. Sam dropped Evan off after they had a brief jam session. Evan was excited about the progress they'd made on his conundrum of a song. Evan revealed he'd recorded the music they'd made that night and he played it back for Sam today; apparently Sam was excited too.

"Want to listen?" asked Evan, taking out his phone. As Cory nodded, Evan played back the recording.

"That's excellent, Evan," replied Cory as the recording ended. "That's what I wanted to talk to you about. I am sorry about that night. I can really see now you were in your groove."

"Again, no pressure, Cory," Evan replied, as a nearby fisherman cast his line out to sea.

"I know, man," Cory began. "Look, you were right Evan. I wanted to be ready but I pushed myself too hard. I think I could have been. I had a lot on my mind that night. I'm, I'm kind of introverted and all that sharing brought to mind some old wounds...Frankie was on my mind heavy that night."

"Aw wow, man, we had no clue," said Evan, rubbing his forehead. "You had like ... a moment huh? Sorry man."

"It's okay," Cory assured him. "I called my Godfather Ken... I didn't really have to call him that night, but I did."

"Yeah, I figured something was up," said Evan.

"I mean, I did have to call him," said Cory. "But I was...I just couldn't deal that night with you guys."

"What did your Godfather say when you finally called him?" Evan asked, looking out at the horizon.

Ken actually echoed a few things that Evan said to Cory, and then some. It was good that Cory wanted to be free. Clearly this trip was doing him good, as long as he paced himself. But it was true; there was no spotlight on Cory to become a renewed musician overnight. In fact, there was no expectation that Cory had to resume music ever again. This time was for him, for Cory, stressed Ken. If that did include music, so be it. Cory needed to find himself again and heal on his own time, to find out what he wanted to run toward, not away from. Cory was undergoing a rebirth, coming out of his chrysalis and rediscovering his life again.

"That's deep, Faber," Evan said, after taking in Cory's recount. "You're so serious. But you're doing what you have to do. And we didn't mean to pry. I do feel I know a lot about you. But you know, share only when you want to share. I can respect that...we're good man. It was just awesome of you to care enough to help a brother out."

"I do what I can," said Cory, looking out over the water. "I'm glad I managed to give you something to work with. I was good for a while there, though."

"Yeah," Evan agreed. "Your sound is just - wow man, it's what I was looking for, but I didn't know it."

"It did feel good to play again," smiled Cory. "I have to work my hands more on those strings. It's like when an athlete stops training for a while and goes back on everything he worked for, and then he tries to run a marathon. No way!"

"I heard that," said Evan. "But it's cool, I can tell you're about your business."

"Oh wow, and Camille?" said Cory, wide-eyed. "You really found something in her, my friend. She's so flexible and at the ready. You just threw her those lyrics and she was ready to sing!"

"Great chemistry!" said Evan, nodding his head.

"Oh yeah, man, you guys could be telepathic one day," Cory enthused.

As he and Cory laughed, Evan caught a glimpse of a familiar face out of the corner of his eye. For a moment, his whole countenance changed.

"You alright?" asked Cory, concerned.

"Yeah, just somebody I used to know," answered Evan. "Let's get out of here, Faber."

As the two friends walked down the pier towards the parking lot, Evan leveled with Cory.

"By the way, my Godfather's beach house is down this way," Cory offered.

"Sounds good, Faber," Evan said. As they moseyed down Sand Piper Road, Evan told Cory about some of his past.

It's true; Evan had been searching for direction for his music, for his whole life for that matter. He hadn't known his father and it somewhat troubled him that his family, and especially his mother, didn't like to talk about the man. Evan had seen people come and go in his life, and like anyone, it was hard when you felt like you couldn't connect to someone.

"It's like those chords you were talking to me about the first time on the pier," admitted Evan. He too, felt he was progressing down a path that very few could understand and at a pace and frequency often times cryptic to him. Thankfully, a few people like Sam, Camille and Tony could roll with him. They were hustlers like Evan. But life was still happening around them and he wanted, needed something more specific, more definite.

"Kind of like life itself getting in the way of your plans?" asked Cory.

It was something like that. Evan, Sam and Ryan weren't musical geniuses but they put in as much work as they could toward their music. When experimentation became more focused and the EP began to form, they had some of the best of times. But it was hard to rehearse and record sometimes and the project took longer than expected to complete. The last song was giving them trouble but they were nearing the homestretch when Ryan became a father and found his new opportunity.

"I couldn't be pissed at him," Evan said, eyes glued to the road as they walked. "Ryan was starting a new life - a family! They needed him more than I did. I couldn't stand in the way of that."

"Yeah, of course Evan," Cory agreed. "But go back. Who was that guy you got rid of?"

BeBe was an old running buddy of Evan and Tony's growing up, but he'd fallen by the wayside. At least that's how Diana had put it. Evan was *okay* with BeBe, but he knew they'd never be close, not like he and Tony were. But why Tony put up with him was anyone's guess. Maybe it was because he partied at a different tempo than Evan. This was clear when Evan, Ryan and Sam had been invited to the university to DJ a party. BeBe and some others snuck in some dope. One thing led to another and Evan found himself running from a police bust. Thankfully, he and his friends weren't caught or hurt, but it was a close call. Evan owned up to his family about it and since he and his friend's weren't suspected of anything, the family realized Evan had learned his lesson. Even BeBe got off scot-free, but that was the last time Evan trusted him.

"His step-dad back there on the pier was a stand-up guy," said Evan. "But, you know, Faber, sometimes ghosts come back to haunt you, even in the decent people… it sucks."

Cory nodded in agreement. He knew that for sure. Listening to Evan vent his frustrations was a welcome change for Cory. Usually he was the one unloading all of his past drama on others. He hadn't been in this position in a long time, that is, the receiving end, offering an ear to a friend who needed it. Most of his friends had long gone.

The fact of the matter, Cory revealed, was that Frankie had been killed after a drug bust gone wrong. This caught Evan off guard. Cory, Frankie and the other members of The Kindred had a good thing going long ago. They had savored local success in Portland, and enjoyed radio interviews, CDs, digital downloads, and a devoted following. But fast life and inner demons got the best of Frankie and their managers. Cory watched The Kindred's dream collapse as his best friend lost himself to drugs too. Worst of all, it cost Frankie his life. After the Kindred broke up, they were under investigation for distribution of controlled substances and a murder scandal.

"Frankie was better than that," Cory lamented. "That girlfriend of his poisoned him against us. But I never thought she'd bring us all down. I know she loved him... she was our friend... we used to believe in each other."

"I don't know man, trust is hard. Sometimes you don't even give people that much. Still, the little that you give, they flush down the toilet like it's crap... that's too bad, Faber, I'm so sorry," Evan said, his voice flustered and shaking his head.

"I know brother," Cory said directing Evan toward the house. It was early evening when they arrived. Stepping inside, they relaxed at the picnic table inside the sunroom, Evan on one side and Cory on the other.

"Sorry, dude," Evan said shaking his head again. "And I see Tony and BeBe together sometimes. Tony's my boy, for real. What's up with that though?"

Cory could see that Evan was getting uncharacteristically edgy and changed the subject.

"People have to learn for themselves," he said. "But, don't let it tear you up, Evan. There are still some of us who are trustworthy. Or at least, there are some left worthy to do battle alongside you to earn that trust."

Evan looked up, surprised.

"Are those more proverbs from the mountaintop, Faber?" Evan inquired.

"Something Ken said to me. "I just paraphrased it a little bit," Cory answered.

"He sounds like a cool guy. Where is he?" asked Evan.

"He's back in Portland. You'd like him," said Cory. "You know what? How's your Uncle Nate?"

Evan raised his eyebrows and thought about it. Rubbing his hands together, his mood completely changed.

"Oh yeah," he began. "My mom told me a while ago he went out of town on business or something. All I know is that he works for himself. Maybe he was invited to a conference or something with types like him?"

"He seems trustworthy," probed Cory.

"Yeah... he is man," said Evan rubbing a groove in the table. "You know? We really didn't see eye to eye, him and me. But he surprised me big time. Like the day after - or really the night you and I met, Faber."

"What happened?" asked Cory, leaning in.

"Bro, I don't know," said Evan, giving a chuckle and taking out his trusty white golf ball. "He's just starting to understand me. You know, I just didn't get some stuff he said that night, but he cleared it up as we drove back home. Man to man. What he wanted to happen out on the pier happened in his truck! He finally got my attention. He was speaking my language. It's like he finally heard me!"

Cory listened to Evan relive the night he connected with his uncle. From what Cory remembered about that night, the little he saw, it looked as if Evan and his uncle had a long road ahead. He was glad things turned around for Evan that night.

"What happened to you in college is fascinating, Faber," Evan said. "But Uncle Nate, and soon my mom, I hope, both begin to realize it's not for everyone. I'm doing the best I can. I'm not out of the race yet. I set a goal to finish this EP and that's what I'm gonna do. I just want to make good music and figure this out. I want my shot at making this dream a reality, but it's that trust thing man."

"What do you mean?" Cory asked.

"I want to make my own way," Evan began. "Look, as you can see I've made mistakes, but I'm focused. I got the right people around me now, and sure, things are moving slowly. But this EP is gonna happen. And with everything from the Internet to DJing to meeting you, I'm more driven than ever to finish this. I put in the work, learn my lessons and I get results. Not as soon as my mom or I would like, but I get them. She and my family were into music once and they were good. Things didn't go as they planned, but I can't give up so easily, Faber. It's in my blood."

Evan was now breathing heavily. He was visibly fired up. And Cory, to his amazement, was fired up too.

"You want something to drink?" he asked Evan, getting up from the table.

"Yeah, sure," Evan said, tucking away his golf ball and following Cory inside.

"Well it sounds like you've got it all figured out, Evan," said Cory, handing him a bottled water.

"Yeah," Evan said, taking a swig of water. "Yeah man, I just know this is the right thing to do, and I'm not alone. I have friends and I network and there are people who look out for me. I know I have skills but I'm not scared to ask for help, or grow."

"Skills plus passion is a recipe for success in my book," Cory said, grabbing a water bottle for himself.

"We're trying," said Evan, taking out his phone. "Oh, I need to call Sam. Hey what's this address, Faber?"

As Evan talked to Sam on his phone an idea occurred to Cory. It seemed that Evan's fire was contagious.

"Hey Evan, where do you DJ?" he called. "Got any gigs lined up?"

∞

Club Soul-Light was the hangout spot for those who wanted to party with their friends. The place was blanketed by darkness. Periodically, light beams danced like tourists on the boardwalk as they navigated the establishment. Music circled the room as bodies rhythmically swayed to the beat. The universal language spoke to its citizens in offbeat cadences. Its tone was that of a feathery tenor with a bottom of full-bodied robust bass. Club Soul-Light's patrons were the 'at ease' nineteen and twenty-something year olds who were vacillating between tourist-boardwalk-hacking careers and the sheer adventures military life promised to offer. Most had the decision made for them simply because the boardwalk did not have a retirement plan.

Cory learned that Evan was a periodic DJ at the club, and once a month the owners changed things up and provided a platform for local talent to showcase their abilities. This was that night. It occurred after several rehearsals that included Sam and Camille. Evan cued things up from his usual perch as DJ, this time accompanied by Sam. Sam, Cory learned, was a musical jack-of-all-trades. Evan invited Cory, toting his guitar, to come up. He smiled, while enjoying Cory's entrance, wondering what the reception was going be like for this 'country-looking dude coming up in here'.

The initial reaction of the crowd included 'boos' and 'hisses', with references to country music and which side of town was more appropriate. The manager signaled the audience to calm down and to show some respect. Then he eyed Evan, for general principle. After plugging into an amp and running through a scale or two for tuning, Cory got the audience's attention.

"We got this," he heard Evan whisper.

Without much fanfare, he attacked a hip-hop riff on an acoustic while inserting a few runs. The crowd settled down with the mounting tension. Feeling the groove, Cory nodded to Evan and Sam who, on cue, found some spice off the synthesizer to compliment Cory's groove.

"This dude is hot," someone called from the crowd.

"Play it, my man, play it," offered another.

Cory hit the change, and the three musicians transitioned into the song that had eluded them for months. Tonight, Club Soul-Light witnessed the unveiling of the band's long search.

Out in the audience, Tony shared in the experience. He was no stranger to the allure of Club Soul-Light, especially when Evan was going to work. But tonight he had a guest with him that caught Camille's eye as she prepared to approach the microphone. Camille had one opportunity that would either go over splendidly, or wind up a disaster -- maybe even cause a rift between her and her beau. She was going to enlist Tony's guest and fellow partier, Jasmine, for a little background vocals.

Camille and Jasmine weren't what you would actually call friends. They met during choir in high school. The two competed for solos and actually had more of an adversarial relationship. They both enjoyed music and had done the usual *hey girl, we ought to get out together sometime* thing, which never happened. Tonight, with Evan and Cory's dynamism and her own energy intensifying, Camille dragged Jasmine from

Tony's arm and took her to the side of the stage. The last time Camille felt this confident and intuitive there was only water and speed involved - but that was a long time ago, another life.

"Why you got me up here? What, I know we ain't singing, girl!" Jasmine frowned in amazement. "What's going on?"

"'Because you're the only one who *might* be able to keep up with me," said Camille as they ascended the stage. "Just flow girl – follow the music, and get on the same page with me. High school wasn't that long ago," blasted Camille.

Jasmine glared at Camille, blurting out insults in Spanish as she grabbed the second microphone. She and Camille were known by their teacher to be the most impulsive and intuitive singers he'd ever had.

"You won't be sorry," assured Camille.

Evan's braids bounced in the air as he swung his head to the beat of the music. Sam, too, shook his head to the beat. Everyone let the sounds escort them to the dance floor. Camille and Jasmine harmonized their vocals to perfection, with enough compromise to accentuate each of their individual talents. Years hadn't changed a thing about the two's chemistry on the mic. Camille led Jasmine along to a chorus that expressed frustration over the lack of an identity and a purpose. Finally, as the song ended, Camille and Jasmine leaned back to back as Cory tore out the final riff. The audience roared; the experiment was a hit.

Evan and Sam had to wait to get to Cory, as patrons lined-up to give the artist his due.

"Man, *that* was happening for sure," blasted Evan. "You came out of the gate running before we even got to the transition for the song!"

"Good thing we decided to keep it simple," began Cory. "I had to convince them that I had a few skills. Then produce a little something that they were comfortable with. I'm not gonna say that part was easy, but using the minor pentatonic scale was a good call, Evan, it expands things a little bit.

"So slick, Cory," Evan enthused clapping his hands together. "Man, they went after it hook, line and sinker."

"But truth be told, folks don't generally follow a stranger," Cory responded, as they all met up by his car. "They like going somewhere new with someone they already know. It's always about taking someone beyond where they've been before, expanding their horizons.

"That expansion you're talking about," Evan offered.

"Yes," Cory continued. "In fact, Evan, I bet your biggest success is not only taking the stage, but also building a platform for others to play from. And you know, take us somewhere new."

"Whoa, it's a little muddy right now from all the reverb inside my head," Sam laughed.

"Not for me. I got it. I'm holding onto that Faber," said Evan. "I think what we got here is the start of something real!"

"Evan, I think so," Cory said, as the two shook hands, acknowledging that something very real indeed had just been forged between them.

Across the parking lot, Camille and Jasmine discussed the results of their musical maiden voyage.

"Girl, I was surprised that you were able to keep up with me," said Camille. "I might have to watch my harmonies just so I can keep up with you."

"Yeah, yeah, mi amiga, whatever," Jasmine said, while winking at Camille. "You are lucky I didn't just run you over with my skills."

"Uh, oh, *friend*? Does that mean that maybe we could call a truce?" asked Camille.

"Girl, it would be the musician's loss if we didn't," Jasmine smiled back at her.

"And the ball player's gain, Baby," said Tony, coming up from behind and sweeping Jasmine up in his arms.

"Come on, Jasmine. I'll introduce you," said Camille.

Camille joined the three men giving them a big hug, while Jasmine gave a Hollywood wave and the guys dapped each other up. After giving the ladies their props and commending Jasmine for being quick on her feet, they packed away the remaining equipment and called it a night.

Track 12:
Contending With Horses

A few days later at the Spencer residence, Cory and Evan sat in Heaven's Gate studio waiting on their friends to arrive. Evan had called a meeting after the night at Club Soul-Light, telling them he had something important to share with them. When Camille, Sam with Tony, and finally Jasmine arrived, Evan flipped over his *ON AIR* sign outside the door. Back inside, he had everyone's undivided attention.

Cory had already heard most of what Evan had to say when Evan came to his beach house. He even forwarded his new big idea to Ryan back in Washington D.C., who wished him luck. Evan appreciated the support from close friends like Tony and his Uncle Nate, and he was proud of the work that he, Ryan, and Sam had accomplished on the newly named *The Mustangz EP*. He expressed gratitude for the addition of Camille and Cory on the final track, which they had titled *As I Walk*. Last but not least, Jasmine, whom everyone was gradually getting to know and whom Evan definitely wanted at the meeting, didn't go unnoticed after her impromptu contribution at Club Soul-Light.

Jasmine was a no-nonsense, what-you-see-is-what-you-get young woman. After their duet the other night, she and Camille made good on their truce and the two became friendly. Camille had never had a close girlfriend, and neither had Tony for that matter, which didn't bother the Puerto Rican spitfire. Camille thought it should, or at least he should give some thought to it. But they were all getting to know each other and forming some kind of cohesive unit as friends and as soon to be band mates.

"Real talk," said Evan. "Jasmine is totally down with lending backup vocals for *As I Walk* and we're gonna record it today!"

A little round of applause erupted for Jasmine, followed by a whistle from Cory in the corner, and a kiss on the cheek from Tony.

"I'm up for the ride guys," she smiled. "Really, it was cool singing with Camille again, singing at all really! It's been *years!*"

After a final update from Sam, excited to be adding a drum kit, and Tony, naming himself their number one fan, the gang went out to lunch to celebrate.

"The Mustangz are complete, y'all," Evan yelled as he led his friends in a toast.

Performing *As I Walk* at Soul-Light would be the first of many monthly open mics that Evan and Cory would team-up to perform. When their schedules permitted, the whole band with Sam, Camille and Jasmine were right along with them supporting on soundboard, percussion and vocals. Rehearsals began to become a way of life. Word spread as various club owners were talking about bookings and there were whispers of plans to take things to the next level to promote *The Mustangz EP*. Evan and Cory took it in stride. But when people began to recognize them and stop them on the street to request a CD or a link to find their music, it was motivation for them to get better organized.

∞

The group had made quite an impression on the music scene in the surrounding Hampton area. One sunny day at the boardwalk, there had been a chili cook-off and other activities. At the center of the boardwalk, just shy of the bronze statue of King Neptune, was the pavilion that served as an amphitheater. The pavilion sat nestled between the street and Neptune's ever-present gaze. A fair number of onlookers watched the activities. The stately hotels hosted those enjoying a meal as part of their outdoor dining experience. Fabric from the hotel awnings provided a drum roll against the air with the wind beating out the rhythm. As the breeze swirled, it created an environment where the wind-transported acoustics allowed the music to be heard for blocks away. On the nearby beach a boy and his dad turned towards the sound as they lifted their hands urging a kite that soared easily on the ocean breeze. Encouragement from clubbers, as well as pressure from Sam, Camille and Jasmine, drove Evan and Cory further out into the streets. Now that they had ventured more out into the open, they questioned whether folks who were not from the 'club' scene were going to appreciate what they were trying to do.

The wind whistled past the sound hole on Cory's guitar and the instrument seemed to moan without any assistance from anyone. Cory had been under the pressure of performing many times. His hands steady and fully awake, he was unfazed by the added stress.

"Man, I'm feeling the flow could really be in the pocket today," Cory suggested to Evan.

"I got you on that one," echoed Evan.

The assistant manager at Soul-Light had agreed to step in as emcee and was coordinating the day's activities. When the sound of funk hit a particular groove during the warm-up, the emcee toyed with the audience; he even jumped down off the stage and tempted girls in the audience with his moves, going so far as to give them the microphone to sing as he howled a few lines. Everyone was having fun.

Cory's steel string guitar vibed fluently. Evan was on keyboards and mixing grooves, head bobbing to the beat as Sam manned the drum kit. This expanded their sound, topped-off by Camille and Jasmine on vocals. There was a synergy evolving and a creative heat brewing hotter than the summer sun.

The crowd started to swell as restaurants gave up their patrons. Nearby hotel clientele began to find their way to the scene. The emcee prompted the crowd to give it up for the ensemble, and the audience responded enthusiastically. The manager announced that the group was making headway on the local music scene. The crowd chanted for an encore and the band yielded, as dancing couples began to pepper the grassy patch under Neptune's careful watch. Taking their last bows, the group retreated backstage to catch their breath before breaking down their equipment.

"Girl, you were slammin'," said Camille, as she hi-fived Jasmine.

"I was," gasped Jasmine. "But no bonita, *we* was slammin!"

Together the two laughed and hugged singing "we da man," when Cory snatched their bottled water and poured it on them.

"I do hereby christen you – ya da, ya da, ya da," he laughed.

"We are turning it up, man," said Evan pumping his fist in the air.

"Definitely hitting our stride, we get better every time," Cory added.

The two continued talking as everyone began packing up the gear. Eventually Cory and Evan were off to themselves collecting everything when the conversation turned to comparing organic styles of production and more structured styles. Evan recalled the music starting off like that for him and Sam when Ryan was still living in Hampton. Evan mused that a lot of music must start that way: free flowing, natural and organic, as Cory put it. Then gradually it starts to take shape, go in a specific direction and *boom,* a structure presents itself for a musician to live in.

"Yeah, Evan, I guess life is just one big education," said Cory as he took a seat in front of the stand where the keyboard once stood.

"Now how is that, Faber?" Evan asked, after handing Sam a piece from the drum kit.

"I dunno Evan, to me it's like which came first, the chicken or the egg?"

"How'd you put that together?" asked Evan, plopping down next to his friend.

"Well, you mentioned structure versus organic...Berklee taught me that when you get the basic structure down first it's easy to flow and to the audience the music seems organic. Don't get me wrong it is, but some organization helped. Then when folk listen to musicians flowing in the pocket they may not realize that there are guidelines for that part too."

"Cory, I know the music, I just didn't apply it to life. Sometimes the structure feels like manipulation."

"Ev, you know better than most - people don't like being manipulated," said Cory flexing his fingers like a magician.

"I hear ya, Faber," yielded Evan.

"It's not just that. It's like people won't let you just be who you are," said Cory, acknowledging a wave from Sam.

"See, that's the kind of stuff that pisses me off," snapped Evan. "Even when they want what you've got to offer, the music, it's like it's got to be on their terms. Everyone's got their terms, trying to control you some kind of way."

"Evan, that's why I respect you trying to get to your terms," Cory admitted. "Even when I would do what I do, back home I'd rather have it on my terms. Structure or flowing in music or even the managing part can be slippery too, not all but still."

"True," Evan said as he handed Sam a case. "Man you've seen some things."

"Yeah, man," Cory agreed, circling the last of the gear. "Otherwise, it's like you're prostituting yourself out. And it's like what you've been talking about, getting control of your life. No matter what your mom or anyone else says, put out what you say you're putting out and the way you say you're doing it."

"Glad my uncle got that message," Evan concluded. "And I'm glad you dealt with those vultures yourself, bro."

"Cool, but just don't forget to make the transitions when the time comes," Cory cautioned. "Not all management is parasitic...when trust is found, they can help you manage your life, not just your career. That's what I'm learning."

"You gents ready?" asked Sam, walking back.

With that, Cory snapped the last case latch into place, and the three friends exited the pavilion under the eternal watch of King Neptune.

∞

Trust was an ironic topic for Cory and Evan to discuss. Shortly thereafter, things changed dramatically one night at the Club Soul-Light when Cory was not with Evan. He had been invited to attend a local family BBQ with Ms. Senor, and Evan was back to doing his solo thing at the club, like old times.

"Evan! Play me something good," pierced through the fade between songs.

"Yo, you know I gotcha one, Tony," Evan shot back through the crowd. "Looks like you got something good right now." Evan eyed Jasmine attached to Tony's side.

"That's what I'm saying," hollered Tony. "We just got to keep her this way."

This night began no differently than any other, Evan with his computer mixing at the club while Tony spun his female flame around his finger.

Evan played the next song, fronting with some verbal hawking to fill the dance floor. "Hey, watcha gonna do with *the I love you?*" he yelled into his mic. "Don't let this song start without the love of your heart."

As the music flowed, Tony nodded his approval while yielding to the call of the living room sized parquet floor as it beckoned he and his partner to stay.

"Do you love me?" Jasmine whispered in his ear.

Tony slipped in a well-worn response. "Just as sure as the sun rises, baby".

He swayed to the beat, "Baby, when I make it big-time, you are gonna be with me."

"Do you really think they'll take you, T?" asked Jasmine, her chin buried in his shoulder.

"There's no reason why they shouldn't?" Tony said confidently as his hand descended the small of her back.

"I was talking with BeBe the other day" whispered Jasmine. "He's pushing everyone to support you in the Hampton Roads Classic."

"Yeah, he's alright. I gotta hand it to him. Sometimes he ain't too smart though," Tony said in a voice low. "Once he got ID'd at school for something stupid, but faculty was confusing him with Evan. And so instead of taking advantage of the situation BeBe goes ahead and cops a plea, totally implicating himself."

"But T, do you think that would've been right?" Jasmine inquired slowly. "Wouldn't Evan have gotten in trouble?"

"Not necessarily," said Tony. "It was a simple case of mistaken identity that could've worked his way. It ain't his fault that he and Evan got similar mugs, but anyway..." Tony turned her with the rhythm of the music hoping that was the end of the discussion. But Jasmine wasn't finished as she pulled Tony close.

"Okay, Tony. BeBe says they're taking money on your showing in the Classic." Even in limited light, Jasmine's stare was piercing. Feeling uncomfortable with the conversation and the focus of BeBe's loose talk, Tony minimized the comment.

"Baby, it's just the fellas having a little fun," he smiled. "No harm, no foul."

"But sweetie, betting on your games is... risky. No it's wrong," Jasmine said, pressing the issue without raising her voice. "If the cops found out it could mess up everything."

"Lookie here now, that's why they ain't gonna find out," Tony said, arms stiffened as he pulled away. As the song rounded the change, Tony grew uneasy about the intrusion into his business.

"Life's about living, and that's what I'm going to do. Besides, I personally may not be able to pass on some sure money like this," he said. Then more soothingly "Now you come on up in here for some more of this loving and let it calm your nerves." Tony's arms gently swallowed Jasmine. His words enticed her but the real satisfaction came when her and Camille's eyes met. Jasmine had landed her man and the look she gave Camille communicated her success.

Across the dance floor, Evan cued up the final series of songs with Camille on his arm.

"Ev, look at that, Tony's getting serious over there with Jasmine," smirked Camille.

"No, that's Tony over there dancing with Jasmine," Evan retorted.

"Why do you have to be so defensive about your boy?" asked Camille, a little defensive herself.

"He's a player" Evan said plainly.

"Player-wannabe," Camille shot back. "I can tell he's feelin' her. He ain't fooling nobody."

"He's got to dangle a little interest, got to keep his game up, ya know," Evan offered, wrapping the cord to a set of headphones.

"Yeah, but Jasmine is not a game, Evan" his girlfriend cautioned. "I've heard her talking and she's real serious about Tony."

"Well, if she'd have a word with the other girls, she'd have an idea that Tony likes to keep his eligibility intact with as many of the ladies as possible," Evan stated.

Camille just shook her head and looked back over at the two dancing.

"And why you all of a sudden defending her?" asked Evan.

"Evan this isn't just some sport we're talking about, she's a person," said Camille, voice full of conviction. "Besides, things are different between her and I now. And I have half a mind to let her know what the real deal is...at least if you don't say something."

"Keep your nose out other people's business, Cammie," warned Evan.

"Evan, Jasmine would be good - for a good man that is," Camille continued. "She's exactly what Tony needs. He just isn't smart enough to know any better, but it can pierce his thick head. I know it can. He listens to you, and Jasmine's one of us now."

Evan could only watch as Tony maneuvered Jasmine on the dance floor. It tore at his heart when Camille positioned him to act out of his comfort zone of enjoying the moment. But contrary to what Camille perceived as his cavalier attitude,

Evan didn't like the situation between Jasmine and Tony either. Truth was, she was right. Jasmine was good; a lot of the girls were good - for a good man. But as long as Evan had known him, Tony wasn't a bad guy, or a good guy. He was Tony.

The song faded to a close as the house lights went to yellow, signifying the last chance for alcohol had passed. Evan attempted to close up shop and find his way to Tony.

All of a sudden there was the sound of glass breaking. Then shots rang out. The pop of gunshots descended on the partygoers. Like a herd of frightened animals the patrons dove and huddled for cover under large tables and furniture. The blasts were sharp, broken by periodic gang calls.

"Yardees reign!" rang out in the crowd.

The assault lasted only a few seconds, which was an eternity to anyone caught off guard by the attack. Then, just as quickly as it began, it was over. The perpetrators escaped through a fire exit, which was satisfaction enough for the patrons.

Cursing, fueled by anger swept through what could have become a tomb for some. Everyone was angry at what had just happened and their inability to do anything about it.

"Are you alright?" Evan asked Camille as he lumbered back to the table that she had hidden under. He had been on his 'mission of responsibility' toward Tony when the ruckus started. It bothered him that he was not near Camille so he could protect her.

"I'm going to be fine," she replied. "I've just got..." her words were cut short by the frantic screams.

"Tony! Somebody call an ambulance!"

Tony and Jasmine were nearest to the gun shots and didn't make it to a place of cover. All eyes focused as Jasmine, down on both knees, cradled Tony's head as a pool of blood began to form from the crimson stream running between his eye and ear, and flecks of glass were mingled in his hair.

Evan, convinced that Camille was fine, raced toward his friend, pushing through the crowd of onlookers, panicking that his worst fears were realized.

"My man, don't do this to me...My man...Tony, say something...come on man." Evan's cries went unanswered. The only thing saving Evan as he slowly slumped to the floor was Camille's shoulder. She caught up with him in time to brace him from the full impact of his fall.

The ambulance attendants were uncharacteristically quick to arrive. Police converged on the club to ask questions, clear the scene, and to try to restore some order. The EMTs hoisted the gurney into the ambulance. Police were attempting to question Evan but all he could see was the blur of flashing police lights as he peered through his tears. Jasmine, feeling lost and unsure, pulled herself into the ambulance and glanced back at Camille. No one's life would ever be the same.

Track 13:
Triad

The lights in all the offices dimmed around him. The night crew commenced their usual janitorial concert consisting of sounds from the vacuum, broom and water splashing from the mop. Jake Daniel LaShea ended his temporary perusal of the Norfolk skyline through his office window. Pivoting on his heels, he misjudged his proximity to his mahogany desk, knocking the monogrammed pen and pencil holder to the floor.

"Ah...blasted desk!" he said, swiveling and bracing his leg. "That was my bad knee."

"LaShea," he mumbled to himself as he fell into his custom-made leather chair. "It's important that you be here. It's important that you do this..."

"Good night, Mr. Jake," called out the petite cleaning lady as she ended her work.

"Night Mrs. Washington," he replied. "Do you need me to see you out?"

"No problem at all Mr. Jake. Did you forget Buck and Steve are with me?" she asked poking her head into his office.

"Oh, yeah" said LaShea, recalling that the crew had grown a few months ago, along with the increased office space to accommodate his expanding business. Where was his mind?

Reaching into his desk, he juggled the blood thinning pills that he kept in containers that were color-coded by the hour. He guzzled chilled bottled water from the bar in his office, which brought him some relief. LaShea thought about his baby girl, Camille, and the family struggles. He protected her and that was his only world for now. He smiled as he caressed the family photo in his hand. *That* was why he had to be here. Not for business, not for pain and gain, he needed to be there for his family.

His music system kicked-in as the LED flashed 12:15 AM.

"Ah – two-minute warning," he said, rubbing his forehead. After working so many late nights, he had agreed to a compromise with Camille to at least warn himself as the night wore on.

"I can't deal with this now. I need to hear what's going on – I need to know that there's some life out there," he mumbled, turning the radio dial to the news.

∞

Diana dabbed Evan's head with a soft-warm cloth while she listened to Camille's version of what happened at the club. Evan laid there on the couch under his mother's care, somewhere between sleep and the realization of possibly losing two of the closest people in his life. It didn't hit him that his own life was a part of the equation.

Ever since her candid conversation with Nate about Evan, Diana made a gallant effort to see things as he saw them, and take her hands off the wheel to see what Evan would do. Things had been going smoothly. She'd even met Cory a time or two when Evan's band came over to rehearse. Evan appeared to be happy and in a good place. But tonight, Diana's worst fears seemed to be validated.

"Girl," offered Diana, "I just knew one day this stuff was gonna go too far. I just knew it. Child y'all could have been killed."

"Ms. Spencer, we didn't know anything was going to happen," sighed Camille.

"That's just it," interrupted Diana. "You never know when this stuff is going down. But I just thank God that you're alright. Lord, give me some space to breathe."

Thunder came as a knock at the door and interrupted their conversation. Handing Camille the towel, Diana made her move to the door.

"Who is it?" she asked hesitantly.

"LaShea," boomed the voice back.

Diana opened the door with a sigh as Evan sat up ready for the worse.

"What's going on?" LaShea spit out. "Spencer, my daughter better be alright."

"Yes, Daddy, we are *both* alright," Camille emphasized, rushing to her father, embracing him.

"I heard on the news that there was another shooting over at the club," he said, releasing Camille.

"The kids really are fine," inserted Diana. "Let me get you some coffee," she said, dashing toward the kitchen without waiting for a response.

"I'm not in the mood for coffee and chitchat," belted Camille's father.

"Daddy, you need to calm down," said Camille, trying to take his hand. But he was too excited to stay put.

"Well, what would *you* do?" LaShea asked, pacing the floor. "You've just heard on the radio that there's been a shooting at a club you've told your only daughter to avoid. And the man of the hour sits here quietly and hasn't said a word."

Camille tried again to take her father's hand and ease him into a chair as Evan pulled himself together to offer an explanation.

"Mr. LaShea, we weren't doing anything wrong," offered Evan while gathering his strength. "I was just working the set. In fact, we were close to quitting when these shots rang out and these dudes come yelling '*Yardees*' in the joint."

"But you shouldn't have even been in that kind of environment," blurted LaShea, interrupting Evan's story.

"Daddy! Give him a chance". Camille clutched her father's shoulder trying to settle him. He meant well and he's always looked out for her; they were all each other had.

But when is he going to trust me, thought Camille. She'd done everything right growing up, always been the model daughter. She was the shining golden apple of her father's eye. So why did he insist on overreacting and jousting, second-guessing her boyfriend? She wasn't hurt but that wasn't enough. He didn't even care that Evan had tried to protect her.

"Yes, please calm down," said Diana, gripping the tray of coffee and nearly slamming it down on the coffee table.

Sure, LaShea had a right to be upset - scared even. But her child, her baby, was in the line of fire also.

"Jake LaShea," blurted Diana, unable to contain herself any longer, "My son does not wake up with a goal of hurting your daughter! Let me remind you, he was in the place too. And don't forget, this is my house...and unlike you, I'm concerned about *both* of them."

"My best friend was hit, too...he's...he's," said Evan dazed.

"I DON'T GIVE A CARE ABOUT YOUR FRIENDS," yelled LaShea, causing everyone to jump. "In fact, that's the whole problem, the company you keep. If possibly you'd had a little more parenting in your life you wouldn't be running with these no-count hoodlums. They run the streets in packs like wild jackals with no guidance, no respect, and no hope...They might as well kill each other so we can avoid expending police resources on their worthless lives".

LaShea was practically hovering over Evan and his mother when he'd finished. Camille had never seen him so upset.

"Come on here, girl. Let me get you out of here," said LaShea turning on Camille.

Furious, Diana wasn't about to let LaShea leave without giving him a piece of her mind. One hand on her hip, she raised her other hand and wagged her finger in front of LaShea at point blank range.

"Jake Daniel LaShea!" boomed Diana. "You've got a lot of nerve coming up in here suggesting there is something wrong with my son and my parenting skills. You don't come up in here disrespecting me like that."

LaShea was done talking. He had his daughter and was ready to make a vindicated exit but Diana cut him off, her back to the door indicating she was not quite done yet.

"If I didn't have the fear of God in me, you'd be wearing that hot coffee," Diana said, looking up at LaShea. "In fact, 'cept for the fear of God, I'd burn your behind and ask for forgiveness later!" Diana slowly stepped from the door toward LaShea, backing him into a chair where he plopped down.

LaShea struggled to rise but mysteriously her 130-pound frame exploded in a burst of strength and the fulcrum called *attitude* shoved his 280 pounds back into the chair.

Not to be outdone, LaShea tried to rise back up for round two and with his right hand he gripped the chair while raising his left arm. Opening his mouth, unfamiliar words escaped as his sentences turned to moans of pain. Suddenly, he began to fall backward. He grabbed his left side to soothe the shooting pain running up and down his arm. Real time became blurry and images lost their shape and form.

Gripping his left arm he moaned, "My chest!"

"Daddy!" shrieked Camille.

"Oh my God, LaShea!" Diana shouted, reaching to support his descent, coffee cups crashing to the floor.

Suddenly Evan was out of his stupor and firing on all cylinders. He snatched the phone and dialed for help.

"Yeah, yeah we're at..." he said, giving his address to the 911 attendant.

Evan, phone between his ear and shoulder, helped guide LaShea's plunge to the couch. The man's chest buckled from inside with what seemed like the weight of a truck parked between his shoulders. The tingling in his left arm was so acute that his own grip became numb and the room began to spin.

"Cammie, I love you," said LaShea with a dry mouth. This couldn't be happening. From barely escaping a shootout to watching the strongest person she knew collapse as the lifeblood clogged inside his body, Camille felt utterly helpless. Why was this happening?

No, not Daddy too...oh God...Mommy I don't know what to do, Camille's mind screamed.

Evan had thrown the phone down and quickly found himself at knee height, hand on temple, checking LaShea for a pulse.

"No pulse...gotta get it going!" he said urgently.

Diana went into full battle mode, moving to LaShea's left side and grabbing a pillow to elevate his feet.

"Evan, what are you doing?" asked Camille frantically.

"Camille, we have got to get his heart going," said Evan ripping open LaShea's shirt to expose his chest. Working in tandem, Evan and his mother began to massage his heart. Diana had taught him well.

Relieved to hear the shrill sound of a siren, Diana burst out the door to welcome the ambulance.

"He's in here, he's in here!" she hollered waving her arms frantically.

The paramedics dismounted the vehicle and ran from the van and into the house. With effortless accuracy, they proceeded to work on LaShea. Camille froze while they prepared the paddles to shock her father back to life. The sound of her own heart was beginning to become audible when she heard the faint tone of the equipment as his heart started and they were able to get a pulse.

As one EMT radioed in his latest status, the other broke away to explain which hospital they were taking LaShea to for care. Diana tossed the car keys to Evan as he pronounced that he would drive Camille. The ambulance blared into the night, with Evan and Camille following close behind.

∞

Evan sat in his bedroom and rotated the white sphere around in his hand. He'd never really looked at the lucky ball that he had used when he bounced them around in a musical therapeutic manner. He wondered to himself what the manufacturer had in mind when they had named the line of balls.

"I guess whoever uses this one is deserving of the title," he muttered to himself. "In my case, the only titles being handed out are for *loser*."

It had been a few days since the nightmare of that ill-fated night. Mr. LaShea having a heart attack and his friend Tony nearly killed. It was surreal. Tony had literally dodged a bullet. Jasmine, when she was able to had updated Evan on Tony's status. She and the Jackson family had been allowed to see Tony, learning that he'd suffered a gash that narrowly missed his right temple. The sound of shattering glass Evan heard just before the shooting that night turned out to be a beer bottle being broken over Tony's head. He and Jasmine had been hassled by one of the Yardees, and then Tony and the attacker got into a scuffle. When the wannabe thug overpowered Tony by hitting him with an empty beer bottle, the rest of the gang took it as their cue to make their presence known by firing into the ceiling.

Evan was glad to hear that Tony was recovering well, slowly but surely. Whenever Evan could reach Camille by phone, he shared Tony's status. She welcomed the news on Tony's progress as she attended to her father. The good news was just what everyone needed to hear. With Tony's condition improving, they could focus their efforts on comforting Camille who was still shaken up by her father's ordeal. It wasn't looking good for Mr. LaShea, but hearing the news of Tony's recovery was encouraging.

Their friendship with Tony dated all the way back to grade school. Evan remembered he and his mother had experienced enough drama in their own lives with the mysterious disappearance of his father. They tried to rebuild and put their lives back together, which meant relocating. When they moved, Evan changed schools. Diana thought that, unlike other changes she had always known, this change would be good. Now, Evan stood at a new school, in the entrance of a new classroom, with only new friends to make and none to lose.

Evan was anything but poised. He was planted like a statue near the first row of seats in the classroom; the teacher encouraged him to find a seat. One student had an empty desk next to him. All eyes were on Evan as he made his way to the desk. His nerves got the best of him and he lost his grip on his books. The classroom erupted in laughter as the books fell to the floor. Everyone made wisecracks, except the young man with the empty seat next to him --Tony Gerard Jackson.

"Man, it could've happened to anyone," he'd said with that winning smile, helping Evan pick up his things. Ever since that moment, Tony had been on Evan's side.

Evan recalled another time when some seventh-graders had been threatening the fifth-graders. They would pick on them and antagonize them until the fifth-graders would fight each other. Then the seventh-graders would laugh, while they bet on who was going to win.

When Evan found himself in a fight with another student, Tony jumped in and wrestled the other kid off of Evan, risking his own skin because he broke up the staged fight. Unluckily for Tony, a teacher appeared who had seen the commotion, causing him to be temporarily suspended. Camille almost got in a fight with the bigger kids over hearing this news. It wasn't fair that Tony got in trouble trying to help Evan. But things turned around eventually when the Principal caught the seventh-graders who were bullying the other kids and expelled them. The three friends were together again.

But, times were different now and maybe his mother was right. Was the dream life really worth endangering his best friend? Could he afford to get lost in the unpredictable music culture? Maybe quitting his whole scene and getting a job, like hooking up with a grocery store chain was the right thing to do. It was certainly more stable, safer. But what about all of the work he and The Mustangz had put into their music? What about his new friends Cory and Jasmine? He didn't know. But now, with all of this going on, he needed answers. If it were possible, Evan would have started running toward the sunset and not stopped. With everything in him, he knew that he was doing the right thing. It just wasn't the right scene.

Evan surprised himself, suddenly longing for the counsel of his Uncle Nate. But he was still away on business. Things with him and his uncle were in a good place when he left. Evan had found a new supporter.

Maybe if I could reach him he'd give me the skinny on what to do, unbiased straight talk, thought Evan as he took out his cell phone.

At that moment the display lit up, it was Cory.

"I thought that I would give you a call and see how you were doing since that drama down at Soul-Light."

"Yeah Faber, how did you hear about that?" Evan asked, rubbing his temple, suddenly exhausted.

"It's in the papers, man," answered Cory. "You okay? Pretty tough to hear about Tony."

"I know. And on top of it all, Mr. LaShea's heart attack," answered Evan.

"Sorry you and Camille are going through this, Evan. It's a lot," said Cory. "Anything I can do?"

"We just have to keep it together, man," said Evan. "Things were looking up for Tony. I don't know how this is going to affect his games. And Camille is shook up by what happened to him and her dad; bad night bro."

"Camille's strong," Cory offered. "You're right though, we need to stay together. I'll visit with you too if you want."

"Thanks Cory, I appreciate it," Evan said, truly grateful. He was glad Cory and Sam hadn't been there that night. He was glad Jasmine hadn't been hurt, being so close to Tony and the thug that knocked him out. He and Camille got off unscathed though Evan was still furious he hadn't been near enough to Camille or Tony to be any good to them. He felt conflicted about having been in the middle of his best friend and girlfriend when chaos broke out, not being there for either of them when they needed him most.

For now Cory just wanted to lend Evan some encouragement and leave the newspapers alone. The sooner they visited their friends in the hospital the better. Cory felt it best to remain silent about the rumors concerning police suspicions surrounding Tony until there was more clarity. The police seemed to think that the Yardees were sending Tony a message; but what about? This was looking very familiar to Cory. But, no, things were different now, right?

Evan would learn the truth soon enough, especially if he and Tony were as close as Evan said, and hopefully before it was too late.

∞

"Yes, it's too bad. He was so strong, it was just his time to go," lamented the nurse, shaking her head.

"Excuse me," asked a middle-aged woman interrupting the nurse in the doorway. The woman sitting on the bed peaked around the nurse to see who it was.

"Ah, Gloria, hello," gushed the woman rising from the bed to greet her friend.

"Well see now I told you, I better get movin' earlier, didn't I, Dorothy," said the nurse smiling and waving at the two ladies as she left the room.

"It's good to see you," said Dorothy LaShea as the two ladies embraced.

"Congratulations, I'm so proud of you," Gloria enthused as they sat down on Dorothy's bed.

"I'm proud of me too. I've got a lot to catch up on. Thank you for driving me home today," said Dorothy, locking her travel case. "You have been such a good and dear friend to me."

The sun was setting on the soothing comforts of Friends House, a regional rehabilitation center for breast cancer survivors. Dorothy was going home. Long ago Dorothy had endured the mastectomy, where they were forced to remove one of her breasts. Although a fairly well educated and level-minded woman, Dorothy found herself battling suicidal thoughts as she wrestled with the healing process. No matter how much loved ones had tried to convince her of her innocence, she continued to believe that it was somehow her fault. She didn't want her husband to feel like he was trapped with, *the monster*, as she referred to herself. So, she went so far as to indicate that if he wanted a divorce, and perhaps it would be better, she would give it to him. After all, how could he continue to love, *the monster*? She resigned herself to an eventual demise and became reclusive, severing ties with family, friends, everyone – all who did not wish to see Dorothy endure the journey alone.

Gloria was a consistent visitor to Friends House. Whereas most people would at least consider visiting the infirmed, Gloria had made it, as she said, *a career move.* She had lost her own mother, who had fought a courageous battle against cancer last year. Gloria fought with her against the disease every step of the way and had moved her mother to the area after careful consideration. She invested large amounts of time and energy caring for her, always encouraged that although the journey belonged to her mother, she would not allow her to walk it alone. It was during this time that she met and became friends with Dorothy.

Gloria was a devout woman and Dorothy accepted her investment of time and encouragement as a friend at the House. The two of them always enjoyed rich conversation. Dorothy had slowly been exposing herself, until they had reached this climatic point.

"You see, what did I tell you?" said Gloria, taking Dorothy's hand. "God does not give His children bad gifts or things to hurt them. He will use everything that we encounter to draw us into a deeper relationship with Him. It's alright to have been angry with Him. You lost a part of yourself."

At this, Gloria gently touched the center of Dorothy's chest.

"But when you are done being angry," Gloria continued, "Remember, He did not put this thing on you. As a Father, He is good. He stands waiting with outstretched arms for your return, just like your husband and Camille."

Dorothy did not consider herself a religious woman. She recalled that her days as a business woman had cultivated an ability to observe people. When they showed her who they really were, she believed them, simple as that; time was money and money was power. But not anymore - she knew what real power was and she hadn't had it in a long time. Her strength and that of her family had been severely tested by cancer. But strangely enough, Gloria's enthusiasm and brief sermons didn't bother Dorothy in this place, especially when Gloria talked about family. Family is what Dorothy longed for. Visits from Gloria had awakened a yearning in Dorothy she had long forgotten -- no doubt dried up by the chemo as she had labored to get well. At least that's what she had told herself, but no more excuses. Like the king in the Bible that Gloria had told her about, Dorothy had gotten a second chance at life. She was cured. She hadn't gotten off unscathed, but she was alive and life was calling her.

All of these things warmed Gloria's heart as Dorothy expressed her gratitude and her renewed strength. She just kept saying she couldn't wait to hug her daughter again.

"Nothing can burn away a mother's love," said Gloria, resolute, "nothing. Your daughter is so blessed to call you mother, Dorothy LaShea. You never gave up. And though I talk a big game, your life has blessed me too; you're like the sister I never had. Oh, I just want to tell everyone you're coming home."

Dorothy and Gloria hugged once more and shed a few tears of joy. It was time for celebration; Dorothy was coming home. And though there was cause for excitement, it was Dorothy's wish that her return home be a surprise.

∞

The following afternoon, Heaven's Gate, pulled double-duty as Evan and Camille sought refuge within its walls from the past week's drama. Camille's once attractive physique had been overwhelmed by nerves and a lack of rest. Bags began to sprout under her eyes and the once pretty young girl was replaced by the shadow of a poster child for a stress relief drug. In an attempt to find solace, her headphones had become a second accessory to her hairstyle as she listened to a series of unfinished musical tracks Evan had on his computer. Evan explored the chords of a ballad in the making while he sat at the keyboard. He also donned a set of headphones as he went to work.

After a pause, Evan pulled off his headphones and, brushing aside a braid, exhaled and watched his girlfriend lay on the couch, still listening to her music. She looked so cold, arms folded like she was trying to ward off a wintry front. It killed him to see Camille looking so helpless and worn out. Surely there was something he could do.

He had an idea. He switched seats and went to one of his laptops and pulled up a playlist of original music he'd been compiling. Waving to get her attention, he beckoned her to take off the headphones and listen to the songstress floating out of the external speakers.

Peace and quiet pounding on my ears
Amongst the crowds the roaring bands
The closer you are, the further I appear
Seems like the essence of your plan
You are never, never, never, ever, alone

"You are something," said Evan, hitting the Stop button. Outside there was a light rain. The two sat in the silence of the moment, Evan's comment lingering in the air. Finally, Camille broke the silence.

"Evan, I just don't know if daddy's going to make it."

"Don't talk like that," he replied, eager to keep her spirits high.

Camille sat up and set the headphones down and shook her head. She had a lot bottled up.

"This is too serious. With every visit the doctors tell me he's not making progress like he should. This was not a one-time event; it has been building up over a long period of time."

"Cammie, we have to be strong. It's a matter of figuring out how to handle this thing," offered Evan.

"We can't, *just figure it out*, Evan!" Camille snapped. "Don't you get it? There are some things that all you can do is react to them. There are no *do-overs* and no Rewind button."

"Calm down, Camille," Evan said soothingly, sitting next to her. Camille looked away; she was trembling, even her voice.

"Evan, my whole world's falling apart. I thought I was strong. I can't take this. Just when it looked like things were improving at school..."

"We can cope with this, baby," said Evan, taking her hand gently.

Camille couldn't take it. Why couldn't Evan see it her way? Cope? She shot up out of her seat.

"No, there's no plan! I need a plan. And even with all the planning I do, it's not working out. First my Nanna, then Mommy? And now this?"

Hot tears flowed down Camille's face. Evan rushed to her, hands cupping her head in a desperate attempt to comfort her, an attempt she accepted this time. They both stood in the center of the studio, the rain outside now falling heavier.

It had been several years since Evan or anyone had seen Camille's mother, Dorothy LaShea. He and Camille were involved with each other, and then life dealt the LaShea's such a devastating blow. Evan was perplexed. Whereas Mr. LaShea had seen very little that he approved of in Evan, Mrs. LaShea had grown closer to accepting him for who he was. When she received her diagnosis, the closeness she and Evan were achieving was suddenly postponed. The diagnosis of breast cancer tracked through their family: first a great-aunt, next Camille's grandmother, and then her own mother.

Mrs. LaShea's prognosis was not hopeful. The damage was pervasive and chemotherapy was presented to the family as the only viable option. Facing this critical situation was further complicated by Mrs. LaShea's gradual withdrawal.

Evan slowly released Camille. She wasn't shaking but he could still sense she was on edge. Without saying a word, she exited the studio; Evan heard the bathroom door close. He walked over to his computers again and just stared, not sure what to do. He nearly flew through the ceiling when his cell phone vibrated in his pocket.

"Hey, Evan?"

"Cory, hey," Evan answered. Cory reported that Tony could have visitors and would be released soon, according to Jasmine, who anticipated seeing all of them at some point. Evan was appreciative but was sorry to report on LaShea based on Camille's outlook. Evan tried to take comfort in his mother's optimism and prayers. She was not assigned to Mr. LaShea's or Tony's case at Suburban Hospital, but she was working Mr. LaShea's floor, and that was enough.

"How's Mrs. LaShea taking it?" Cory asked.

"She's not in the picture right now, Faber," Evan said cryptically.

"Aw man, I'm sorry," Cory said earnestly.

"Oh no, she's not...dead." Evan was treading into dangerous territory and he spoke as intentionally as he could without blowing the LaShea family secret. It was not public knowledge that Camille's mother was away for emotional and personal reasons, despite being in remission for some time.

"No offense, it's family business. But Dorothy's fine," assured Evan. "They'll deal with it."

Camille returned from the bathroom with tissue, wiping her worn eyes. Patting her pockets she exhaled irritably, having forgotten she had misplaced her phone. This was not the time to lose her lifeline with her dad in the hospital, and she reminded herself to look more closely for it as soon as she got back home. She was about to enter the studio, but at the sound of her mother's name she stopped and listened.

"I do wish her mom was here though, Faber," Evan admitted. "Cammie's glad Tony is alright but he's got people and Jasmine."

"Camille's got you, Evan," said Cory, almost like he was asking instead of telling.

"True man, but I've never seen her like this... her family's been through a lot."

Camille entered the studio steel faced as Evan mouthed that he was talking to Cory.

"I need to get back to the hospital," she said, getting her purse not waiting for Evan's response.

With his hand over the mouthpiece, Evan signaled for her to hold-on. Instead of waiting, Camille walked out and slammed the door without saying a word, the *ON AIR* sign falling to the ground on the other side.

"I gotta go," said Evan, ending the call.

Dorothy and the nurses grunted a little as they worked together to shift the bulking weight of LaShea from one side of the bed to the other. He had begun to stabilize after the emergency bypass surgery and now the recovery loomed ahead.

"Careful with that leg," the nurse ordered. "That's where they had to borrow a vein. It's still a little sensitive."

The mechanical adjustments on the bed were a big help, but it's difficult when the patient really cannot communicate with you. As the three completed their rituals, Dorothy found herself in one of those vinyl cushioned, art deco hospital chairs, staring out the window. Where was her daughter?

"Dorothy?"

Dorothy turned sharply toward the doorway. Astonished, Diana Spencer entered the room. They hugged each other as Mr. LaShea lay sleeping totally unaware of his wife's return.

"Oh my God, when did you come home?" asked Diana, holding Dorothy's hands tightly.

"I came home yesterday evening to hear that Jake had had a heart attack," Dorothy answered. "I wasn't even thinking that you'd be here, Diana!"

"My shift started a little bit ago, I didn't work last night," said Diana. "You look well. Have you seen Camille?"

Dorothy had always enjoyed fashion and would step out in-style when she had known better days. She wore a designer charcoal pantsuit with a cut that accentuated her figure and height. The outfit was highlighted with a mauve silk top and matching shoulder scarf, not overdone though; she would never over do a thing. Never one to be pretentious, Dorothy had kicked off her matching charcoal shoes to get comfortable.

"The nurses can't reach her, they don't think she's been home either," said Dorothy swallowing hard. "She wrote to me she'd be home this summer. One of the nurses said she had planned to come by tonight"

"Yes, yes she's definitely home," Diana nodded in agreement. "She's been spending a lot of time with Evan, naturally. Oh, in fact, he told me they were coming in. They'll be here in a few minutes since the rain let up."

Right then Dorothy's friend Gloria came with coffee, accompanied by another nurse.

"Diana, Dr. Patel needs you," the nurse said.

"And Diana, this is my friend Gloria. She brought me here," offered Dorothy. Diana shook Gloria's hand on her way out.

"I'll be back. Camille's going to be so happy to see you Dorothy. She needs you." And with that, Diana was gone.

Dorothy and Gloria sat together watching Mr. LaShea, Dorothy's coffee cooling next to her. This was not what she intended to find when she came home. When she and Gloria arrived at the house she once called home, it was deserted. Today was usually the day LaShea worked from home. But it appeared no one was home and Dorothy had no need of house keys while at Friends House. If it hadn't been for the neighbors telling Dorothy about LaShea – well, she didn't want to think about it. She was just happy to have found at least half of her family and anticipated her precious daughter arriving soon.

"He looks so peaceful lying there sleeping," Dorothy whispered as she stroked LaShea's hand.

"Yes," began Gloria. "His doctor has him heavily sedated. They say he needs the rest."

Dorothy's green eyes took in the subdued figure of her husband. Her freshly done shoulder length hair fell to his chest as she leaned over to kiss and caress the side of his face. A tear ran down her cheek. She had always wanted to look her best for him and even though he couldn't see her, she had returned to the state that he once knew so well.

"I missed you," she whispered.

Before the cancer, she had always been career-minded. Although her husband's career provided handsomely for the family, Dorothy insisted on pursuing her own interests. This created a unique sort of tension in the household; the family did all that they could to define themselves. Camille and

Dorothy's relationship was most affected by it. Dorothy was not the typical homemaker.

It was the curse of a *good thing* taken to extremes. Dorothy and LaShea, as she and everyone else loved to call him, met while in college. Both were overtaken by their aspirations. They were kindred spirits. They belonged to the right Greek organizations, invested in strategic campus extracurricular activities and later joined the proper associations and civic organizations. The challenge in all of this was that LaShea thought Dorothy would relinquish her desires when they married and had a family. She thought it was outrageous: the idea that she would somehow give up who she was. As Camille grew from a toddler, Dorothy tried to balance being at the top of her career and motherhood. The tension reverberated through the family. As things heightened, her cancer diagnosis put things over the top. It had become unbearable. Dorothy was dreadfully sick and experiencing a nervous breakdown, losing her drive, zest, and control.

Camille actually took after both of her parents. She possessed the zeal to succeed. As a young woman, with her mother away, she made Daddy her charge. LaShea rewarded her attempts to manage the home. Daddy and his little girl became even closer. Sadly, this drove a wedge between the three as Dorothy felt that she was unfairly judged when it came to homemaking, whereas, Camille was given the benefit of the doubt.

"Mommy?" came the familiar voice of her baby girl. Dorothy turned to behold the gorgeous image of her only child as Camille stepped into the hospital room flanked by Evan. Camille's face began to blur as tears of joy welled in Dorothy's eyes.

<u>SIDE B</u>

Track 14:
Help!

By now, Cory's many trips to Evan's house made it easier for him to navigate the countless turns. The car came to a halt along the gentle sloping curb in front of the house. Cory skipped the doorbell, remembering it didn't really work, and pounded out a rhythm using the doorknocker and his fist.

"Right on time," said Evan exiting the house and locking up.

"Thought I'd treat you to one of your own concerts," Cory answered. "Let's go see Tony."

"I got something you should hear," said Evan as they walked to the car.

Tony was getting stronger every day. Jasmine said his winning personality was back and he was up and about taking walks through the hospital. Jasmine would stop by the hospital later today but until then no girls were allowed; Tony missed the fellas. As Cory rounded the corner making his way for the hospital, he and Evan listened to the rough cut of *The Mustangz EP* on Evan's MP3 player. It was a real treat for Cory since he had only contributed to a couple songs including the song *As I Walk* he and Evan had performed together.

Over the course of officially forming, playing local venues and cutting the CD, The Mustangz had accumulated various contacts and their network grew. Production duties were entrusted to tried and true contacts Evan and Sam made. Their hard work was paying off. Soon the EP would be released for everyone. Evan tried not to allow life's recent events surrounding Tony and Mr. LaShea to dampen his spirits.

"Yeah, I loved this one," said Cory, bobbing his head. "Man I missed out on the early recordings."

"Thanks, I try," said Evan, increasing the volume. "We tweaked it, you know?"

"No, I mean it man. That's really got some flavor," Cory pressed. "A lot of people's music ain't really saying much, or their delivery distorts everything. You, on the other hand – well, for instance, I was noticing before today that your style is to present an attack, when most would opt for a musical rest. Replay that last song."

"Man, I just always liked doing that," Evan enthused. He always felt he should be able to get a little wild in his musicality. Sometimes when he'd listen to music from others, he imagined that he'd take it up high instead of going low and vice versa. Finally, when he chose to take up music, the keys and turntables, he felt like God, totally in control and free to explore whatever mood he wanted.

"Yeah, well man it's tight. That's playing in a different realm," Cory added, beating the steering wheel. "See right there – the listener and the musician are in a natural relationship. It's just like people, there's a give and take. It's not just giving to the listener, spoon-feeding them the next natural progression. Your stuff is different. You force the listener to interact, to give, by setting them up to expect the natural progression, then BAM! You attack with something totally different."

"You're not just saying so?" inquired Evan. "That's exactly how I feel in my head. Does that make sense?"

They pulled into the parking lot of the hospital, which surprised Evan, who was so engrossed in the musical analysis that the drive hadn't taken long at all. He disconnected his MP3 player from the car stereo but, instead of going in right away, they got to the heart of the conversation. As they continued to talk, a theme emerged regarding Evan's style. A lot of material on the album, including some of the lyrics, was like two athletes performing martial arts. Where traditionally, one would attack and the other would defend and parry, the opponent responds by going on the offensive too and attacks back, right in the middle of what is coming at them. It throws off the first attacker, making the timing on everything totally wild. The listener is the first attacker who is being constantly advanced upon by Evan, the second attacker, when normally there would be setups, rests, or defensive stands.

"You, my man, do that with music," Cory said as they exited the car. "Music in a rut is predictable. Your style is fresh, by advancing, using unusual cadences; you're forcing the listener to be engaged. It's special man."

"Faber, you are too wild," Evan said smiling brightly. His fear that others couldn't comprehend his blend of music had slowly been fading as the band and the EP were coming together. But to hear Cory tell it, even though they were bandmates, was like hearing it from someone who was a fan. Stopping in front of the automatic doors of the hospital, Evan looked at Cory, taking his words to heart. Little did he realize he was rubbing his trusty white golf ball between his hands like he was about to start a fire. Trusting his gut was paying off.

"I'm telling you Evan, this stuff is gonna serve you well," Cory smiled back and they went inside.

The front receptionist directed them to the third floor, East Wing. They were only too happy when the elevator they were riding in spewed them out right across the hall from the wing they needed to visit.

"May I help you young men?" A voice greeted them from behind the nurse's station.

"Perhaps, I can be of assistance," intruded the voice of a patrolman, obviously posted to track what visitors came and went.

"Look, we don't mean no harm," Evan exclaimed. "He's a friend of mine and I..." the officer interrupted, asking for identification from both of the young men.

Cory's calm head prevailed, as they both offered identification and began to explain their connection to Tony. After a brief phone call, the officer allowed them in.

"Tony, that's some security guard you got out front," Evan said.

"What's up Ev? What's up Faber?" Tony welcomed them and smiling widely as he lay in bed. "Yeah, well you know man, only the best for me during my stay."

"Yeah, well check it out. Ryan and his girl Raquel send love from D.C. man," said Evan, walking over to the bed and shaking Tony's hand and Cory did likewise.

"Let me find out my brush with death reverberating all around the world," Tony laughed. "I do feel stronger."

"Something like that, yeah," Cory agreed, smiling.

"So, T, after all you put us through, I could've killed you myself," Evan began. "There's stuff in the papers, the news. You got police posted? What's going on?"

Tony looked over their shoulders toward the door. Evan and Cory followed his gaze. The officer happen to peak in over his shoulder, then continued to survey the hallway, planted firmly like some kind of watchdog. At that, Tony's two friends decided to take a seat.

"Well..." Tony began his story. "I saw an opportunity to exploit my immense ballin' skills with my creative intellect. I mean, why should they be making money off of me? I ain't no punk and I wanted some of my own action! So, I said, hey, I can take this thing to a higher level and make a little bit off my ability to play the weather man."

"The weather man?" Evan asked.

"Yeah, my ability to forecast – jumpers raining from the sky," replied Tony as he mimicked a jump shot with his arms.

"You saying you planned to predict the scores and control the outcome of the game and make money from it: the Point Spread?" Cory questioned.

"I prefer to think of it as diversification in capitalism," answered Tony cheekily.

"From the looks of it there was nothing diverse about them coming after you," said Cory. "You were the only one attacked; minor injuries all around, probably just chaos though."

"That it, Tony? Now you got yourself in hot-water while others almost had to pay for your creativity!" Shot Evan. "Man, you know Cammie and Jasmine were up in that place? What were you thinking?"

"I had nothing to do with that!" exclaimed Tony.

"We've been like brothers for a long time, Tony. But I swear, if anything had happened to Camille – you'd had to pay for that!" Evan blared, pointing and leaning forward intently.

"Ev, my man," Tony stammered.

"And them dudes you was dealing with didn't flow with your plan," Evan interrupted. "Tony, those were the Epps Yard fools from across the way. What's happened?"

"The point spread and my personal status collided," Tony inserted.

"They collided? What do you mean?" Cory asked.

"I guess I saw stars, man," Tony admitted, rubbing his eyes. "See, we were supposed to win, as we always do, but by five. My people like a close game. But then the coach and the bench tell me that Jonesy's got a chance at a school record for assists. Well, I got to help my boy out and who better to dish the ball to – but my hot hand? It was totally unselfish on my part."

At this, Tony smirked and shook his head. Evan and Cory exchanged glances, piecing it together.

"So you win by more than five 'cause you had to score for Jones to get the assist record?" Cory summed-up.

"The least that I could do," replied Tony as he shifted in the bed.

"And they blow the place up because you wrecked the point spread," Evan concluded. "Suit and tie guys are using them as what, enforcers?"

"Actually, BeBe could have intervened but he just didn't have the skills," said Tony sitting up.

"BeBe?" Evan scoffed, standing up beginning to pace slowly.

"But why are you talking so freely with the Man just outside the door?" Cory asked.

"You are very smart my man," interjected Tony.

"The coppers have been after these business people, your suit and tie guys, for some time now for – shall we say: *higher-crimes*," exclaimed Tony. "They already know my story, they want the bigger fish."

"So what's next?" asked Evan.

"Well, *the man*, as you put it Cory, has asked me to help them throw a big net in the ocean, you know a sting," answered Tony.

"And what about you?" inquired Cory.

"If I can help them pull off the big catch, they are willing to disregard my lesser infractions," answered Tony, eyeing Evan.

"So, are you gonna help them?" questioned Evan.

"It is currently in the best interests of my future to cooperate," Tony continued. "But I know you got my back no matter..."

Evan spun his back on his best friend, breaking his sentence, and stood in front of the door. The physical separation was more than obvious. Years of friendship were finally on the line. Evan had too many realities to deal with and they were all crashing in – triggered by his best friend's troubles. What was wrong with Tony? How could he be so reckless, so stupid and throw in with the likes of BeBe, this fully matured street gang and the mobsters that set them loose?

"You with me, right Evan?" asked Tony, looking from Cory to his best friend. "Don't make me have to beg man. We been through way too much together for it to change. You know I was always there for you."

Just as Evan turned to respond, the door yielded to the patrolman who had been stationed on the other side.

"Visiting hours are over."

Cory rose and joined Evan at the door.

"Ev?" Tony asked again. Evan gave him one last glance then silently turned away, conflicted.

"Good seeing you Tony," Cory offered. "We'll see you on the outside real soon."

As the two quietly left the room, Cory touched Evan's arm.

"You're boy's changing, man. He's talking about cooperating – of course he has to. But it's a start. I just hope that the mask starts to come down. You could be the one to help him see this thing through."

Evan shrugged and jerked himself away from Cory as they found themselves back in front of the elevator. The two disregarded a creaky old lady who spoke with the patrolman stationed at the door.

"Evening gentlemen," nodded the officer.

The drive home gave Cory and Evan a chance to digest the situation that Tony had created. Both men debated the severity of the set of circumstances, which somehow triggered an avalanche of events that were now all crashing together. Evan questioned the level of loyalty that Tony was requesting of their friendship. It was like Tony didn't even see how his actions affected his own friends. Cory listened closely to Evan's side, all the while encouraging him to remain true to his friend, in spite of Tony's stupidity. Cory felt that there were chinks in Tony's armor, the façade of arrogance that he wore, and that this recent turn of events had the possibility of loosening him up a little bit more. Cory also reminded Evan that Jasmine could play a critical role in helping unveil the real Tony Gerard Jackson and, from what Cory had observed, having Jasmine by his side could only be a good thing.

On other fronts, Evan confided to Cory that Dorothy LaShea had come back to her family just when they needed her the most. He had seen this first hand.

Back at the Spencer residence, Evan and Cory saw the chain of events as an opportunity for them to channel their emotions through their music. They each committed to chronicle the past events in song and allow the music to heal, where possible, any damage that may have been done. They both knew that pain provided one of the best inspirations for creating great art. The wounds were worth the price of unleashing a masterpiece.

Track 15:
Girl Talk

Finally, the gang was together again, united by catastrophe but strengthened by love and an affinity for family. Today they were gathered in Mr. LaShea's hospital room to comfort Camille and her mother. The calluses on Cory's fingers spoke to the time spent bending strings in the name of the muse, his labor with The Mustangz having reawakened his skills. By now, he almost blindly went about his business on the guitar, as if it was all that there could ever be. The bond between Cory and the instrument was inexplicable. Evan, leaning against the wall, smiled as Cory transitioned and the tune became that which Evan had recently played for Camille back in the studio the night her mother came back into her life.

Cory arpeggiated more precisely to slow the tempo, and expressed the lyrics in a drawn out fashion to reduce the pace. Evan's eyes grew wide with pleasant surprise. *I didn't know he could sing too*, he thought. Next to him, Jasmine, wrapped in Tony's arms, shot the same look at Evan. *Wow*, she mouthed, as Cory's voice melodically soothed in silky hush tones, massaging every auditory sense in the room.

Hospital waiting rooms are traditionally sterile, without personality or cause; however, it now played center stage to Cory's concert. The bland walls and overbearing furniture seemed an unlikely ambiance for his audience, who were drawn together in support of one in need. They huddled together around Camille and Dorothy to allow the acoustic medicine to soothe them as Cory sang on.

As I walk this road before me Lord
Searching to find my way
I get an empty, empty feeling Lord
You just might turn and walk away
But you must understand, I've not been here before
Will you walk with me Lord or am I going it alone?
Still you say...

Camille and her mother sat on the bed holding hands. Cory's playing was beautiful, and Camille smiled weakly when the tune became familiar to her. Evan had played the track of her singing it; this was before he informed her of her mother.

She paused to pull herself together. She'd have to deal with that and Evan later. What mattered was that her family was finally back together. She exhaled deeply and slowly hummed in time with Cory until she found herself mouthing the small lyric he repeated. Drawing her mother's arms around her, they rocked side to side as one while Camille allowed the music to penetrate her soul and minister deep within her being.

"Man, how does he do that so well?" whispered Tony.

"It's a gift. Don't you know anything?" Evan shook his head.

"Shh, guys...I think it's really special." Jasmine whispered back.

"Whatever," was all Tony could say.

Tony was back, altered only by his missing high top fade and the addition of stitches on the side of his head, the physical reminders of the shootout at Club Soul-Light. The emotional scars were still healing, or at least for Evan stagnating. What Jasmine played off as classic Tony/Evan banter was in truth a deep friendship that, like Tony, was buffeted and up against the ropes. This, too, would be dealt with later.

Cory strummed and strummed and gradually ended his playing. Camille looked from her father to Cory and smiled, extending her hand. Cory took it, shook it warmly and smiled back.

"Thank you, Cory," said Dorothy, nodding toward her sleeping husband. "I think he likes it.

"My pleasure, Mrs. LaShea," Cory replied. "Lyrics are like people. They're always at their best when in the right company."

"I know where I can get some refreshment," Tony whispered in Jasmine's ear and made his way to the elevator.

While the others talked quietly with Dorothy, Camille and Jasmine were talking amongst themselves in the doorway. Dorothy had moved back home and she and Camille were doing well. Life was surreal for Camille right now, made even more so by the sudden and shocking return of the LaShea matriarch. Camille was overjoyed not to be alone. The family had come together in their darkest hour with Camille at the epicenter, bolstered by her mother's return.

"Girl how is he?" asked Jasmine, looking back toward Mr. LaShea.

"I'm glad that he's resting," Camille replied, folding her arms. "But I don't like the way the doctors and nurses seem to be observing me. Not in a bad way, just sort of, well – like they have different expectations than I do." Her eyes started to glaze over and she forced a smile. Camille couldn't give up now. When she saw her mother the night she came back in her father's room and locked eyes with her mother's emerald orbs, it was like a sign from God. Her Mommy had fought cancer and won, and now she had come back from the brink of emotional destruction to be with her husband and daughter. Camille was convinced that together she and her mother would bring her father back, too.

Jasmine caressed Camille's shoulder, easing the tension as she guided her to the couch near the others. Sam, sitting on the armrest, moved Cory's guitar so the ladies would have a place to sit.

"How are you holding up, Cammie?" Sam asked, lightly plucking the guitar strings.

"It helps by just having you all here, Sam," answered Camille.

"Babe, you know we can't let you go through this alone," offered Evan.

Jasmine stroked Camille's hair and pushed back the strands revealing the tracks of earlier tears. "We got your back." Camille dropped her head onto her friend's shoulder, nodding her head.

"It's hard; Camille..." shared Cory. "But you and Mrs. LaShea have each other. Your family is amazingly blessed right now."

"Baby, your dad's a very strong man," Dorothy added. "If anyone has the capacity to pull through, it's him." Dorothy rose from her husband's side and joined Jasmine and her daughter on the couch. Camille, curling up between both women, suddenly recalled a long forgotten experience with her father. Although her eyes welled as she shared the story, her genuine smile graced the listeners as she began.

"I remember a time once when I was a little girl. Daddy had taken me to the beach, Sandbridge. We loved to go there; the waves were great and it was always nice and quiet. He had gotten me lemonade and we sat on a bench together. He would take my straw and suck just a little lemonade into it and then plug his finger over the hole so that it stayed in the straw. I would tilt my head way back and he'd unplug the straw and let the lemonade flow into my mouth. It was so simple, so vivid - feels like that happened just yesterday. I wish that we could've had more moments like that." Her tears, Camille realized, were of pure joy, as if she'd forgotten the struggle that still faced her father. She could picture the sunshine and taste the lemonade from that day. Her mother leaned over and kissed her on the cheek.

Just then the elevator doors opened. It was Tony who, feeling somewhat insecure about his gesture held his head low. In a few strides he was within arms distance of Camille and extended a can to her. "It's lemonade, it was all they had. I hope that's okay with you. And here's a straw. Here ya go, Mrs. LaShea. Sorry it took so long, ran into some people."

The others sighed and smiled in unison. Jasmine raised an eyebrow.

"What?" Tony's palms rose as he shrugged his shoulders.

"It's perfect, Tony," Jasmine bounced to her feet and planted a kiss squarely on Tony's cheek.

"There's a lot of support here," Tony continued, rubbing the back of his neck awkwardly. "That's all you really need, right? Is someone to go through it with you. It sure helped me and my family, trust me." Jasmine squeezed Tony tighter. She was so happy everyone was together supporting Camille. As Tony kissed Jasmine on her forehead, he eyed Evan. He was right, Evan thought, but things were complicated right now and the past couldn't be wiped away so easily. Besides, Camille needed him right now, Tony would have to wait. Or maybe he needed Camille. One thing was for certain -- no matter who was to blame for this mess, he couldn't deny that he and Camille had become distant lately.

∞

One lazy afternoon, Camille and Jasmine were sitting on a park bench on the campus of Hampton University. The girls sat close to the water as if they would toss in their worries and cares. The sun slowly bowed to embrace the ocean, a last stanza to the symphony of another day. Jasmine had joined Camille, her mom, and Gloria for brunch earlier and spent the day talking and getting to know the LaShea ladies. It was good since Camille and her mother had a lot to catch up on, but it was a real treat to be able to introduce them to their new gal pals. Their minds were never far away from LaShea as he fought hard in the hospital. He was having complications that were prolonging the healing process but his doctors assured Camille and her mother that their man was undergoing the best care they could provide.

Getting away was good for the ladies. Thinking on only positive things for a change, they enjoyed a fine meal in the early afternoon, told stories and laughed while the professionals worked on Camille's father. Finally, the ladies split up. Dorothy and Gloria returned to the house to relax, which left Jasmine and Camille to venture elsewhere and see what the rest of the day had to offer. After driving around for a while blasting 90s pop and R&B and trying to remember the lyrics, they found themselves at Hampton University. Both friends felt as if they'd known each other all their lives. They did to some degree, but they both knew they were never close friends by any stretch of the imagination. This got them talking about high school and how life had shaped them.

"I think people got this superficial impression of me," offered Jasmine. "They see this Latina, and yeah what's the politically correct term, um, spicy way about me. But there's much more to me than that."

"I guess I never thought much about it," Camille said softly.

"Camille, isn't there more to you than what people see? I know there is," said Jasmine, cocking her head to the side.

Both girls kicked back to finally express their thoughts, which they hadn't discussed before. The scent of salt water wafted in the air. Behind them, some guys were walking and throwing a basketball. Jasmine turned her head to take in the sight and smirked, "Yeah I'm loud and rambunctious. Well, I was when I was a girl. I drove my parents crazy. But I had a cousin who was really weird and into books and swords and stuff. Well my parents put us together for a summer and I learned to Fence."

"You what? You fix fences?" Camille asked, eyes rolling.

"No, silly. I mess around with fencing – you know sabers, sword fighting, Camille," said Jasmine, poking Camille in the arm.

"You are kidding me – like pirates and junk?" Camille chuckled.

"No, like Antonio Banderas with his fine self. Like Zorro!" Jasmine emphasized, shaking her head. "I was a little hyper, but not like my cousin, though. He had ADHD. Heck, now he's like a geek celebrity if you look him up online. But it helped us to concentrate and learn how to incorporate some finesse. He's my favorite cousin. I remember him calling it *physical chess*."

"Daaang," Camille gushed. "I can see you now. Don't they wear all white with funny masks? You really liked it, huh?"

Reminiscing, Jasmine smiled and turned back toward the water. "Yeah. I learned lessons from it that I can apply to life. Everything's not all about charging with the foil..."

"Foil? What the heck?" interrupted Camille.

"It's the standard sword, girl. Shush! I'm trying to be deep. It's about proper footwork, maneuvering, understanding form. Sports like that really showed me how dramatic and exciting life can be if you stop to see what's really going on. I go for what I want and do it with style, just like when I competed. And protecting yourself is so important. You can't just let anyone in. But when cool people like you show up, you gotta strike and get them on your side."

"Wait, time out," said Camille, making a "T" with her hands. "Are you saying you wanted to be friends in acappella?"

"Oh no, no way girl. I was trying to destroy you," said Jasmine without missing a beat, to which Camille shoved her aside playfully.

"But I didn't want to be a bull in a china closet. There are rules and standards for confrontation - form," Jasmine continued.

"I would have never guessed that in a million years," Camille said.

"What, that I fence or that I can be like a bull in a china closet?" They both fell back laughing.

"Both honey. That is so cool. Yeah you brought your best in high school. I remember you," said Camille, nodding her head. "The discipline your cousin taught you paid off, for real." Jasmine nodded in agreement. A light breeze skated across the water, brushing the girls' faces and tossing their hair. It was peaceful by the water's edge and Camille was finally decompressing with Jasmine by her side.

"I know you've got Evan, but you got me also," Jasmine offered, touching Camille's hand softly. "I know it's scary now, but you're safe with your friends."

"Maybe that's my problem," Camille mused. "Thing is, I wasn't always so much of a safe and predictable person."

Another breeze caught Jasmine's hair, blowing it into her face. "What do you mean?"

"I had everything planned out. Before my mom got sick, my dad and I used to go to the beach," Camille began.

"Yeah, you were telling us last time we were with your dad at the hospital," Jasmine interjected.

"There's more, before the lemonade. We would go down to Sandbridge because my dad was teaching me how to surf."

"Go ahead, you are kidding me!" asked Jasmine, playfully pushing Camille on the shoulder.

"Yeah, in Sandbridge there was something about the unpredictability of catching a wave and living on the edge that sucked me in," continued Camille grinning. "We called it walking on water."

"Wow, Camille the Surfer Girl!" Jasmine exclaimed.

"Daddy even helped me join an association. There's a network of African American surfers," added Camille.

"I guess when your mom's health started to get bad," Jasmine said slowly, "You hung up your board?"

"I needed as much stability in my life as I could get," said Camille with a far off look.

The two stared out over the water as a boat turned up the channel. Jasmine found out about Mrs. LaShea's bout with cancer but was still in the dark about Friends House. Camille had a slightly queasy pit in her stomach and it reminded her of Evan.

"So, we both had a little more going on, huh?" Jasmine said with her elbows propped on her knees and her face in her hands.

"I wouldn't tell Evan this," answered Camille. "I would not want to scare him off. I don't know, but I guess there's a little bit of under current or rip tide. There's the old part of me that understands the spontaneity of the music, the adventure. But the *present* me with all of this craziness needs some sort of stability for the future, now more than ever… there have been too many surprises."

"Except for your mom," smiled Jasmine, to which Camille conceded, nodding her agreement. "But Camille, where's the surfer girl? Life dealt you some hard blows. Is being *Miss Boring* and predictable who you really are? You might need surfer girl to handle the rough waters, everything ain't predictable."

"I know that. But I'm not ready to let go of that part of me yet. What's predictable is safe," said Camille firmly. "Surfing was a long time ago. I don't know, I guess I've grown comfortable with it."

"You've grown comfortable with me as your singing buddy, too," Jasmine added. "Just saying."

"Hey, let's take a break from my troubles," said Camille, folding her legs. "But I want good for you too, Jasmine. I see you and your boo, Tony."

"I know. I want it right also," smiled Jasmine, biting her lip mischievously. "He's got a good heart. I know those Yardees at the club really scared him, even though he tries to act all big."

"Nothing gets past you," said Camille, exhaling softly.

"I could swear sometimes he's off on his own," Jasmine continued. "But I don't know with who, or what. I notice he gets funny calls."

"Uh oh, he's going to make you kill him," said Camille, waving her index finger like a sword.

"Girl, who you telling?" said Jasmine, playfully leaning into Camille. Evening had set in and the two continued to talk as they walked back to the car.

"I won't kill him yet. I need proof he's being a bad boy, just to be sure," said Jasmine.

"Maybe that's what sets you apart Jasmine. You'll probably one day see what you hope for. The rest of us aren't sure we can see that for Tony anymore." Camille hoped for the best and that her friend would use his second chance wisely, and not hurt any of them. But what Evan said echoed in her mind: Tony was Tony.

"Oh, I'm not blind girl," Jasmine concluded. "But Tony just needs to believe in himself... maybe a little less. He needs faith, not all that smack he's been talking. He's too grown for that. You should see him with his family. But that's what all men need."

"You know that's right," Camille added as they both laughed in unison, high-fiving each other.

That's right, that's all they need, Camille reflected on Evan. *We're the ones to give it to them.*

The only thing Camille worried about was whether she and Jasmine were giving two men who had grown up to be thick as thieves a little too much faith. Only time would tell what kind of name these boys would give to love in the eyes of Camille and Jasmine, whether it be a good name, or a bad name.

Track 16:
Memories

Dorothy LaShea was attempting to handle the setback of LaShea's heart attack as best that she could. Camille was trying to find the positive. But Dorothy had personally traversed the doorway of death and she was sensing familiarities that she'd rather not. None of the visits had been the same anymore. Each visit was unique and pointed toward an impending scenario. Today, Dorothy's visit would be the light at the end of the tunnel.

The peace of the hospital room helped to soothe Dorothy's nerves. Her hand gently stroked LaShea's forehead, delicately avoiding the various tubes and monitoring cables that were now the tether anchoring him to this life. It had gotten to the point that the nurses very quietly went about their work, knowing that it was not the family invading their purpose of duty but rather, the nurses were clearly invading the patient's only solace, his family.

"He'll need your comfort," the nurse mused out loud.

"He's always got my care," offered Dorothy.

And with that the nurse exited, suggesting that she would make sure that the two of them would no longer be interrupted.

Relying on her deep love for her husband as a guide, Dorothy considered the peacefulness of the room but also noted the coolness, which was odd, because there was no breeze. However, there were only light sheets draped over LaShea.

As she adjusted the sheets, her mind drifted…

"I can't stand the cold, baby," LaShea bellowed.

"Well honey, this romantic camping trip is going to have some inconveniences," Dorothy replied.

"Now, I can take it, don't get me wrong," he replied. "It's just that I don't like being cold. It would be the worst punishment for me to die in the cold."

Early on in their relationship, she and LaShea enjoyed the routine of sharing a bottle of wine and a simple meal while camping out by the ocean. The pure black sky with its rich, thick blanket covering and stars for night-lights had been their ceiling. But one thing LaShea disliked was waiting for the coolness in the sleeping bag to dissipate while it warmed up from their body heat. The two enjoyed rubbing their feet together and snuggling in the double-large, overstuffed cocoon.

The light from the window brought Dorothy back to reality. The hospital room, as nice as it was, was nothing like the escape of the beach that she had just daydreamed of. But the need was the same. Without much thought, Dorothy gently gathered herself in the bed with her husband to provide him with the much-needed warmth that only she could give.

Dorothy was saddened as she considered that there had not been time for conversational goodbyes. Despite all of her efforts, LaShea was leaving. As time passed, gentle warmth began to permeate the bed and a sense of satisfaction affirmed her. Dorothy's thoughts guided her to that place again. She released the thoughts that God had somehow shortchanged her and Camille by taking away LaShea. She merely thanked God for the time she and LaShea had shared. Her family was whole again.

"I do love you," emerged from her lips, and she thought of her dear LaShea and how he would have never left or forgotten her during her pain. He had been good to her. She thought of how he had invested in Camille during her absence. Although work was driving him to an early grave, he had promised that he would be there for her, and he had been.

Dorothy had chosen her mate well. LaShea and Camille, already two peas in a pod, grew even closer during this season while hoping and praying that their loved one would regain herself. LaShea never sought the refuge of another woman and Camille was forced to grow up a little sooner to take care of the both of them. Together, they made quite the team. LaShea vowed he would never leave Dorothy. He promised that he would get Camille through college as they both had planned prior to their horrific discovery of the cancer.

LaShea uttered a barely audible moan. Dorothy, lying next to him, inched closer and rubbed his cheek with her finger as she whispered in his ear. He opened his eyes, peering at his wife for the last time. For a moment, the subtle twinkle of recognition shimmered in his eyes. Tears of joy filled her eyes, dampening the sheets and his cheeks. The warmth of their love was immense. The window sheers, which had until this moment simply stood as solemn sentries in erect posture, now silently gestured in the breeze, 'goodbye.'

∞

The scene at St. John's Methodist Church was bright and carried the classic style of Dorothy, a woman intent on properly honoring her husband. The red bricks of the building collected and held the warmth of the sun, and a gentle soothing breeze wrapped itself around the congregants. The clouds were gracious enough to periodically shield one's eyes from the glow of the sun. Men in crisp dark suits served as ushers and stood like soldiers among the floral arrangements. They guided the celebrants into the church building as each paused to offer encouragements to Camille and her mother. Camille slouched in her seat, hands wringing and wet, eyes red and swollen from crying. Dorothy was poised. Her posture was firm and straight, her eyes were focused. Shoulders back, arms open, she embraced the well-wishers. Seated next to her was her friend Gloria, who was honored to sit with the family to lend support. Camille glanced back toward the middle of the church and found Jasmine, who slightly cocked her head, intently returned the gaze. Camille accepted the strength offered by her friend, and recognizing the gesture, rose and stood alongside her mother. Together, they accepted the greetings of those that came past.

Evan was seated a couple rows behind Camille with his mother and Uncle Nate who returned from his trip the evening LaShea had passed. Tony sat with Jasmine, Cory and Sam on the other side. Ryan and Raquel sat behind them cradling their baby girl, Zarah. Each was there to offer support to Camille, each to reconcile his and her own humanity.

A semi-circle of assorted flowers created a serene presence in the building. The arrangements of freshly cut flowers stretched their stems towards the ceiling with buds open, revealing their blossoms. They seemed to reach out to the attendees. From this garden of color emerged the grand casket, stately perched on a caisson of royal purple. The casket was silver and majestic with ebony handles as highlights, ready for the time when the pallbearers would hoist the capsule to its final resting place.

"Today we celebrate the life of Jake Daniel LaShea," began the minister. "Oftentimes we are here to support the family and encourage them. Today, a family has come that has experienced more than a lion's share of life's challenges. And on what some would have supposed to be a sorrowful day, we celebrate. Today, God has seen fit to prepare this family, and they offer support to us. But is it them, or is it really the hand of God reaching out to us all? We know the answer to that. Dorothy was lost to everyone: family and friends, for a season. Now she has returned much stronger and we have all gained her for a lifetime. We cannot mistakenly judge the events that brought these circumstances about. Sometimes you don't know what kind of sacrifice had to be made in the past for you to experience the benefit afforded to you in the present. But the sacrifice is worth it. He cares enough about us to ensure everyone and everything is in its place, because it is a benefit to witness the entrance of the Lord's own to his rightful home. We are saddened, but He has made us witnesses to Jake Daniel LaShea entering into his rightful home."

In what seemed like a matter of minutes to Dorothy and Camille, the minister had concluded the service.

"Let us pray."

With the procession over and the graveside service concluded, the Hampton soil crunched under the feet of the parishioners as they made their way along the path from the burial site back to their cars. The warmth of Evan's embrace protected Camille as she allowed him to support her those few yards, which seemed like a journey of miles. Mrs. LaShea held his arm on his other side with Gloria taking her other arm. The ladies' tears were intermittent now, but Camille thought it was still good to have Evan to lean upon.

Jasmine, Tony, Sam and Cory were already gathered back at Cory's car. The conversation between Cory and Tony was a distant drone in Jasmine's ears as she peered through the half-open window. She captured the sight of Evan as he paused with both women, one on each side, to look back at the grave one last time.

Jasmine watched as Camille lightly kissed Evan's cheek before she entered the limousine. Mrs. LaShea laid her hand upon his arm for support as she lowered herself into the seat, and her hand remained as she beckoned him to join the three ladies in the car just before the chauffeur closed the door. Ironically, he had now become the caretaker of Jake LaShea's two most valuable treasures.

Track 17:
Your Services Will be Required

The recent turn of events, Mr. LaShea's funeral and Tony's involvement with both gangs and the police placed the gang's friendships in a somewhat awkward position. Everyone was hoping to take a breather to regroup, as Evan, Camille, Jasmine, Tony, Sam, and Cory relaxed for lunch in a park off General Booth Road. Things were getting back to normal. Tony's wound had healed and he was now bandage free - although his high top fade was gone.

General Booth was a winding road and outside the normal bounds of their traditional beaten paths. It opened to a quaint little park on one side of the road, which had slots for a handful of cars to park. There was a swing and sliding board for smaller tykes and a few other accessories. The neighborhood offered much needed quiet space. The idea was to get a handle on where their collective lives were. They were soon reminded that they were still on a collision course with trouble as a patrol car pulled up and its occupant unfolded his massive frame to exit the vehicle. The officer lumbered toward the group.

"Afternoon folks," grumbled the sheriff while wiping his nose and mouth with an overly used handkerchief.

"Something wrong, sheriff?" Evan returned.

Tony shifted uneasily on the picnic bench while Jasmine tightened her grip on his arm and tried to settle him.

The sheriff tucked his handkerchief away and clutched his belt buckle. "No, you all enjoy your lunch. But I would like a word with you, Mr. Jackson."

Tony felt his stomach rise up through his throat as he lifted a leg over the seat and joined the sheriff. Jasmine, gathering herself to offer support, rose with Tony as he brushed himself off.

The officer held up a hand, "Uh, just Mr. Jackson, little lady."

Tony looked back at Jasmine and nodded to reassure her that it would be alright. Camille glanced up to see for the first time what appeared to be traces of an increasing need for connection between the two of them. Clearly Jasmine's worries over Tony's strange calls were justified, but the present situation was far more serious than *other* girls, or anything of that sort.

Evan leaned over to Cory, "We can only guess what this is all about, can't we?" Cory nodded in agreement. Camille looked from them back to Tony, concern written all over her face. Since when had her clique of friends become so secretive?

The sheriff adjusted his holster as both he and Tony stepped just out of hearing distance of the others, and the two proceeded to talk. The eye contact was serious and Tony glanced back only once. His usual cockiness seemed to be on a sabbatical. If this weren't enough, the small group's uneasiness built even more when the conversation went on a little longer than what would have seemed the normal length of time, whatever that would've been. Heartbeats also escalated as another man, in plain clothes, stepped from an unmarked car and joined Tony and the sheriff. There was no wondering that the other was undercover, the nondescript Crown Victoria gave him away. After what seemed like an eternity, the two officers finally returned to their vehicles and drove off allowing Tony to rejoin the group.

Jasmine ran to his side, "What's going on, T, what'd they want?"

"They said that there may be an upcoming need for my services." Tony did the best imitation that he could of the classic Tony cavalier attitude, but it was obvious that his cockiness had long since departed.

"Yeah, well what's that mean?" asked Sam, throwing up his hands in frustration.

"Yeah, Tony?" echoed Camille sharply.

Tony caught her tone but focused on Jasmine. Tired of feeling on the outskirts with his own friends, especially with Evan, and fully aware he was sweating bullets, Tony sat

Jasmine down and told everyone the long story. He left nothing out, everything to do with BeBe, the high rolling tycoons whose pockets he helped pad, his debts and cooperation with the police all came tumbling out like a flood.

"So they have bigger fish to fry and Tony's part of the bait," Cory seriously injected.

Tony peered at Cory while Cory returned a penetrating glance. The others were only fixated on Tony and missed the exchange.

"They wanted to know the names of people I've been hanging around with and if they have any connection with a money laundering ring," Tony reiterated.

"Do they suspect us?" Camille stepped toward both Tony and Jasmine.

"We were always on the list," Cory said, looking at Sam and the others.

"He's right," offered Evan. "I don't know much about this stuff, but I would've scoped us out a long time ago...but we're probably way too obvious."

"Oh, really? And how do you know so much?" demanded Camille, arms folded. "You and Cory seem to suspect a lot."

"Look Camille, we didn't want to put his business out there. I'm pissed about this too," Evan answered. "We're trying to figure this out."

"Oh, now you want to honor people's privacy?" asked Camille indignant, turning her back on Evan. He looked at Cory confused, but Camille just sat down and fumed.

Tony sat down on the bench and continued, "Apparently, a good way to spread money is through multiple exchanges of hands. Nobody really cares about the penny bets on basketball point spreads. It was simply a means to a larger end, of having clean money exchanged for the fake stuff."

Cory's sigh was somewhat audible while he stretched back to take in the sky as if help would somehow fall from above. This was starting to feel a lot like the business with Frankie and the band back in Portland long ago. He rubbed his face with exhaustion at the thought. Was history repeating itself?

Evan paced intently and eyed Camille, "Tony, you need to get yourself out of this stuff – man what were you doing?"

"What were you thinking?" added Camille as she rose with Evan.

"Look, I didn't know any of this was going on," Tony shot back.

"The police and the Epps Yard gang sure did though, bro," added Sam shaking his head in disappointment. "You played yourself."

"Are they asking you to do something?" Jasmine rubbed his shoulder. She too, was angry that he'd kept this from her. But ganging up on him wasn't helping anything.

"They said they'll be in touch." Tony dropped his head.

"So we just wait?" asked Camille, standing up and pacing in the park. "No plan?"

"I just wait," Tony corrected her. "They plan."

"Just like in basketball, you let the game come to you," Evan concluded as he bounced his golf ball off the tabletop and into his hand.

∞

It had been several weeks since Evan and Cory visited Evan's studio. The recent events were quite a load and had driven them to Heaven's Gate. Today, as usual, the two of them were squarely in the zone, this time joined by Sam, hours after Tony had dropped his bomb on everyone. Cory had picked up his guitar and was expressing the collision of his thoughts through the music while Evan played the part of recipient, dribbling his golf ball to the rhythm of the sound. Sam added a few strings on Evan's keyboard and additional percussion on the beat machine.

With no one to disturb them, the three began steps on the original journey that had drawn them together; only recent events could have nurtured them to this launching pad. Everything was in sync. Having put aside his golf ball, Evan had the right balance while listening with his headphones, securing his backwards baseball cap. Cory had his favorite Martin guitar, which included a nice preamp that he adjusted for optimal input into Evan's mixer. Today, his only interface was a chorus pedal with a vibrato rate set halfway to avoid melancholy, which created a moody accompaniment as if there were multiple guitars. Evan preferred a pronounced mid-range tone with crisp treble, instead of a ringing twangy sound that usually accompanied acoustic guitars.

After Sam captured a few loops on the digital recorder, Evan setup the keys to enhance the natural flow of Cory's chord progression. This permitted Cory to pause, exchange roles with Evan, and listen in on the composition that flowed from his heart. When Evan wanted a guitar riff to recycle, he merely re-inserted what he had already captured on the board. He could also expand or compress Cory's finger picking for a more massaging effect.

The three worked like chefs subjected to a small kitchen. Each man promised some unseen friend in a distant room a dish to end all dishes; each man arranging and discussing, compromising and replaying the music; each man trying to maintain the integrity of their personal taste while creating a complete meal, a dish which properly reflected their collective style. The Underfed Angels concert with its food theme came back to mind, making all of them smile. Out of this give and take a new oneness, a new sound was emerging. It was something that was born out of each man respecting the other, allowing one, Evan, to take the lead in producing the collective sound, even though he was also a participant. Cory brought the body of the sound on guitar, versus keys, which were used to provide accents and seasonings. And lastly, Sam laid a foundation of beats with such a driving pulsating pattern that they threaded each man's heart to the next. He was truly a master musician. You could count on "Sam the everyman" to be where you needed him.

Cory took note of this, nodding to the beat. As painful as it was, Evan couldn't let anything happen to his best friend, even though he was still angry with Tony, and his passion came through in waves in the music. He didn't have all the answers, but that had never stopped him before.

Tony's problems were on everyone's mind and it caused an incredible sound to gush forth from their souls through the music. Cory clearly remembered the downfall of his friends thanks to the mistake of just one. Fear nearly gripped him again. His godfather had been with him every step of the way on this journey in Hampton Roads. Ken couldn't be more proud of the news regarding Evan Spencer and *The Mustangz EP*, but most of all he was proud his godson Cory was back in control, in charge of his emotions.

Cory couldn't allow the past to devour his new life any longer. They would fight, Cory decided. He, Evan, Sam and Tony all bore witness to the power of that concert back when they all met together, guided by angels or some strange force. They couldn't allow the bond to be severed or for Tony to be swallowed up by his weaknesses, especially if he wanted to change. But what could they do? How can you starve your doubts when the fear fuels them? The music screaming from the studio was the sound of the young men's resolve to find out.

Track 18:
Wired for Sound

Ambling through the mall became Jasmine and Tony's shared pastime. The cool night air released a mist of rain as they crossed the threshold along with all the other shoppers.

"A drink would be nice," Jasmine broke the silence.

"Yeah, I'm game. Let's hit the shop over there," responded Tony, leading the way.

Tony gathered their drinks while Jasmine watched the carousel hurling its miniature occupants along.

Children are so joyful, she thought – *so carefree.* A man in a wheelchair paused to watch his youngster as two ladies joined him, drowning their cares with high-end coffee and ice cream in waffle cones. Jasmine wondered whether she was being too carefree with Tony. Did he even think of her as his girlfriend? Did he see any of them as friends anymore? It's like they were all getting in the way. And Tony appeared to be in denial of the downward spiral he was obviously careening down.

She remembered her talk with Camille about form and discipline and channeling her energies. Was she practicing what she preached now and taking her own advice? Or was she the victim of Tony's flailing blade, his immaturity landing him a lucky point? Surely she hadn't forgotten how to govern her heart, the most important part of herself, the muscle that mattered the most.

"I used to love the teacup," she mused as Tony joined her. "It's not like the stationary ponies on a carousel. The wheel between the seats, in the middle that spins you faster in the opposite direction of the overall ride makes it more fun you know? You get that extra umph."

However, the concerns of recent events had created a counter spin of their own and it was not a thrilling motion.

Tony's cell phone went off. In order to read the number better he shielded the overhead light.

"Tony, who is that?" asked Jasmine with an arched eyebrow. "This cloak and dagger stuff is pushing me over the edge."

"Just a friend," Tony said, putting his phone away.

"I want to know more about this friend," Jasmine demanded.

"She's nothing for you to worry about," Tony assured her.

The intensity was killing Jasmine. With one rip, she grabbed the phone from Tony and redialed the number. "What are you doing?" Tony yelled.

Jasmine pushed him back with one arm, ready to resolve this thing and confirm her darkest fears. Camille had warned her.

A creaky voice greeted her on the other line, "This is Grace, can I help you?"

"Grace who?" Jasmine screamed. "Girl don't let me get my hands on you!"

"It's Grace Goldstein. Will you be joining us for Bridge?" inquired the voice totally unfazed by Jasmine's aggressive tone.

Jasmine looked at Tony. "What? What Bridge?"

"Will you be joining us for Bridge with Tony? Are you calling in for him?" Grace sounded completely harmless and altogether serious, albeit, confused.

Tony had heard enough and pried the phone away from Jasmine. "No thanks Mrs. Goldstein, it was just a little misunderstanding. I'll see you at our usual time." And he hung up rolling his eyes.

"Oh my God! Tony, what was that about?" Jasmine exclaimed. "I've had it up to here with your secrets, first the gambling and then the police and now this!"

Tony set his drink down and tried to calm her down. "Jasmine, remember when I was in the hospital? Well, when I was able to get a little breathing room, I couldn't go too far or off the floor. The patient a few doors down was in to have her gallbladder removed. Mrs. Goldstein and some of her Bridge Club would come up and visit her. The coppers loosened my leash and let me hang out with them. One day a lady couldn't make it and they needed a fourth for Bridge so they convinced me. They taught me how to play. It's kinda hard to learn but I'm getting used to it. Since I was new, our bidding system had me not playing hands, so a lot of times I was the *dummy*."

"You must be kidding me." Jasmine's eyes rolled with a smirk. "You've been playing cards?" Jasmine was in more disbelief now than ever. A girl could only take so much nonsense.

"Yeah, it's really cool. In the beginning my partner, Grace, and I would be on defense a lot. That's when you are bidding contracts when you know you couldn't make the trick. I think that's called a *sacrifice*."

"Oh my God, T. So what, when you went to get Camille something to drink and 'got stopped by some people'..." Jasmine began.

"Oh, that. Yeah, Grace's friend, Frieda, was getting out so I popped by to say goodbye to the Bridge Club ladies." Tony concluded.

"This is stupid, Tony," said Jasmine, slapping her leg exasperated, though she couldn't deny she was a little relieved. No more drama.

"Well, did you really think that I would leak something like that out? I got a rep ya know." Tony grabbed Jasmine and pulled her close with a grin.

"Tony, I'm serious," pressed Jasmine. She didn't want any more secrets. She was just as mad as the others when Tony spilled everything about the gambling ring and working with the police. She just didn't show it that day. She wanted to take on Tony herself, one on one. If they were going to be together she had to be able to trust him. But more importantly, he had to know he could trust her. Why did he seem insistent on going it alone?

"Dudes with family and friends as good as yours don't have to make decisions alone, Tony," said Jasmine, caressing his face. Her fingers found their way to the scar on his head where the bottle broke. She kissed the scar tenderly.

How'd I get to this place, he asked himself looking into her eyes.

"Jasmine I..." he started but a second ringtone interrupted his train of thought.

It's funny how one, seemingly trivial sound that's heard daily can set things in motion. A car horn can save an unwitting pedestrian's life; a child's cry can communicate fear or pain; and a cell phone ring can invoke emotions of concern, especially when it's from a particular number. This unique chime caused just such a reaction in Tony and his behavior revealed that this call was not as light-hearted as the first.

"Who is it, Tony?" Jasmine was careful to ask.

Angling the LED for less light and more clarity, "It's BeBe," offered Tony.

"Just be careful", Jasmine cautioned.

"Yeah," Tony agreed and answered. "Sup man?"

"Tony, my man, heard you were out of the hospital. They put you back together?" BeBe's voice had never sounded more duplicitous than it did right then. Just when Tony thought things could never sound clearer, low and behold they did.

"I still got what I went in with – what you got going on?" he asked.

"The word on the street is the high rollers were only trying to send you a warning when they dispatched the Yardees to your hood. It was more a show of care and concern for their business interests." Tony wiped a bead of sweat from his brow.

"Yeah, well they gotta funny way of showing the love. I ain't trying to roll like that."

"I've been contacted to draw you back into the camp – to offer you a truce of sorts, extend an olive branch." This was good. Thanks to the police, the gambling ring was more relaxed about Tony. Since he wasn't suspected of anything and would start his training for the Classic, an upcoming basketball tournament, BeBe and the high rollers were back to business as usual with him. He was back in.

"What do they have in mind?" Tony asked.

"Well, you know there is still the Classic?" BeBe replied. "What about it?"

"The thinking is that you are still the man. In fact, your uncooperativeness during the last transaction may have actually removed some of the attention from you. They see how that small setback can actually work in everyone's favor. You gettin' this?"

Jasmine held Tony's hand ever so lightly, periodically moving in closer to get a better ear on the conversation.

"Man, I don't know" inserted Tony.

"Big T, you ain't got no choice," BeBe continued. "You see, these are serious people, and they've shown they will come gunning for you - some of that 'OK Corral' stuff. You're in this thing whether you wanna be or not. Good news is they've found a reason to like you."

"Yeah, but I ain't so keen on you being the 'brainchild' of this thing," Tony countered.

"Look, you ain't challenging my intelligence!" yelled BeBe, voice cracking. "I wasn't the one going native and then dodging bullets."

BeBe was silent for a moment. Tony paced back and forth and looked toward Jasmine. She just sat there, arms crossed. But instead of a scowl, her faced seemed to say, *end this*. Tony found the strength to keep it together. It was time to put this whole fiasco to rest.

"Representatives from both sides need to hold court, the Little Rascals and their parents, so to speak," BeBe explained, regaining his composure. "We'll get the Yardees on lock. Look, I'm supportin' you. They also want to assist you with your finances."

"What do you mean?" Tony inquired, whirling around.

"Your *almost* betting scheme was entertaining to them. It showed guts, but still it was small in their eyes. Vandusen, well, he'd like to elevate you and to do that, you'll need some sort of collateral and they are willing to front you some." Vandusen was the one controlling the Epps Yard gang. He'd herded several kids from the crew to act as his enforcers. Now interested in making money at the Classic, he was taking Tony's old gambling plan to another level.

"You saying they are going to front me some money?" pressed Tony.

"Not exactly money and you will have to play a more substantial role than just shooting a ball. You down or what?" This time it was Tony's turn to be silent as BeBe waited for his answer.

"Court, huh?" he asked finally.

"Yeah, here's where you need to be boy," began BeBe. When Tony had all of the logistics, the call was over.

Jasmine's heart was pounding. Like any woman, she wanted to know details and she wanted to know them now.

"What did he say?"

"He's talking about me and the parties involved having a little conference," said Tony, sitting down next to her. His eyes were forward. He was thinking.

"The men that were shooting at us?" Jasmine pressed.

"No," Tony said offhandedly, brows furrowed.

"Well, what? Who else is involved?"

Jasmine was seeing a new dimension of Tony. His normally cavalier exterior was now peeling away like the layers of an onion. She watched as he rubbed the inner-side of his thumb from nervousness where a callous had formed, something she'd never noticed before. His eyes started to dart back and forth and his head bowed, under the weight of the information he'd just learned. The façade of jokes and one-liners had disappeared.

"Hey, let's get out of here," Tony said. They rose together to go to the car.

As they walked, Jasmine purposely leaned in toward his chest. His heart pumped violently, she felt his rib cage expand and contract.

Tony reflected on BeBe and his place in their lives. He had been his and Evan's running buddy. But as they got older, BeBe got into more and more trouble and was even arrested a few times. Then there was that time at the university when Evan was doing music for a campus event and there was a drug bust. That's when things started to change for Tony, at first he thought for the better. Evan could be so narrow-minded. He had his music and everything, including the loyal girlfriend who supported him. If it wasn't music related, Evan didn't take any interest in it; he was such a stickler. BeBe and Tony got into all sorts of shenanigans and what Evan didn't know wouldn't hurt him. Although they were practically brothers, they were going in different directions, and that was fine. But now Tony wasn't so sure he was in control of any direction he wanted to go in. If the money didn't have him, the gangs wanted him, and if they couldn't reach him the police could. No matter how powerful Vandusen appeared, this wasn't worth the price. Tony's life wasn't his own anymore, and if basketball, Evan and Jasmine, weren't in it, what kind of life was it?

While making their way back to the car, Tony began to slowly break down the call for Jasmine. She knew from their encounter in the park that this day was coming. But now it was actually here. As they sat in the vehicle, Tony gathered himself. As he concluded, he hung his head.

"We're going to make it through this somehow," she encouraged. Her hand met his and just like the carousel, she felt their world turning. The kiss they shared was anything but simple, and for the first time in a long time, they both felt like they were rightly in control.

A second call came through, only not as ominous as the first. Tony held a second cell phone, a burner, and as he answered his back and head were slightly more erect.

"Did the wire pick all of that up?" asked Tony.

"We got it," responded the police detective.

Track 19:
Places Friends, Places Please

The LaShea home was a modest Tudor that was set back on a lazy cul-de-sac. Since Dorothy's departure, it had a sterile feel about it, an aura of impermanence. Even the way the pictures were hung on the wall gave it a *we'll get back to it* feel. Incomplete themes permeated the bathrooms, hallway and dining area. The dusty hand towels in the guest bath were neatly hung but had never been changed. It wasn't that the place was untidy or messy; it just didn't seem like folks had used it for living – just existing. The occupants of this house had never moved forward.

"Mommy," stated Camille as they toured the house, "have I told you how wonderful it is having you back home?"

"I know, sweetie. It's wonderful to be home," Dorothy sighed as the two held hands.

LaShea and his daughter had been mentally preparing for the unthinkable – the possibility of Dorothy dying. The irony of it all was that now she was back home and he was gone. The hallway mirror captured a view of the mother and daughter, hand-in-hand strolling its corridor.

"Your hands seem worn, Mommy. Are you alright?" Camille asked a little concerned.

"I'm fine. Sometimes it takes a while to get something out of your system. Your Grandmother used to say that one's hands tell the story of their present state because they are most used to touch another life. Either they are giving or taking life, but it is the hands that are pierced with either our pain or the pain of others." Dorothy accepted and gently rubbed in the scented lotion her daughter offered her as they examined the bathroom.

Camille, a little overcome with emotion, felt the warmth of her mother's hands as they embraced her faced and wiped away the tears. The blur of her mother's face came into focus between the tears and they embraced. Throughout the evening, they laughed and cried, bowed their heads and recycled the ritual, both unaware that nightfall had come.

The next morning Camille was awakened by the smell of bacon and eggs as she pulled herself from the sofa in the rec room. The two never made it to bed, but merely drifted to sleep on the plush sofa.

Dorothy held the butter dish as she monitored the toaster, "Girl, do you want cinnamon on your toast?"

"Oh Mommy, you're wonderful. Of course I'll take some," gushed Camille, snuggling under the large quilt on the sofa, enjoying the warmth from it.

"You know what I really wish we had was some orange juice. Girl, I drank so much orange juice while I was at Friends," said Dorothy.

By now Camille was rubbing the pattern of the quilt out of her face as she swished a toothbrush round in her mouth.

"I could use some, too," she echoed. "Was it nice there, I mean, at Friends?"

"Sweetie, the place was aptly named," answered Dorothy while using the spatula to slide the sunny-side-up eggs onto the plate. "I met some wonderful people there. Speaking of friends, how are yours?"

"We're okay. Jasmine and I are getting closer. And there is really something happening between her and Tony – as long as he don't act a fool. And singing with the guys has been great."

"I can't believe my little girl has cut a CD!" Dorothy beamed proudly, crunching on some toast.

"It's like when Ryan left and Cory and Jasmine joined, we all found our places," Camille mused. "Evan and Cory have a good vibe. It's like a major progressive move forward for Evan's band. Heck it is a band!"

"Wow, so some people left but you gained new ones and it's perfect now," pondered Dorothy. "Wild how that works."

Camille extended a hand and Dorothy did likewise until both leaned in and their hands joined. "I'm just glad to have you back whole," said Camille.

"Yes, whole," Dorothy agreed.

It wasn't long before the two felt that they were, as Dorothy would say, "Being summoned by the shopping gods." Just as one would suit up as a competitor in an athletic event, dressing for shopping was just as important. The two gathered a basket of newly laundered clothes and also perused their recently dry cleaned items.

"What do you think of the orange chiffon to complement these cork pumps? Or the neutral lace instead?" asked Dorothy.

"Either will work, maybe the chiffon. The ballot is still out on the pumps, but then again they do work and they're good for a lot of walking," offered Camille. "For me, I'm feeling jeans." Camille assumed the role of mannequin for herself, while pressing the jeans against the front of her legs.

"Girl, I love the little dolphins on the back pockets." Dorothy quickly pulled out a knit V-Neck hip riding top, a brightly colored multi-layered silk blouse with billowy sleeves and a white lacey number, cut to mid forearm. "Now, here are a couple of tops for consideration."

Piling into the car, Dorothy and Camille basked in the scenery on their way to the shopping mall. Traffic was non-existent. Most people were already at their destinations by the time the two of them had gotten started. The sun was high in the sky with only a few clouds for decoration. Catching-up with their lives was a nice distraction and the mother and daughter were forced now to walk to a beat of their own making, without the help of Mr. LaShea. It's hard to regain a stride you never really had. Each seemed to possess a new zest for life and a desire to set course on a new beginning; LaShea would've wanted it that way and they knew it.

Later, it seemed like the bags were towing them as they made their way from the last corridor to the main entrance of Peninsula Town Center and the afternoon sun beamed through the doors. Two giddy ladies with bags for appendages as they shimmied toward the entrance. "I'm feeling ice cream from *Jimmy's*. Is *Jimmy's* still there?" asked Dorothy.

Jimmy's was a small non-chain ice-cream shop off the main strip. The décor greeted you with black and white photos of various events in and around the Hampton Coliseum. At one time it was a hangout spot for the students, including the LaSheas. Although the flavors were not as numerous as the major chains, the ambiance was relevant community, which sometimes drew a local crowd versus tourists

Sitting with their ice cream, the two shared their thoughts.

"Honey... you know your Daddy was only trying to keep you safe that night, right?" asked Dorothy as she spooned her ice cream.

"Yeah, it's just... well...I don't know," Camille stammered, peering into her frozen treat.

"What is it, Camille?" Dorothy pressed.

"I wished he'd tried to hear our side of the story," answered Camille. "I wanted him to know that Evan - well, those dudes wouldn't have hurt me."

"That retribution thing with the Epps Yard boys and all," Dorothy added.

"How did you know about that? I hadn't mentioned it to you," Camille's attention rocketed from her ice cream and pierced her mother.

"Oh honey, news travels," responded Dorothy matter-of-factly.

"No Mommy, there's more to this." said Camille, putting her spoon down.

Dorothy placed her dish on the table while clearing her throat, "Honey, I spoke with Evan's mom."

"But, how could you have talked to her?" Camille inquired, cocking her head to one side.

"Cammie she works at the hospital," said Dorothy. "And it was really good to see a familiar face near your father."

"But I didn't even get to talk to you," Camille said, her voice rising, "I needed you." Camille's eyes began to fill with water.

"Camille calm down, Honey," said Dorothy, soothingly. A few people were beginning to take notice.

"I just can't believe he went behind my back like that. I knew I heard him talking about you," yelled Camille.

"Sweetheart you're not making any sense. Heard who talking about what?" Dorothy was at a loss. She had never seen her daughter so upset.

"But Mommy, we're a family and he just goes behind our back? It was no one's business. How could they reach you and not tell me?" Camille's ice cream hit the floor as she shot up from her seat and ran to the car. Patrons turned as the dish impacted the floor. The manager eyed Dorothy as he made his way towards the table with a mop in hand.

"Don't worry, I'll pay for the dish," offered Dorothy.

"I know you will," replied the manager without as much as making eye contact. "$13.50".

"Here," Dorothy said extending a $20 bill. "Keep the change."

Dorothy attempted to comfort Camille as she sulked during the drive back to their home. It was getting dark as they rounded the cul-de-sac and turned into the driveway. Camille ran into the house while Dorothy made trips to bring in the packages. Tossing her keys down in a dish by the door, Dorothy joined Camille who was on the sofa clutching an overstuffed pillow.

"Baby, I know how you feel."

"No, you don't," Camille spouted like poison. "It was hard being without you and somehow my boyfriend gets to talk to you and I don't? Go figure."

"Evan loves you baby. But no one was cracking our family secret. They didn't find me, I found them." explained Dorothy.

"So you went to *see* them!" yelled Camille, getting excited again.

"I wanted to surprise you and your father," said Dorothy, taking Camille by the shoulder. "But it was too late. You were already at the hospital. Our neighbors told me what happened to your father. I ran into Diana on the same floor of the hospital. It was pure coincidence."

"When I reach out and try to love someone they leave me," cried Camille.

Dorothy sat down as close as she could to Camille. "Baby that's not true and no one was keeping anything from you or running from you."

"I loved Nanna, and she was taken from me, then you got sick. Next was Daddy and it's like I keep reliving the same movie over and over again." Camille choked on tears and hid her face. To Dorothy, her daughter resembled her 4-year-old self all over again, trying to fight the tears.

"Baby, it's gonna be alright." Dorothy stroked her daughter's hair.

"I'm sorry," Camille sniffed, releasing her emotions. "I'm sorry Evan. I'm sorry Daddy that I couldn't be with you at the end."

Camille fell into her mother's loving arms. Dorothy turned down the lights as the peace of another evening embraced the two women.

∞

A few days later, Evan and Cory were listening to their latest track, the creation of their collective talents from the other night with Sam, when Evan's cell phone vibrated so loud it interrupted them. It was Tony.

"Go ahead, man," Cory urged.

"Yo," Evan said simply, to which Cory made a face at him.

"She said I should give you a call," answered Tony

"Oh, it's Ton-ay," Evan half joked, while he looked up at Cory.

"Jasmine said I should give you a call – you know for some honest to goodness backup," Tony continued.

"What?" exclaimed Evan. "Since when do you listen to Jasmine?"

"I do – man, I do now, probably should get your help."

"What's going down?"

"I've got to meet with these dudes who've been banking on my games," Tony confessed.

"The actual dudes? For real?" Evan rose up from his chair and Cory stepped closer.

"Yeah man, coppers got a plan," Tony said. "This is it."

"So, where and how do I fit into this?" asked Evan, as Cory nodded his head in agreement with the question.

"You still my boy, right?" pressed Tony.

After a brief pause from Evan and a punch from Cory, Evan relented. "Yeah, man."

"Alright, that's what's up," said Tony, genuine excitement in his voice. "Coppers gonna be hidden, I need somebody who's got my back. I don't wanna be nobody's collateral damage."

"Now I ain't doing no cops and robbers Tony," Evan cautioned.

"Huh?" Cory asked with a shrug.

"Not asking you to carry no piece – just ..." began Tony.

"He – we want your support Evan," Jasmine interjected, whispering into the phone.

"Jasmine, that you?" Both Evan and Cory were surprised by her voice. Tony wasn't playing games with her after all.

"Just be near – for the both of us...please?" She asked.

Evan held the phone away from his face and looked at it. This thing was getting more real by the moment. And Tony was actually listening to Jasmine; she was on the line. Camille had been right about them – maybe trouble was finally bringing him to his senses.

"Let's meet up, Ev," Tony offered.

"Ok, but I need to see Camille first. It's important," Evan said firmly.

"No sweat, I'll text you," Tony answered and the call ended.

"I'll drive," said Cory, who had finished packing up his guitar and pedals.

Cory and Evan navigated the roads to the LaShea's as evening descended on Hampton Roads. Wheels splashed puddles of rainwater as they rounded the bend. A light was still on in the house when they arrived. Evan was determined, whether or not the light was on. He thought that he'd respected Camille's wisdom. But he didn't realize the kind of insight she had until he sensed Tony's change in regard to Jasmine. He also remembered Camille's words about Tony as he exited the car and approached the door.

"You were right about Tony," Evan said, as he and Camille sat in her bedroom. "He's working with the cops to right this thing. It's going down tonight. He called me a little while ago."

"So this is really happening?" asked Camille. "Does his family know?"

"I figure as much? Maybe? He's over 18; they might not have to know. I don't know how it all works, to be honest," Evan admitted, brushing a couple of his braids aside.

"I know my mom hasn't said anything," he continued. "Neither has my Uncle Nate since he got back in town. He always hears things. But this ain't something everybody needs to hear, I guess, detective work and all."

"Maybe he just felt boxed in?" said Camille, looking down.

"Boxed in?" probed Evan.

"That's why he told us everything. It must have gotten real for him. I mean we can't do anything but..." Camille rubbed her neck and looked into Evan's eyes. "I guess he felt bad about what happened at Soul-Light."

"Yeah, that was scary as all get-out," nodded Evan.

Camille nodded in agreement. They were quiet for a moment, simply taking in the recent turn of events.

"It's always about Tony," chuckled Camille. "Not a party without him."

Evan smiled. He leaned forward and brushed a strand of Camille's hair back. Her hair was still damp from her shower earlier. Evan met Camille's gaze and his hand rested gently on her neck. They felt like they hadn't seen each other in years, as ludicrous as that was. Evan's face slowly inched toward her's.

"Evan," Camille said suddenly, causing him to jerk back slightly and remove his hand. Camille smiled a little and took his hand and placed it on her cheek.

"Evan, I'm sorry," Camille began. Pausing to collect herself, she started again.

"What I'm trying to say is thank you, for everything. Thanks for all of the love and support, with everything, with my mom and my dad and the funeral. I know the band hasn't been together much for a while."

"Oh don't worry about that. We guys made do," Evan added.

"Well still," Camille continued. "I know I've been weird lately with all the changes in my life. But you never ran away. I can trust you."

Camille's voice trailed off. She had pressed herself against him and they shared a tender kiss. Everything was getting back to the way it was. Camille was right, a lot of life changes had occurred in all of their lives. But some things, such as Evan and Camille's connection, were reverting back to their original order as evidenced by their lengthy passionate embrace. The night was still young, and there was plenty of time for one more dynamic change.

Track 20:
Holding Court

Tony leaned over the railing at Little Island Pier as he waited for Evan and Cory to meet him. His arms were covered in goose bumps from the crisp, night air. As a breeze blew in over the water, not a vessel could be seen. It was overcast and the moon was full, which made Tony feel like it was perfect for night-stalking creatures such as the Wolfman or the Lochness Monster to jump out at any minute. The night seemed ominous. But then again, what he was about to do was no walk in the park; he didn't make a habit of leading police stings.

In a few hours he and BeBe would meet up with Vandusen, the head of the racketeering ring. When all persons of interest were accounted for and the confessions were caught on tape, the police would descend on the meeting, shutting down the ring permanently. Tony could possibly return to basketball if all went as planned.

As nearby fishermen cast and reeled in their rods, Tony began to feel like live bait. The only difference was he knew what he was getting into and expected to escape unharmed. But it wasn't like that with real fishing; fishing was a gambit, a sacrifice. A fisherman close to him was checking his line under one of the pier lamps when Evan and Cory arrived. The three friends dapped each other and hugged, then took a spot leaning over the pier staring out into oblivion. Tony was in the middle, flanked by Cory on his left side and Evan on his right. They stood silently, listening to the continuous loop of snapping fishing lines and lapping waves below, until Tony at last broke the silence.

"You know, I was thinking about Ryan today," he began. "Off in D.C. doing his own thing with his family and new baby. What the heck did he do for a living, anyway?"

Evan rubbed his chin trying to come up with an answer. Cory squinted his eyes and offered a guess. "Consultation or something?"

"I don't know," said Tony, shaking his head. "Point is he's off doing his thing, kinda doing better than some of us here. Some of us got girls, jobs or a thing we're into. But Ryan. He's what I wanna shoot for." Evan and Cory nodded in agreement. Even though Cory had only met Ryan a few times, anyone striking out to make something of themselves who can still find time to hang out with buddies was impressive.

"Ryan's little girl, Zarah, was a cutie wasn't she? Did you see her, at Mr. LaShea's funeral? Evan asked.

"Yeah man, I did," Tony agreed staring at the ocean as another breeze blew in. They looked happy man, I mean really happy. Sorry you had to lose him like that Ev, I know he did good stuff with you and the band."

Evan waved his hand away as if sweeping Tony's statement aside and off the railing. "Nah, don't sweat that T. I mean, thanks, but we all made peace with it. Our little boy Ryan's all grown up." The three laughed as Evan wiped away a fake tear. As they settled down Evan realized Tony was rubbing his hand a lot.

"You okay bro?" Evan asked, patting Tony on his shoulder. Cory looked over, giving all of his attention to Tony and Evan. Tony exhaled, shook his head and looked at the jet black sky above, the full moon hidden behind some clouds.

"I'm just ...I'm scared guys," Tony admitted, rubbing his head. "How'd I get to this place? What went wrong?"

"Life, man," Evan offered simply. "We can't go back Tony, but you're not alone. You and the cops are gonna squash this tonight, remember that."

"You're back in control, Tony," Cory offered, elbowing him gently.

"I just keep asking myself why I didn't stop with this nonsense back at that college party. We almost got pinched big time with BeBe that night." Tony kept shaking his head as if trying to wake up from a bad dream. He knew things could turn around, that he could get his life back. But he had to get through the night first.

"I - I almost wanna bail on the cops," he said. He exhaled deeply as if he'd been holding his breath for hours.

Evan inched closer to Tony and wrapped his left arm around his friend's neck.

"Chill man, chill. It's gonna be ok," said Evan, trying to soothe him. By now Tony was shaking and Evan was getting a little bit nervous. Cory stepped in and offered his encouragement.

"I've been where you are, man," he began. "You're trying to make sense of things. Sometimes in the beginning, life seems like a big party and you think you're invincible and your skills take you far. Next thing you know, it's all gonna come crashing down if you don't make the right choice. It sucks. I was too late man. I made the choice way too slowly and it cost us." Evan listened intently as Cory wove the tale of Frankie for Tony. It felt good to have Cory here.

"We mess up, Tony," Cory continued. "We think we have all the answers but sometimes someone else is holding all the cards. By the time we look at all the options and try to figure it out, it's too late. But it's not too late for you." Cory grabbed Tony's shoulder and looked him in the eye.

"Just think about that. It's not too late for you. It's not too late."

Tony's cell phone chimed in his pocket. He slowly pulled it out and saw a text message from Jasmine, which simply read, *I love you*. Standing so close to him, Cory and Evan saw the message, too. As Tony adjusted himself he dropped the phone over the railing.

"No!" he yelled, which drew glances from the patrons on the pier. But the phone bounced and, before it hit the water, Evan quickly caught it.

"Oh God," breathed Tony, accepting the phone back. "Ev, thanks."

"The girls were always falling over themselves for you," Evan joked, and everything resumed normally on the pier, except for Tony's laughter.

"What? What's up?" asked Evan.

Tony couldn't contain himself. He crouched to his knees and shook with laughter until he turned and propped his back against the lower rails to get himself together. Evan and Cory still confused and a little freaked, sat down next to him as Tony fought to get his words out.

"It - it - it's just so crazy. You know, most of the girls that came after me wanted you, Evan!"

"What?" Evan asked, confused.

"Well, like the last few...Sheila, Ciara, Kirsten..." Tony stammered. "When I was done with those girls, they always had to get the last word. Some of them were like, 'Why did I trip off your dumb butt? I should've got with Spencer.' They didn't even want me."

"Well ain't that something," Cory mused.

"What do they have to do with this?" pressed Evan, still in the dark.

"They settled for me man," Tony revealed. "They knew being with me was a waste of time, but they knew they couldn't get with you."

"You don't have to belittle yourself, Tony," said Cory.

"No man, it's not like that." Tony continued. "I was in your shadow Ev, always was. I couldn't be the good boy you were with the music hall of fame family. But if it wasn't for you and Camille there would be no Jasmine and me."

"Dude you'd *been* going after her, though," said Evan, shaking his head.

"Yeah man, but she blew me off and then got buddy-buddy with your girl," Tony explained.

"Jasmine wanted Evan?" Cory gasped, cocking his head.

"Nah, she just wanted a friend. But I was friends with you guys already and I wouldn't leave her alone," Tony shrugged. "I don't know. It's like I caught a break, thanks to you. Kind of like you catching that dumb phone...and it's Jasmine!"

"Oh okay, if it makes sense to you," said Evan, grinning.

"I don't know man, maybe I'm flipping out. Maybe it's the pre-sting jitters," Tony said, wiping his face. Tony turned from Cory to Evan and just sighed. He was finally starting to feel calm.

"I love that girl, you know," he said. "Can you believe that? Me? In love? Like in those stupid movies?"

"Congratulations," said Cory, smirking.

"Jasmine is one of a kind, T," said Evan. "And I'm not just saying that because she's one of my singers."

As Tony laughed one of his phones went off and he mellowed out.

"Yeah, I'm ready," he said and ended the call. It was time. "I just wanted to be with my guys, and make sure we were cool." They got up from the pier floor and started walking back toward the parking lot, their friendship intact and renewed.

Men were already there and waiting when they approached the parking lot. Tony immediately recognized them as his police contacts. Tony turned to Evan and Cory and hugged them both. Evan returned his best friend's hug, squeezing him extra tight, in case there was any doubt that their bond was iron clad.

"Be in touch?" inquired Evan.

"No doubt," answered Tony. "Thank you guys. We're gonna set it off at Brigg's warehouse tonight!" And with that, Tony turned to meet up with the detectives.

Now it was only Evan and Cory standing in the parking lot.

"We'll hear about the arrests on the news in no time," said Cory optimistically. "Tony's got this under control. The cops will watch his back." As Cory unlocked his car and began to get in he paused and stared at Evan.

"Don't worry, Evan," he said.

"Yeah the cops will be watching his back," said Evan, opening his door with a strange look in his eyes. "But who's gonna be watching their back?

∞

Unlike the ocean, the alleys of the Hampton Roads area were non-therapeutic and sadly cool. The vehicles that cruised near them, oftentimes messengers of darkness, scuttled from one place of destruction to the next.

Tony had agreed to meet Vandusen's men behind the large Brigg's warehouse with police cover, in a space for moonlight to oversee the whole operation. But the night was still overcast with a light rain. The police had instructed him to stay out of the shadows and to draw as many suspects into the light for possible identification, but they didn't count on it raining. It was getting fairly late and Tony's heart raced as BeBe pulled-up. But Tony wasn't afraid anymore, he just wanted to end this once and for all and get his life back. Bebe parked his large Lincoln near a street lamp, just shy of the moonlit opening. In the background, forms shifted back and forth.

Offering to drive Cory's car back home from Little Island Park seemed like an honest gesture by Evan. But he slammed the accelerator and sped off to the warehouse in pursuit of Tony.

"He's got police support," Cory protested as they sped down the road.

"Do this for me, Faber," Evan pleaded. "I just want to see that they end this. He's my oldest friend, man. I know a shortcut and I know that area, we'll be in the clear."

Evan wanted to support his friend and he knew Tony would have wanted them to be there somehow.

"I want to make sure that BeBe gets his," Evan said through gritted teeth. "These thugs aren't gonna trash my friend's life. They're not taking him out like this." Cory held on tight as Evan sped along, narrowly missing a red stoplight. Before he knew it they had screeched to a halt near the warehouse.

"This is insane!" said Cory, jumping out of the car behind Evan. "Evan give me those keys!" Evan stopped in his tracks, slowly turned and tossed the keys to Cory. Cory looked them over, then faced Evan and shook his head.

"Doesn't matter, we're here now."

Evan nodded. "We're just gonna watch, Faber. I'd have done the same for you and Frankie."

"Watch it, Ev," Cory warned him. "This is nothing like me and Frankie."

"My bad, man. Look, Tony...he's better than this," Evan said, throwing his hands up in the air. "And I'm gonna see him make it right. I love that boy. Stay here if you want, but I need to see this." Evan turned and ran for the warehouse leaving Cory looking on in horror.

Two men flanked BeBe as they strode coolly across the parking lot to talk business. Tony did likewise. He flashed his best Tony Jackson winning smile as he approached them.

"We are pleased to finally meet this future NBA superstar," offered one of the men, dressed in a suit.

"Yes, it is an honor," insisted the other, wearing a turtleneck and jacket.

"Yeah, well I appreciate it and everything, but I almost didn't make it that night at Soul-Light," exclaimed Tony. "I thought we were friends, Vandusen?"

"Not to worry," Vandusen, the man in the suit, interjected, "Although they were amateurs, they were only instructed to make you aware of our presence, that's all. It was a show of force to remind you who's in control."

"Is this how you always do business?" Tony asked, following instructions and moving to a key question. "I mean, I heard that The Epps Yard Crew hit the Players Club last month...only a dude didn't walk out of there."

"You have many questions, Mr. Jackson," answered Vandusen, staring.

Water danced nearby as a second car swerved onto the scene. Undercover cops were positioned all along the escape routes. The streets were abuzz with hoodlums hooting, hollering and shoving, but anyone from the streets would recognize them as typical wannabe thugs roaming the streets harassing everybody in sight.

BeBe made a move back towards their car taking advantage of the open door.

"Remain calm," Vandusen commanded the man fiddling with his jacket.

Evan crept out amongst the faceless nightlife, unable to tell cop from crook, but the need to differentiate hadn't occurred to him at all. He didn't realize he was in a hornets' nest. He watched as a fumbling drunk staggered out of the driver's seat of the Yardees truck while the passenger leaned over the top of the car. From the back seat, another thug rolled down his window and hurled obscenities.

"It's in control," Tony heard in between the drops pounding against his earpiece. The police were watching like hawks.

"Yardees reign! Yeah man, pow, pow, pow," hollered the drunk.

The man with the turtleneck and jacket warned him that they were uninvited guests at the meeting. BeBe was enough representation for the Yardee foot soldiers.

"We should've been paid more," the drunk retorted.

"Paid more?" Vandusen exclaimed. "You *are* amateurs!"

Evan began to move dangerously closer to the group. It was not unusual for those on the street to *own the street* and tonight was no different. Unfortunately, in the light of a nearby street lamp, Evan resembled BeBe. The Yardee shotgun-man knew BeBe was connected with this meeting and Evan's appearance mixed with the gunman's erratic behavior and whatever he drank and/or smoked earlier set him off.

"Last month was an accident. We told you that!" he screamed, slowly raising his gun.

"This is MY operation. Now put that gun down," screamed Vandusen at the top of his lungs.

The police heard what they needed to hear. The captain raised his hand to signal the strategically placed detectives who were masquerading as people of the night.

"I said put that gun down. I paid you well," Vandusen shouted.

"Then it was BeBe who short-chnged us. He trying to cut us out boys!" screamed the Yardee in the back of the truck.

Just then, Tony's listening device began to lose power. Evan and the first Yarkdee were in a position to see Tony's back left side begin to flash red. The blips were rapid in real time but for a few moments the final flashes seemed to count off time like the slow militaristic cadence of soldiers marching to their demise.

"POLICE, FREEZE! POLICE, EVERYBODY ON THE GROUND!" yelled the hidden police captain through a megaphone.

"He's wired!" yelled the thug in the passenger seat.

Evan lunged toward the group while the officers who were impersonating prostitutes, gamers and pimps swarmed from inside the perimeter surrounding the warehouse. Vandusen retreated behind the car door and entered the vehicle with BeBe as one of the other Yardees spotted Evan, who appeared muddy in the dim light.

"BeBe!" he pointed, mistaking Evan. The Yardee partner realigned the shot for Evan, who was totally exposed and unaware of the gunman; his only focus was Tony.

Tony fell as his ears popped from the sound of shots ringing out from the direction of the Yardee's truck. The man in the jacket tried to shoot back but his nerves got the best of him and he missed his target. Next thing he knew, police descended on him, tackling him to the floor. All bystanders fled as the police revealed themselves.

"Holy - Evan?" Tony screamed as he and Evan lay flat.

Suddenly, BeBe and Vandusen both burst from their car and opened fire. Evan and Tony covered their heads while police returned fire. The whole place erupted in gunfire and BeBe and Vandusen's screams echoed throughout. Vandusen's arm exploded as a bullet from a policewoman posing as a prostitute took him out of the firefight. Another round hit his leg dropping him to the ground.

Evan followed Tony and they began to crawl behind his car when the sound of a revved engine came careening around a corner.

"What?" a voice screamed.

As Evan and Tony peeked over the hood, Evan's eyes grew wide as he watched Cory's car come flying into view - right at BeBe.

"AAAAAAAHHHHH SCREW YOU COPS!" BeBe yelled, shooting into the car windshield. A splatter of blood hit the inside of the windshield and the car spun out of control, forcing BeBe to leap out of the way.

"CORY NO!" screamed Evan. BeBe who was still on edge, turned in the direction of Evan's voice and fired a shot. Tony pulled Evan down again. As they lay on the ground they could see from underneath the car that BeBe was several yards away. More shots rang out until finally, Evan saw BeBe's knees hit the pavement and his body slump over.

Evan broke cover and ran straight for Cory as the police fully converged onto the scene.

"HEY FREEZE DON'T MOVE!" screamed the policewoman.

"GOOD GUY!" yelled her partner, having recognized Evan with Tony weeks prior.

"INFORMANT! HE'S WITH ME!" Tony hollered back racing after Evan.

The police checked for survivors and arrested Vandusen, along with the man in the turtleneck and jacket, and the two other Yardees in the truck. But BeBe and the drunken thug were dead.

Evan ripped open the drivers side door and Cory spilled out onto the pavement. Evan noticed the blood on the windshield and some on the headrest and yelled for help.

"Get help! Get help! Call an ambulance – Cory's hit!"

"Oh God," Tony sobbed, helping Evan and an officer with Cory.

He's better than this was the last thing Cory remembered Evan telling him before he ran off. Cory had heard that before. He had uttered those same words to Frankie the day he left him to die at the hands of criminals, alone with no support and no friends. Cory reasoned that the last person Frankie saw should have been him. He couldn't be there for his best friend long ago, but tonight Cory wanted to be there for his new found ones.

Cory's mouth was dry; moving his tongue was labor. A song lyric went through his mind. Evan knelt down and cradled Cory's head. He was talking but Cory could not hear him. Blood mixed with the tears in his eyes and he couldn't see anything. Cory realized that he missed his family, his godfather, and his friends back in Oregon. Then there was his friendship with Evan. He'd have to get their songs out. He never got to tell Evan what Ken said about him.

Evan sounds like the real deal, Ken said over the phone. *He delivers every time, doesn't he? Like his name's sake?*

Street sounds became audible again. The red light on Tony's backside remained solid and then slowly faded out.

Track 21:
Transcendental

The pastel sandstone walls of the humble structure enveloped the mourners as they filed into the church. A Southwestern motif with multi-toned, vibrant colors adorned the windows and doors, which let in light of a burnt orange hue that simulated both sunrise and sunset. No crucifix or other religious icons were present to challenge the occupant's motives. It was a sanctuary that embodied heaven, without assumptions, and earth, with the evidence of man and his intended cooperation with nature. Palms trees were placed in what seemed to be strategic locations around the sanctuary. Their green fronds were like fingers as they waved in the breeze of the overhead fans.

A petite woman gently made her way to the speaker's platform. She welcomed the guests and described this as a time of transition. She encouraged those in attendance that it was a celebration of Cory's life and reminded them how he had touched all of their lives. Her joy was inexplicable and her posture was one of victory, not lament. She concluded her greeting with a few words from one of Cory's songs. Her voice was life giving, her pitch was undeniably true. The words seemed to touch everyone's soul. Inspired, others came forward to exchange their personal insights into Cory's life. They came from near and far to testify about the impact that Cory's life and death, had on the musical community. Some of the musicians who stepped forward used their instruments to convey what was in their heart. Others offered a poem.

An older man of average build, wearing basic garb and an air of importance, strolled humbly across the platform. Apologizing for his weariness, he stroked his bald head and wiped his brow. His brown shoes were well polished and his dark trousers were neatly pressed with the cuffs falling precisely to the top of his shoes. His shirt was meticulously folded into his trousers and showed no signs of wrinkle or distress.

He thanked God for Cory's assistance in helping him come to know about God's Kingdom, and described his son as the one Cory had befriended in Portland. Although he was eventually killed, his son had expressed that he'd developed a stronger sense of self and even grown closer to his Creator, crediting Cory as a key player in this change. Although, it sadden him to think that Cory did not realize how much of an impact he had on his son's life. The lives of these young men revealed to him that there were key influences of relationship: timing, message and impact. He admitted that he had wanted his son to succeed so much that he had distorted things and impaired his son's progress. After stepping back and watching events unfold, he explained that his eyes were finally open. As he completed his story, he began to unfold the strap of a leather bound book.

"I ask that you review 2nd Chronicles 5:5 - 6 with me. 'And they brought up the ark and the tabernacle of the congregation, and all the holy vessels that were in the tabernacle, these did the priests and the Levites bring up. Also, King Solomon, and all the congregation of Israel that were assembled unto him before the ark, *sacrificed sheep and oxen, which could not be told nor numbered for multitude.'"

At the end of his reading, the old man shut the book and quietly wrapped the leather binding. Folding his hands on top of it he closed his eyes and all was silent for what seemed like an eternity. Then, lifting his eyes toward the attendees, he spoke again.

"I emphasized the phrase 'sacrificed sheep and oxen, which could not be told nor numbered for multitude'. More often than not, we fail to realize the measure of sacrifice that must be made for us to experience a particular benefit. We tend to think... well I know that I have, we think inwardly, and we adopt a narcissistic viewpoint. But we don't know what kind of changes Hampton Roads had to go through to be prepared to receive Cory. We don't know what kinds of changes his new friends had to experience to accept him. I was considering, you cannot measure the sacrifice required for true purpose to manifest. The reason may be because it's not a one-for-one exchange. An apple tree does not look like an apple seed. In fact, unless the seed is planted and dies, there won't be an apple tree. And so friends know this, we who were touched in our relationships with Cory should be encouraged to step into our collective destinies no matter how strange or painful the transition, destinies that have been prepared in advance for us and may one day lead to *where the streets have no name*... Thank you."

As the older man concluded, a young man stood up and walked toward the casket. Laying his hand on it, he smiled and whispered, "The Grammy goes to...thank you, Cory."

The nurse's face slowly came into view. It glowed as the light shone brightly behind her head while she was leaning over. Cory's head was throbbing and the lights hurt his eyes. But hearing the nurses and his friends was worth braving the splitting headache.

"He's coming to," they kept saying. "Cory's waking up."

Track 22:
Discussions with the Past

All of his new friends were overjoyed to hear that Cory had only suffered superficial wounds in the firefight at Brigg's warehouse. The bullet that came through the windshield simply grazed his scalp, and the doctors expected he'd be fine in no time. Ms. Senor stayed by his side on his first day at the hospital. Whenever she needed a rest she turned things over to Evan, but the garden of fresh flowers in the room reminded everyone of her presence. As Cory healed, the police cleared him and Evan from their unofficial involvement in the sting that night. As far as the police were concerned, Evan Spencer had gotten lost and wandered into police territory when he noticed his best friend meeting with some shifty characters just when all hell broke loose. Cory Faber, looking for Evan, drove into the same police situation and was fired upon by suspects. Tony's cover was safe, Cory's wounds were anything but fatal and the bad guys were arrested, though sadly, a young man lost his life.

Cory was glad to hear that Tony's business with the police was concluded. He soaked up some rest and relaxation anticipating his godfather and his parent's flight down to get answers and clear details on what happened. For now, he heeded instructions to rest. In time, he'd be walking around with a clean bill of health.

Cory's family wasn't the only ones who wanted answers. Tony's family could put their fears to rest about his illegal dealings, but he'd have to work to earn their trust back too, just as he had with his friends. He assured everyone he was a new man, up to the challenge and unafraid to face the consequences of his actions.

But Diana Spencer needed peace of mind. The idea of her son caught up in a police sting, taking on criminal rings in the dead of night was not her idea of letting go, as Nate had pushed her to do. Evan endured intense grilling when the real story finally came out amongst the group about the affair at the old warehouse. How could he be so stupid? And so reckless? He had interfered with a police investigation! It could have been argued that Cory wouldn't have gotten hurt if it hadn't been for Evan being so bullheaded. Nate got the same earful sometime later.

"So what? You just leave on your 'Spirit Walk' to discover yourself, lecture me about my son, and I am the one who needs to let go?" Diana demanded in the living room with her big brother. They hadn't talked since that night at dinner when she felt Evan was slipping away like a wet fish.

Nate was doing all he could, trying to understand his sister's anger and confusion, without pressuring or censoring her.

"I know it was reckless and maybe Evan got off too easily. But the point is he got involved in Tony's thing to help him. This was never about rebellion, Diana."

Diana shook her head, fuming. "This has gone too far Nate. That mess at the Soul-Light was on Tony! Getting that place shot up? The news drove Jake LaShea to his grave. I thought Tony and Evan were supposed to be friends. What's he done for EVAN lately, huh? Getting everybody caught up in his mess!"

"Tony's making up for it," Nate urged her. "He put his own family through a lot too. He's got good people in his life, but he put those murderers away, *real killers*, and their associates. Tony's got to think about how his actions affect other people. All the kids do, no matter what."

Nate folded his hands together. Diana overreacted about a lot of things, but this was worse than the college drug incident, and it pained him that he wasn't around when Tony got hurt in the club shooting. But it seemed that maybe something else was eating at his sister and fueling the anger she had over her son's recklessness. What point was she trying to make? Evan was helping people! He was stupid about it and could have left it to the police; surely emotional support should have been enough for Tony that night.

Come on Sis, give me something, he thought.

Diana, jaws clenched and arms folded tightly, paced back and forth briefly in the living room before sitting down again, eyes watering.

"Where have you been, Nate? Where have you been all this time?"

Nate sat up perplexed. "I've been with my partners in the business, it was a summit."

"Nate?" Diana said methodically, eyes tense. "Where did you go? Huh, where did this *new* Nate come from?"

"Diana..." Nate said lowering his eyes.

"WHERE?" she screamed. "I'm not in the mood for games! Everybody is making all these life changes. I nearly lost my son twice while he's off saving the world with his music. And you? You were supposed to guide him away from all of this... to *protect us*." Diana's head twitched as she spoke. It was like Nate was on trial. Diana wasn't as angry anymore. It was as if she was stalking her own brother like prey, the living room turning into her hunting grounds; she was circling him like a lioness.

"Go ahead Diana. Say what you need to say," Nate offered, not fighting it. He deserved what was coming to him. He knew this day could come.

"So... you and Evan," Diana began slowly. "You two all buddy-buddy now? Where was that over 20 years ago, big bro?" Her words were laced with venom and Nate winced when she uttered them.

"You were always there for me, Nate, always watching my back. You'd have done anything for me. Or was I mistaken? Huh? Maybe it was all for YOU."

"Diana, I love you and I love this family. I'd never let anything happen to us," Nate said earnestly. "You were so young and our family had been through so much."

"Don't hide behind the family, Nathan." Diana pointed her finger shaking with rage. "You loved music just like the rest of us. It flowed in your veins no different than it did in mine. I was happy and you weren't. I found someone and you were alone. That man LOVED me!" Diana began to sweat as tears fell from her eyes. Every muscle in her face was tense as she tore into her brother.

"What changed?" she demanded. "You always thought you knew better. You would've done anything to look good for Daddy. I held onto the music tighter than the rest of you and you just had to take it away - to take him away. Now what? Now you need a new challenge? You drive my son away from me, too?"

"No!" Nate interrupted unable to take anymore. Diana paused momentarily, perhaps grateful for a breather. Nate tried again more softly.

"No, I don't want to drive Evan away from you, honey. I don't want to decide anything anymore; that's why I took my hands off the situation. He's your son and he's a man that knows what he wants."

Diana fidgeted absentmindedly and the two were quiet for a moment. Both of their minds were racing, and after shaking her head as if to dislodge something absurd, Diana probed further.

"You still haven't answered my question, Nate. What changed?" Nate just sat there and rubbed his tired eyes.

"Okay here's another question: who was in love back then? Me or you?"

"Diana what do you want from me?" Nate demanded.

"Nate, you see it so clearly now," said Diana softly. "I know I throw fits and I get in Evan's face and smother him. I'm not stupid; I'm his mother. But I had a choice long ago, and you took it from me. Now you want to give it back and it's too late."

Nate rested his palms on his knees, taking in the suddenly frail image of his little sister swaying in her seat.

"You never even said you were sorry," she whispered as fresh tears flowed down her face. Nate's countenance expressed pity as his sister sat there, heartbroken all over again.

"You let him come in, play my heart strings. Nothing so beautiful had ever come out of my life as when I'd loved him, next to Evan. But then you just drove him out. You all did. Now you're switching on me again, and my son is happy. He's right where he needs to be. So tell me Nate."

Nate looked away as it all dawned on him; he started to cry softly. What could he tell her?

"Why do I feel like I have been *cheated*...Again?"

Track 23:
The Time for Games Has Passed

Cory's acoustic melody floated over the rooftops of the nearby beach homes as he sat on his upper deck. Guitar in hand, his gentle strumming ushered in high noon. He wore a clean bandage where the bullet had grazed him. His buzz-cut was the work of the nurses who dressed his wound. His mom freaked when she saw his shaved head when they talked online. He had to admit, he missed his shoulder length blond locks. He was thinking about this, among other things, as the sun rose higher in the bright blue heavens above. The thunder of jets pounded the sky.

Frankie would have laughed me to scorn if he could see me now, Cory thought, lightly strumming the guitar strings. He remembered Frankie hassling him from time to time about his long hair, calling him names like Pretty Boy and even Rapunzel. His jokes were over the top, but once Frankie got started there was no stopping him.

What part of shoulder length did he not understand, Cory mused, smirking to himself.

Cory's thoughts drifted to his mom and dad, who were very grateful to have heard from him and overjoyed he was alright. His mother wasn't thrilled to hear her son had been shot. Thank God for Ken, because Cory didn't know how to break that news to his folks. He left it to Ken to explain the gritty details. Cory overemphasized *car injury*. He was certainly having an *exciting* time in Virginia they thought. First his car was stolen, and then he was shot at trying to help a friend. But all was well and he assured them he was safe. Cory had video chatted with his parents the other day and showed them his bandage. It was good to see their faces again. He could count on one hand how many times he had talked to them since coming down to Virginia. He just needed space for a little while from everyone involved with Frankie's case except Ken, of course, who was right in the thick of it. His mom made him promise to stay in touch more often and he wasn't about to argue. The recent turn of events with Tony, Evan, and the gambling ring was a stiff reminder that family was everything. That, and the dream he had in the hospital, was still on his mind. He paused his guitar playing for a moment, lost in the vision, when he heard footsteps.

"Hey Faber," said Evan, smiling.

"What a pleasant surprise. What's up Evan," Cory replied, setting down his instrument and hugging his friend. The hug lasted a second longer than Evan had anticipated. After slacking somewhat, he awkwardly embraced Cory tighter.

"Sorry," he laughed when they released each other and sat down.

"No it's fine. It's just good to see you, buddy," Cory answered. "So...how's our favorite basketball star?"

"Tony's good," Evan began. "There will be a court hearing soon to square this whole mess out. He's laying low for now until the police tell him otherwise."

Cory picked up his guitar again and started plucking out a few chords. "He's going to be okay though, isn't he?"

"He'll be fine, I think. His full cooperation should take the case far," said Evan, shielding his eyes from the sun. "Number one priority is making the case against that Vandusen guy stick. That's all I know."

"What about Jasmine?"

Evan leaned back to get more comfortable when a cloud blocked the sun, giving him some relief. "She's okay. She's by his side. His whole family is. My mom and I were talking to them, lending our support. I'm just glad this thing is done. I don't think it's looking too good for Vandusen though."

"Good," said Cory, eyes closed basking in the shade the cloud provided.

"Yeah... so how are you?" Evan asked. "We barely recognized you without the hair. You and Tony look like twins."

"I bet we do, Evan," Cory joked sarcastically, rubbing his buzz cut. "He probably cried every night for his beloved high-top fade. Faded for good." They both got a good laugh out of that one.

"Maybe I'll get a faux hawk when I heal up."

"I don't know, man, Cammie said the long hair was sexy, made you look artsy or something," shrugged Evan.

"Did she now?"

"Her words, but then she flipped it back on me and said that's why she loves me so much," Evan continued with a grin.

"I can see it," Cory nodded. "The braids give you that earthy, conscious Afro Soul demeanor, you know? Like you're gonna say something deep any minute."

"Well yeah, I've been known to spit a few words of wisdom now and then," Evan gloated, sitting up straight. "I am a fairly decent lyricist, if I do say so myself."

Cory laughed while searching for a chord on the guitar that he couldn't quite figure out. Soon the sun peaked out from the cloud, beaming down on them again.

"How is she and Mrs. LaShea?" Cory asked, closing his eyes again trying to get the tune right.

"They're good, too. They said something about looking at the books for Mr. LaShea's business," Evan answered. "You wanna go into that room downstairs and get out of this sun?"

They descended the steps and walked inside to the sunroom. Cory set his guitar down and turned the ceiling fan on. They sat down at the picnic table and Evan went to his favorite habit of dribbling his white golf ball.

"You and your lucky charm are inseparable, aren't you," Cory remarked. "I don't think I've ever seen you without it."

"Yeah, it's my muse, I guess," Evan answered, rolling the ball on the table top from hand to hand. "That is to say, it gives my head and hands something to do when I'm not in Heaven's Gate working on songs with you guys. But you didn't answer my question. How are you, Cory?"

"I'm alright, I guess," Cory answered giving Evan his full attention. "Head feels a little sore from time to time, but I'm great otherwise."

"That was a crazy night, bro," said Evan, eyes wide as he rolled the ball from side to side. He lost control of it and it nearly rolled off the table but Cory snatched it before it hit the floor.

"Nice hands," said Evan.

Cory looked the ball over and bounced it on the table.

"You dream much?" he asked Evan.

"All the time, Faber," answered Evan. "Did you dream something you want to talk about?"

Cory bounced the ball to Evan, who caught it. Evan then slid down so that he was sitting on the opposite end of the table from where Cory sat. He rolled the ball to Cory and, as they talked, the ball sped from corner to corner like a small tabletop game.

"It's a miracle we got out of there in one piece," Cory began.

"Dude, you were like a madman driving out of nowhere like that," stressed Evan, chuckling. "What was going through your head?"

The ball rolled back to Cory, who held onto it for a little while as he thought about Evan's question.

"When you ran after Tony to the spot, I was driving away man. Then my mind went back to that car ride with Frankie back home. Everything flashed through my mind again, mainly our success and of course, the girls. That one groupie latched onto Frankie hard man, and then the guys started lying and acting weird. Then Frankie came clean about the drugs and it all led to that car ride. You know what? I really don't remember if I knew he had the dope on him that day or not anymore. My Godfather might've had to arrest me if I'd been there. I just remember feeling like my best friend was throwing everything away."

Evan sat quietly, hands folded together, as Cory spoke. A lot of Cory's tale sounded so close to what they had been through with Tony. It was like they lived parallel lives.

"I saw his dad in the hospital," said Cory.

Evan blinked, dumbfounded.

"Frankie's dad came to see you?" Evan gasped. "But how did he know?"

"The dream, Evan, I saw him in the dream," Cory offered, correcting Evan. "It was like he was giving a eulogy, or a benediction. It was surreal to see Mr. Johnson. It was like he was really there. He said all these amazing things to me."

"Wow, he spoke to you?"

"Well, that's where it gets weird," Cory said, picking up the ball and rolling it to Evan. "I dreamed there was a funeral. But what I thought was Frankie's funeral turned out to be mine!"

As Cory spoke, Evan lost the ball and it bounced lightly on the astro turf and rolled into a corner.

"Like an out of body experience?" Evan asked, sitting down again with the ball in his hand. This time he held onto it and listened closely to Cory. The time for games had passed.

"I remember Mr. Johnson saying things about sacrifice, preparedness, and how proud he was of me. I never saw my body, just a casket. I assumed I was in the audience, you know? But then, I heard Frankie's voice. It was like it was coming from somewhere else, muffled you know? I just kind of felt... dead."

"What did he say, Cory," Evan asked, leaning over the table and frowning intently.

"Our saying, *the Grammy goes to* and then 'thank you, Cory.' That's what he said. He told *me* thank you." Cory's voice broke slightly. Evan continued to lean in as the story unfolded.

"Evan, I swear man, for a while it was hell without him. Everything got screwed up. We had plans, dreams!"

"I know bro," Evan agreed. "Trust me; I know what it's like."

"But it was like he and his dad were actually here with me," Cory pressed. "I can't explain it. The last time I saw him we fought in that car. Next thing I know, he's gone forever. We were really pissed off at each other. No matter how kind his dad was back home, I always felt..."

"Guilty?" Evan offered. Cory nodded and shook his head.

"And I guess I didn't want to feel that again. I didn't want to leave you behind at the sting, Ev. Next thing I know I'm angry and driving like crazy hoping I'm not too late to back you guys up."

"You showed up right on time. Otherwise you'd have blown the whole operation, dude," laughed Evan, elbowing Cory. "We are a bunch of knuckleheads for real man, just running into stuff like we own the night or something."

"Tell me about it," Cory chuckled, as his spirits began to rise again. He and Evan sat quietly for a moment and just processed things.

"I'm really glad you're okay."

"So am I, man. Hey let's go inside and get something to drink," Cory offered. They walked inside and Cory went to the kitchen while Evan sat on the yellow sofa.

"Is this thing from the 70s or something?" Evan asked.

"Probably? I don't know man, my Godfather would know." Cory came into the living room with cold, bottled ice tea mixed with lemonade. Handing one to Evan, he sat in a matching yellow chair near the sofa. They sat back, drank, and enjoyed the air conditioning, all the while pondering their discussion.

"Except for the scratch, you are okay if you think about it," Evan said, rubbing his head. "You're here with new friends, making music again. Heck, I don't know what would have happened if you hadn't helped me complete *As I Walk* for the EP. Tony is ok and taking care of his business and Sam is in a good place on the drums. He's even marketing some things for us. A lot of good has come from you being here, Faber."

"Yes, how about that?" Cory said as they thought over the times they had together. The bonds between all of them had been tested but they had come out stronger than ever.

"It was nice of Frankie to say *thank you* on our behalf like that," said Evan with a smile.

Cory looked over at him with a confused look. "What?"

"Frankie said *Thank you*". "You meant a lot to him, man. I don't know it's just nice. It's as if he spoke for all of us. But since I'm sitting here now, I can say it. Thank you, Cory. For everything you've done."

"I was just trying to figure this all out, Evan," Cory said, arms wide. "I just wanted to find myself and my own purpose."

"Exactly," smiled Evan. "And I can tell you we are all glad you did. Just Faber being Faber."

"Well, you're welcome, Evan," said Cory earnestly. "And thank you, for letting me be me."

Track 24:
So Close and Yet So Far

Diana stood in the hallway that connected the living room and the kitchen, looking up at the ceiling. Dangling above her head was a rope loop-handle that was connected to a small door. She slid a step-stool underneath the opening and grabbed the rope handle, pulling the snug door down. Aiming a flashlight to illuminate the small crawl space, Diana climbed into the attic.

"Ouch", she snapped, having hit her head on the corner of a small desk. Diana's nostrils flared as a musty smell combined with the aroma of mothballs stung her sinuses.

"Where are you?" she muttered. Diana's heart skipped a beat when her eyes rested upon the black hatbox she was searching for. Reaching for it and sitting down at the desk that had nearly decapitated her a moment ago, she opened it cautiously and, like Pandora's Box, a wave of emotional relics rushed out to greet her.

Hidden under some documents lay several pictures of Diana in her younger years. There were also photos of Nate, their parents, and Evan's aunts, uncles and cousins. They had captured sepia-toned images of varying degrees of bliss in the Spencer family, but most displayed their love of all things music. There were pictures of family karaoke outings, the family at concerts, a cousin playing the drums, and another playing the saxophone. Finally, Diana found images of herself with her eyes closed shut and mouth smiling wide while singing into the microphone. In one of these snapshots was a handsome and well-built man who favored Evan. He held Diana tightly planting a kiss right on her cheek. Placing this photo behind the others in succession, another photo showed Diana and the man fully enamored in a passionate kiss. Diana sighed deeply, eyes drawn in sadness.

"Mom, I'm back from Cory's!" she heard Evan holler. Startled, she dropped the box and everything tumbled out. A few photos and documents spilled through the attic door and down into the hallway. Evan heard his mother gasp as he rounded the corner into the hallway.

"What are you doing up there, Ma?" he asked, bending over to pick up a couple of the photos and the documents.

"Baby, that's, that's really," Diana stammered.

"What's this, bills?" Evan asked, examining the papers. Suddenly, his eyes grew wide as he took in the fine print.

"This - this is a recording contract," he gasped. He flipped through more and more pages but the name on the front meant nothing to him. Diana looked on from above like a vulture, half obscured by the darkness of the attic.

"Is this for me? Who is this guy?" Evan asked excitedly.

"It was..." Diana began, barely above a whisper.

"What did you say? I need you to explain this mom!" Evan yelled, beaming. He had never seen a musical contract before.

"It was... it's your... father's Evan," said Diana. Evan gazed up at his mother wide-eyed. "Why... why haven't you ever mentioned this?"

Diana looked again at the old photo of her and Evan's father. They were in love back then, no older than Evan was now. Diana's eyes felt hot and her jaw clenched.

Ask your uncle, she thought bitterly.

"Mom, please come down here. You're saying my dad made it in the business?" Evan held up the papers imploringly, head cocked to the side like a confused puppy. Never in his wildest dreams had he ever guessed his father had achieved success or become a star of some kind. Heck, seeing as Diana rarely ever spoke of the man, Evan had wondered sometimes if his father was long dead.

"Your uncle," Diana began. "That contract wasn't good enough for him and your grandparents. No one was good enough for me. So your father left me, you and the music." Evan could tell his mother was holding back tears but he was still amazed by all of this. Sitting on the stool below, he looked over the rest of the papers until he found a typed letter addressed to Uncle Nate, separate from the contract. Diana sniffed, still holding the photos. She peered over again at Evan as he read the letter to himself.

"That's your father's surrender to Nate and our family," said Diana, her bitter words seasoned with sarcasm. "Sure, he returned once to see you but, as you can see, he didn't stay long." She wiped her eye and held up her left hand, spread her fingers, and massaged the empty ring finger, and added.

"Even if he is just a few miles away."

Her acrid laughter floated down to her son, head hung as he finished reading his father's letter to his uncle.

"Mom, how could you and Uncle Nate keep this a secret? And why would dad...?" Evan slapped the papers against his legs as his voice trailed off. He looked into space, shaking his head irritably. He was angry, enraged even. But something, a little something in the back of mind bubbled to the surface.

Something just ain't right, he thought.

"So why are you telling me this now? Huh? Or were you ever going to say anything about this crap?"

"You watch your mouth, young man," retorted his mother, pointing down at him still seated in the chair.

"Or what?" Evan yelled causing Diana to catch her breath. "Y'all were just gonna keep me in the dark about him, about his record deal? About him coming back while I've been out struggling BY MY SELF? He could have helped me! We could've been together!"

Evan stood looking up at Diana, breathing heavily, arms tense and sweat forming on his brow. Diana held his fiery gaze, finally looking away defeated. She whimpered, unable to hold back the tears.

"Oh now you've got nothing to say?" demanded Evan. "Of all the times to be quiet you pick now. Okay, that's fine, that's okay. Maybe I WILL go see Uncle Nate and get some answers from him." Evan was a whirl of motion as he crossed into the kitchen. Diana could hear as he shoved at the chairs, slamming against the table.

A photo of Evan, Diana and his dad fell to the floor in his wake, brushed by the wind of the door slamming. He was no more than a toddler in the photo of his family posed on the golf course. Evan's dad held a golf club in one hand and hugged Diana fondly with his free arm. As she cradled Evan a white golf ball could just be made out in Evan's tiny hands.

BOOM! BOOM! BOOM!

It sounded like the police were at the door as Nate rushed through the hall and flung it open.

"What's going on?" he started to demand, but Evan's barging in cut his words short. His nephew strode into the hallway leading into the living room but stopped and whirled around, his breathing raspy.

"Okay..."

"Evan what's wrong with you, what's happened?"

"This is what's happened," Evan said thrusting the papers into Nate's chest and shoving him backwards. Nate righted himself and glared at Evan who glared right back unfazed.

"You watch it, Evan."

"So you drove him out?" Evan demanded, swaying angrily from side to side.

"Who out, Evan?" Nate yelled.

"My dad. That's his recording contract, Unc!"

Nate looked over the papers perplexed. At the end of the stack was a dotted line with the name of Evan's father in print but the contract lacked his signature. What was this other sheet of paper?

"Yeah, your dad was a good musician, Evan." Nate began.

"But not good enough for you?" yelled Evan. "Not good enough for Grandpa or anyone else? You just had to screw up Ma's life? Dad came back for us!"

Nate gestured defensively and tried to calm Evan down. "Where did you get this, Evan?"

"Mom, she just dropped this on my head back home," spat Evan, throwing his arms out exasperated. "She made it sound like you all exiled dad and she pretty much didn't fight for him either. All this crap she gives me? She could've used that attitude back then to keep us together."

As Evan stopped to fume, Nate perused the letter that was under the contract. Now and then he looked up from the letter at Evan. As he continued reading he mouthed the words.

'Nate, I love your sister dearly and would not want to offend your family or disrespect them in any way. I also have music as my passion. But I love Diana too much to lose her. So, I'm going to set my music, my passion, aside rather than make her a widow of it. But you and I both know my education isn't much. Even still, I've sold all of my equipment. I've resigned myself to do whatever it takes to make my new family work – no matter the cost, no matter the sacrifice. It won't be easy, but if it means a steady paycheck, I'm just thinking of the woman I love. Please don't hate me, Nate. I don't think you know this, but Diana and I are expecting a little one - yes, she's pregnant. I swore that I would not disrespect your family and I won't – we'll marry when I return. Here's the money to help her get things ready. Can we call a truce? You were right, Nate, about everything. Diana should not have to learn, what are really my own personal lessons, or pay for my stubbornness. You and I both know how passionate she can get. She will understand one day, and I hope my son will too. I'm finally starting to get the big picture. I'm trying to focus on securing a future for others, for the ones I love. Thank you for teaching me that Nate.'

Best,'

When he finished he sighed deeply and looked his nephew in the eyes.

"Evan? I've made a lot of mistakes in the past and done and said things I'm not proud of. Yes, your Grandpa and I and others in the family were close knit. And yes, we disapproved of your father."

"Why?" Evan glared daggers at Uncle Nate.

"We didn't want your mom to be disappointed if the music didn't pan out. We were only looking out for her the best way we knew how. We'd lost so many of our family to this business, to the money and power, and the corruption. Sometimes it's just too much."

"Wasn't that her choice?" Evan asked, folding his arms.

"She said the same thing," continued Uncle Nate. "She was so sure of herself, of their love. She was so defiant. She couldn't stand that I held my fears over her head."

"Oh gee, can you blame her," Evan shot back. "And now that's what she's been preaching at me all these years. So good for you, you got what you wanted. But none of you tried to help me or teach me, knowing what you did about music."

Nate looked back at the papers in his hands and shook his head. "I didn't know about this letter, Evan. This is the first time I'm seeing it. It's addressed to me but she clearly kept it from me. When your father left, he and I weren't on good terms at all. We had a fight before he left. And honestly he just disappeared. As far as I knew, he didn't make a thing of it, well, except for this letter, obviously. I really wish I'd done things... I wish we'd ended things differently, your father and I."

Evan relaxed his clenched fists and, with a sigh, leaned against the wall to process all of this. He just never knew what to think of his dad. He'd been a ghost for most of his life and now he'd found out the man was only a few miles within reach. So close and yet so far, and it devastated Evan.

"Evan, I'm so sorry," Uncle Nate offered, stepping closer.

"And I guess Ma is bitter because you changed your tune after all these years?" Evan inquired. "No more bossing me around, pretending to be my father? Guiding me?" Nate hung his head as Evan emphasized "Guiding me" with his fingers acting as quotations.

"You did all these things to her?"

"Yes, Evan," Nate admitted. "It's not so cut and dry, but it's how things turned out. But, at the end of the day, your father made his choice. You read the same words I did and I think he eventually thought he was doing the right thing."

"Despite your help?" Evan shot back, folding his arms again and facing the wall.

"Yes, despite my help," agreed Nate.

"This is too much," said Evan, voice breaking and knees buckling. Uncle Nate hurried to his nephew's side and braced him against the wall. At first, Evan resisted the help. Then, rethinking it, he used his uncle's shoulder to prop himself up. His back was against one wall, and Uncle Nate was leaning against the other wall, facing him.

"Evan, forgive your mother," Nate said softly. "Don't turn into her. Don't let your anger turn into resentment. You've got her drive but don't claim her pain, too. Whatever it takes."

"Now I see why this family is so broken," said Evan, voice hoarse as he peered at the ceiling, searching for relief. "We've got so many secrets... no trust. That's why none of them are ever around."

"Evan, this is between your mother and me, this is not your burden," said Nate evenly. "You have accomplished so much. You've got amazing friends, and a young woman that loves you, and they all have an interest in music and in you and where you're going. You're the catalyst, Evan. From what I've seen and heard, since even before leaving, I can see you're all focused and bonded by mutual passion for art and for each other."

Evan closed his eyes tightly as if it would block out the truth. "So much of this just doesn't make sense... my dad is here somewhere. I don't know what to do." As hotheaded as he could be, Evan was accustomed to being in control of strong feelings like these. But now the emotional floodgate had been opened by the truth that his father was closer than he thought, cared about him, and had come closer to fulfilling his dreams than Evan had. His father, *his father*, had been offered a real recording contract. Evan was so amazed by this that he cried silently against his uncle's wall. No moans, not even a whimper. Just the heaving of his chest while tears flowed like lava as he tried to suppress the emotional onslaught.

Nate stepped closer and embraced Evan as he sobbed. "He did it for you," He whispered. "You've got to believe that in the end, no matter how complicated things got, your father was thinking about your future the best way that he knew how."

Evan wept out of sadness and anger for feeling cheated out of the chance to know the man.

Track 25:
Guardians & Hunters

The rumbling of the engine came to a halt as Camille shut the car off in the parking lot of Little Island Park. She'd spent the day with Evan and learned the latest about his dad. He told her about the argument he had with his mom, his dad's record deal and the goodbye letter to his Uncle Nate making amends, to finally learning he lived in Hampton Roads all this time. Lately, Cory allowed Evan to stay with him at his beach house to get some space. He didn't like his friend and his mom being on the outs but he wanted to help anyway he could and hoped Evan and his mom would get through this. Evan and Camille exited the car and slowly walked to the playground hand-in-hand. Having exhausted the subject, they were now solely focused on each other.

While Evan gently pushed Camille on the swing set, fantasies of him and his father doing the same thing fluttered through his mind. What was wrong with him? He never saw himself as some sappy little boy crying for daddy before all of this came out. But he wondered was it so sappy to wish for something you'd never gotten the chance to have; something new and good? All Evan really remembered was his mother and his uncle growing up.

"Come on," said Camille, removing her low top sneakers and taking him by the hand. "I want to show you something."

It was like she had sensed him drifting off again. That had been happening more and more. Just the thought of his dad being somewhere nearby made Evan paranoid, like he would spot the man any minute. Heck, he could be on the pier fishing right now! It was like those fugitives in the movies, like the one filmmaker Dennis Harley made before *The Good Fight* that Evan had seen with Camille months ago. The character was always looking over their shoulder wondering when they'd be found out, and they were jittery and nervous and always losing focus. Sure Evan would feel the same way if someone were out to kill him, too. But there were no movie villains tracking him to the ends of the earth.

But that's the problem isn't it? No one is looking for me. My dad sure isn't, thought Evan.

"Did you know?" began Camille. Evan was a little embarrassed, having almost forgotten she was there until she squeezed his hand and spoke up. "My dad used to bring me here to surf. Started off with boogie boards first but I got pretty good at it."

"No, you never told me that," Evan answered brows raised. That was genuinely interesting, the idea of Cammie surfing. As they walked along the beach, three kids ran past, one flying a pink kite shaped like a dragonfly, another dragging a boogie board that was too big for her, both being chased by a third child who was laughing.

"Oh, that was you right there?" Evan pointed at the kids, mocking Camille. "Well, you were probably much cuter. Do you still do it?"

"Not for years. I sort of got distracted. But I'm thinking of taking it up again." She led him to a large log lying on the beach where they sat and watched the kids play. As adults joined their children, the sun peaked out from behind the clouds, shrouding the family in sunshine.

"Maybe I could show you how to surf sometime," Camille added, holding Evan's hands. Evan appreciated the sentiment. It would be nice to come back out to the water to try something new with her. He imagined Camille and her father splashing and laughing when she was younger, and he grinned as he thought about Mr. LaShea and lighter times.

"You miss him?" Evan asked softly.

"All the time," Camille answered, leaning into her man. "Mommy and I have our moments."

"How did she deal with it?"

"I think we both have etched more of the good times into our heads," said Camille, caressing Evan's face. "Mommy more than me, I guess. Daddy took such good care of her before she left."

"He was something," agreed Evan, looking out as a dog rushed by into the water. "I miss him too."

One of the little kids was running around with a juice box while Evan and Camille watched her little feet kick up sand. Running up to them, she paused innocently and stared at the couple. She gave Evan a bright smile as he waved to her. She plopped the juice box down and giggling, ran back to her family.

"Oh, well that was sweet," snickered Camille, watching the girl who was now long gone and hugging the leg of an older woman.

"She didn't even open it," Evan chuckled, holding up the box with the plastic straw still notched onto the side of it. "Shall we?"

Evan opened it, popped the straw in place and took a sip. "Mmm lemonade," he said.

"Hey, don't hog it all," teased Camille, snatching it from him and sipping herself. Then pulling out the straw she paused with a funny look on her face.

"Open your mouth," she said in answer to Evan's puzzled look. "Lean your head back and open your mouth." As he did so, Camille held the straw over his mouth and a quick stream of lemonade flowed over his tongue.

"Fun trick," Evan said, looking up at her. The sun shone behind her head like an angelic halo and, for a moment, Evan had trouble making out Camille's face as it darkened in contrast to the beautiful corona lighting her hair like gold. But even though he couldn't see her clearly, Evan couldn't remember the last time Camille had looked so beautiful.

"You're the brightest thing in my life, Cammie. I love you," he said, pulling her close. Camille braced herself with her hands on his knees as they shared a kiss. They didn't move from that spot for hours and just watched the sun set beyond the pier in the distance. Evan hadn't felt this calm in a long time and sitting there on the beach with Camille raised his spirit.

"Grandma, look," they heard one of the children say in the distance. "It's heaven, that's where Mommy and Daddy are!"

I guess Heaven's Gate is calling me, thought Evan. *At least my heaven is on earth... where my mom is.*

Though some things were unclear in his life having her there to go through the unknown with him began to ease his mind. For today, Camille, his guardian angel, had held the uncertainty at bay. Evan would not be beaten down by the past so easily.

∞

Evan called on the same resolve he had experienced with Camille on the beach, when he, Tony and Cory attended the hearing to give their final testimony about that night at Brigg's Warehouse when Vandusen was caught. This was it. Evan indeed showed great strength as he related his account of the night before the courtroom as his friends looked on. Despite Evan's own problems, Tony was very impressed with Evan. But Evan was *present*, as it were. He gave his testimony and when he was done, took his place next to his friends on the bench seating. A nod from Tony elicited the same from Evan; he even managed a *thumbs-up*. Evan was just glad his time in the hot seat was over. Before he knew it the jurors announced their verdict and the case was closed. Vandusen was guilty as charged with a sentence of many years in prison awaiting him.

"We won, man!" beamed Tony as Jasmine excitedly wrapped her arms around his waist.

"He's going away for a long time," Cory added, slapping Tony on the back.

"Congratulations, man," said Evan, shaking Tony's hand. The worst of it was over. Evan had his two best friends back, pulled from the edge so to speak.

As Tony's friends and family exited the courthouse, Evan looked to Tony and asked, "So what now?"

"Soon it'll be my turn to settle with the coppers, man," Tony exhaled softly. "It won't be as bad as Vandusen, but I gotta make this right by my family and by my basketball team. I owe a lot to the players and my coach. I want them to see my integrity is still intact. I still love the game but I know the consequences. My next court date comes later."

"I'm really sorry, Tony," Evan said sincerely. Basketball had been Tony's life and now it was possible it might be taken away.

"Don't sweat it," said Tony as he and Jasmine got into the SUV with his family. "You guys are my team now. I'll see you and Cory at the restaurant."

After the celebratory dinner with Tony and his family, the four friends drove back to Cory's place where they were greeted by Camille and Sam. Together they enjoyed a calm night atop Cory's roof deck. As the stars began to form in the night sky, they all laid about as Cory strummed a few chords on his acoustic guitar. Off and on, Sam tapped out a beat from his seat by either slapping his knees or the top of the bench or banister. Jasmine hummed back and forth with Camille while Evan and Tony sat quietly, each warmly holding onto the girl of their dreams. This was good for Evan who was still feeling melancholy from time to time. He hadn't felt this stuck since before the band had come together, back when he was struggling to find his way musically and other musicians who were like-minded and serious like him. It was as if the stories that both his mother and uncle told him about his dad had somehow managed to suck the wind out of his sails again. Evan wasn't even sure if he wanted to meet his dad now or even look for him. Thoughts ran through his mind as he played with his lucky golf ball. His arms wrapped around Camille as she lay across his lap. She plucked the ball from his hand interrupting his thoughts.

"Sorry, my head was somewhere else," he said. Everyone chuckled and Camille reached up and caressed his face.

"It's so good to be together again," Jasmine cooed.

"Glad you're feeling better too, Cory," Sam added. The others voiced their agreement.

"Yeah, I'll have a scar, but my hair should cover it up eventually," said Cory, rubbing his hair, which had grown beyond the buzz cut. "But, you're right Jasmine, I'm glad that whole Yardees thing is behind us."

"They can't get me without a fight," laughed Tony. "I know now, there's no such thing as easy money."

"If you could do it all over again, would you?" asked Evan, somewhat out of the blue. Everyone fell quiet, unsure of what Evan was getting at or what Tony's answer would be.

"You had your reasons," Evan continued. "And what's done is done. I remember you calling us your new *team* earlier. But if you could reset and change anything, what would you do different about all of this?"

Tony sat for a moment with Jasmine lying against his chest. She rubbed his arm and after a moment, Tony kissed her on her forehead.

"Honestly, I don't know Evan," Tony answered. "I don't know but it feels like they might be taking basketball away from me. I want to say I would do it over. Pass BeBe and Vandusen by and win the Classic, maybe make the NBA. But then maybe I wouldn't know you all cared as much about me as you do, the way you and Cory risked your lives for me. Maybe I wouldn't have learned what's really important in Tony Gerard Jackson's life. Like staying safe for my family and having their trust, or falling in love - real love. That's kinda feeble, Ev. I'm sorry, but I guess what I'm trying to say is you're right. What's past is past and like my boo said, it really is good to be together with you all. I've learned my lesson and this is my reward. There's no place I'd rather be right now. Let the chips fall where they may."

"I'll drink to that," said Cory, reaching into the cooler next to him. The others requested another round of cold drinks and, as Sam took his, he offered his condolences to Tony.

"For what?" Tony asked.

"For your friend, BeBe," Sam said a little awkwardly. "I know it was complicated and he was doing dirt with you, but a life is a life."

"I remember when we were kids," Camille began, as the others pondered Sam's words. "Tony, Evan and me, I mean. I remember that time you two got in trouble for fighting because the bigger kids were betting on you and pushing you around. You remember that?"

"Yeah, I remember," said Tony wide-eyed. Camille could feel Evan's chin rise and fall as he nodded in remembrance.

"How come BeBe never got picked on?

Everyone sat in the quiet, not quite sure what Camille was saying. "Oh you're actually asking them?" Cory inquired.

"It's just I don't really remember BeBe caught up in that. Tony, he was the same age as you and Evan, he was at recess that day," Camille elaborated. "And they weren't going to make us girls fight."

"Girl, I would've had your back. You already know," Jasmine said, folding her arms.

"He was hanging out with the older kids a lot after that," Tony offered. "I don't know. I don't want to speak ill of the dead."

"No, no it's just," Camille stammered trying to find her words. She didn't wish to stain BeBe's memory any more than it was, especially since he couldn't defend himself. "He was just always difficult to figure out. It's like a question mark hovering over him...just something I was thinking about. I still wish things had gone differently, that no one had to die."

"Yeah, me too," Tony nodded. After a long pause he added, "And we're not stupid. I mean Evan stopped hanging out with him a long time ago for a reason. BeBe...after all of this, I guess it was just hard to connect. Maybe that's how he felt. Overcompensating? I never really knew him well, not like I know you, Evan."

Evan nodded and squeezed Camille a little tighter. From the little they knew about BeBe growing up, his family was well off. Why he might have gone from betting in the schoolyard to racketeering with gangs in his adult life was anyone's guess.

"I saw his stepdad a while ago," said Evan. "Cory and I were at the fishing pier over at Little Island Park. I didn't talk to him, though. But...yeah."

"I hear his family is taking it badly," Sam offered. "His stepdad wants to form a rally or something to fight the Epps Yard Crew's drug influence and other gang related issues. It's tough because BeBe was an only child. I heard some people saying they hope his mom finds peace, her bad heart and all."

They sat there again in silence absorbing the results of the case and BeBe's family. Soon Cory was lightly playing his guitar again, tending to the ambiance. Evan thought it was nice how BeBe's stepdad was fighting for his son's memory. As bad as he turned out, BeBe was still someone Evan and his friends grew up with and the community had lost a son. Things could have gone so differently. But what was it that drove BeBe to do the things he did? He had come from a well-to-do family, and his mother's new husband had always tried to be there in his younger days. Everybody loved BeBe. What happened to him? Was that what his own mother had been afraid of, that Evan would turn into BeBe?

Evan still hadn't spoken to his mom since the attic incident and finding the letter from his dad. As Cory continued to play the guitar, Evan reflected on a talk he had with Cory after he'd learned the truth. *Pace yourself.* That's what Cory had said. Evan and his mother both thought they were right, and they were both confused. It was painful to learn that his dad had been kept from him; at least that's how Evan saw it. And it hurt just as much to think about all of the secrets and manipulation going on in the Spencer family. Everyone may have been doing what they thought was right; including his mom, but it didn't mean Evan had to like it - or understand it. That was how Tony had put it. He was a little more vocal about the revelations but did his best to keep things in perspective. But Evan just couldn't shake the idea from his head: why didn't his dad fight for him more? BeBe's biological father was long gone but that didn't stop his stepdad from fighting to make his son's death mean something. BeBe hurt a lot of people running with the Yardees, and yet his family hadn't given up on him. It just bugged Evan and he felt as if he'd never know the answers or learn anything satisfactory in his own situation. He was doing the exact opposite of Cory's advice. He was running headlong into an emotional storm and the unknowns felt like they would sweep him away.

"You okay?" Camille asked, looking at him with her big brown eyes. She tossed his golf ball up in the air and, as he tried to catch it, she tickled him in the arm.

"No fair, stop playin'," laughed Evan, dropping the ball as it bounced off the floor into Jasmine's lap. There was certainly no big decision he felt he needed to make. He simply knew the truth now. As Cory played, he struck a tune that Camille was familiar with and she stopped to listen.

"Oh you haven't played that song in a while. Have you finished it?" asked Camille, propping herself up in Evan's lap.

"Not yet. It still needs work. It's something I started with my band back home," Cory replied.

"Maybe we should play around with it," offered Sam, clapping his hands and rubbing them together.

"Yeah what do you think of that, Evan?" Cory asked, laying down his guitar and exposing his tattooed forearm. From Evan's perspective, it appeared as if the little man on Cory's arm was throwing him the sphere atop his shoulders, spilling musical notes and all. It was a friendly image that gave him an idea.

Track 26:
Still Waters

"Are you going to be okay?" Cory asked. He and Evan sat on the hood of Cory's car in front of his mother's church. After having concluded the court hearing with his friends, receiving clarity from his uncle and spending some time away, his head was clear enough to engage his mother again. He'd apologize for the way he had acted. He wanted to deal with this issue together and so did she; she missed her boy. Today the church was holding a potluck dinner celebrating the pastor's birthday.

"I'll be fine. I just don't want to deal with this on my own," Evan answered.

"You're never alone, Ev, never," Cory insisted.

"I mean alone, without Ma. Look, after everything I just can't handle any more surprises or problems between her and me. I've been doing my thing with you guys and I think it's time for me to face this, you know? Like take a page from Tony's playbook. Own up and see where Ma is going to take this, see what else I need to learn."

Cory patted Evan on the back to reassure him and nodded in agreement. Difficult as this was, Evan wasn't running from the confrontation anymore. Still, there were no monumental decisions he needed to make except to face his mother again. How bad could that be?

"Thanks man, I'm just tired. Things were going so well."

"We love you man, but yeah; this is something your friends can't take on with you. I think you're definitely doing the right thing. You only get one family."

Evan stuck out his hand and Cory shook it and they embraced. Then, slinging his duffle bag over his shoulder, Evan walked across the parking lot to the church entrance.

Once inside Evan crossed the lobby and entered the fellowship hall where the party was being held. The place was abuzz with music and laughter as families dined together and told stories. Kids ran to and fro through the aisles and there was a cake at a table that had to be for the pastor.

"Evan Spencer!" a voice shouted. Evan spun around half startled by the booming voice. It was none other than the man of the hour, the pastor himself.

"Hi Pastor," said Evan, shaking his hand. The man was so large and muscular that his hand swallowed up Evan's and his grip, although friendly, was like a bear trap.

"It's so good to see you Evan," the pastor enthused, smiling.

"You too and happy birthday, Sir. I saw the banners outside."

"God Almighty must have sent you across my path for a reason, Evan. I was about to sneak some of that birthday cake. But you stopping me is just a reminder I need to adhere to the program. The cake cutting isn't until 5:00."

"It's not an easy road but sticking to the program is the best one, Pastor. Don't get in trouble with your wife by starting things off too early."

The church leader threw his head back with a booming belly laugh. When he settled down, Evan asked, "Have you seen my mom around?"

"Oh, she's been all the ladies can talk about in Women's Bible Study son. She said she was inspired by you the past week in her studies."

"She was?" asked Evan, adjusting the strap over his shoulder.

"My wife said your mother was deeply inspired by the passage admonishing the runners to keep pace with the footmen or be left behind. It was connected to her family life she said, about letting go and letting God. As challenging as it was, she said she felt that God was using you as a guide for her path to understanding your family more deeply. You know you only get one don't you Evan?"

"Yes indeed, that's what they tell me," replied Evan, smiling warmly. "Ma and I are both looking for ways to bring our family closer together. We're all we've got, after all."

The pastor smiled and slapped Evan heartily on the back. "Amen, amen. Well keep up the good work. Keep pace as your mom says. Oh, and good luck with your band. I expect great things. I think I saw your mother over there." Evan followed in the direction of the pastor's finger across the vast hall.

Evan remembered that the passage his mother quoted was what inspired his band's name in the first place. Was it coincidence that during this difficult time in their relationship the Big Man upstairs would...never mind. Evan believed in God, sure, but he didn't want to over analyze the situation. The important thing was that he came to iron things out with his mom. Judging from the way the pastor talked, family would win out in the long run provided Evan and Diana found a way to stay united instead of letting the past dry up their bond. They'd been through too much and his mother was tougher than she looked.

"Watch out!" someone shouted. Evan ducked just in time for a football to narrowly miss his head.

"Boys, what did I tell you about sports inside?" came a stern voice from across the room.

"It's ok. I got 'em," hollered a young man several years younger than Evan running up behind the boys with the football. "Guys outside!"

"Wow dude, hey, I recognize you. You've grown," said Evan in surprise.

"Oh hey, Evan. Long time, no see, man," came the reply as they shook hands.

"You got big, man. How old are you now?" Evan asked, slapping his young friend on the shoulder.

"I turned 15 last week," the young man answered while playing with a coin.

"What's that in your hand?"

The coin danced in between the teen's fingers flawlessly as if it had a mind of its own. "Oh, this just gives my hands something to do when I'm not practicing."

"Practicing what?" inquired Evan, curious.

"I play, well, I play guitar," came the shy response. "Me and some friends have a little band going. I heard you have one too. That's tight!"

"Yeah, we're trying. You any good?"

Evan watched the coin continue to flip up and over his friend's finger and knuckles as he answered, "I think so, if I keep this up. Practicing sucks sometimes and my wrists get tired."

"You think that's hard, wait until the calluses show up," Evan chuckled.

"Not a problem," spouted the youth while clapping his hands together. "I can at least make those disappear." As soon as he said so, his coin was gone and he showed off his empty hands.

"Well, if the band doesn't take off you can always go on the road as a traveling magician," Evan gawked. His eyes and smile grew even wider as the coin was plucked from behind his ear.

"Or, I'll just enthrall *your* fans and take them for myself."

"Big words. Ok, you got some fight in you," Evan said, putting up his dukes jokingly.

"The boys need you outside, Mojo" directed Evan's mother coming toward them and wiping her hands on a towel.

"Later, Mojo!"

"Cool seeing you, Evan. Maybe you can give me guitar lessons," hollered the 15 year old over his shoulder as he ran out through the door.

"Yeah I know a guy," Evan yelled back. Turning to his mother he set down his duffel bag and, after a pause, he and his mother embraced each other lightly but lovingly. Then, taking her son's hand, she led him out of the fellowship hall.

"Follow me; I know a quiet place where we can talk."

Behind the building was a pond that was home to all kinds of waterfowl and aquatic life. Sometimes after service, and under the watchful eye of the adults, the kids would try to catch frogs. There were six benches that formed a ring around the water's edge. Evan and his mother found a spot far away from the boys and their football game. Sitting comfortably sipping colorful fruit drinks and enjoying the mild weather they were silent until finally Evan spoke up.

"I'm so sorry for all of this Ma, for leaving the house and gettin' all up in Uncle Nate's face and just..."

"I'm so sorry too, baby," said Diana, patting Evan on his leg. "Like I said on the phone, we both got emotional. What did we expect?"

"I don't know. What did you expect?" he asked.

"I never intended to drop a bombshell on you," Diana began. "I didn't think you'd be home for a while that night anyway..."

Evan watched as a small frog leapt toward the water in front of them and splashed into the pond.

"Did you intend to tell me the truth, ever?" he asked softly.

"I really don't know, Evan," his mother whispered and swallowed hard. "I imagined that if you never asked, I'd never have to tell you... and you'd never leave me. But you left anyway."

"Leave you?"

"I was scared. Scared I would lose you too, just like your other uncle, and your great aunt, and your father..." Diana caught her breath as the faces of her loved ones materialized in her mind, each one taken by music in one way or another. Loan sharks had gotten Diana's eldest brother, her father's first born. And drugs, depression and a lack of creativity had worn Evan's great aunt's mind to nothingness ages ago. They were all musicians and had gotten into trouble trying to make it big in the industry. Some even turned up in the tabloids occasionally. And then of course, there was Evan's dad.

"You didn't think that maybe I'd be successful and make you proud, Mom?" Evan pressed.

"I hoped your father would, that we would together," his mother answered sincerely. "But Nate and your grandfather...they wouldn't have it, they couldn't bear to lose me too. Oh baby, we were all so scared. We thought there might even be a family curse."

"Is that why you got into church so much?" Evan asked, inching closer to her on the bench.

"After we were on our own I just wanted to have some order in my life again," said Diana, patting Evan's leg again as if to drive the point home with each tap of her palm.

"They seem like nice people, as usual," Evan pointed out, quietly finishing his drink. "In fact, they all seem to know about me and The Mustangz."

"Word travels fast, I guess," Diana said. "And I might have mentioned it to a few people in the congregation."

"Do they still treat you okay here?"

"They do. Being here makes me feel refreshed and clear most of the time. I think God has truly been faithful," Diana replied.

"He has been busy, I guess," said Evan, rubbing his hands together contemplatively. "So much has happened to all of us, to Cory, Mr. LaShea, Tony, my music... dad."

"Evan? Anything you want to know about him, I'm ready," said Diana firmly. "It's actually good to have it out in the open now. I'll never make this mistake again, honey. I'm supposed to protect you, and that's what I'm going to do. Not me, you. I know that now. You have your uncle to thank for that."

"I don't need protection anymore, Ma," Evan said, wrapping an arm around her.

"I'm always going to want to protect you, Evan," his mother said, looking up into his eyes, "Always."

"Yes ma'am. I'm glad you and Uncle Nate are doing better," Evan said as a small fish jumped out of the water.

"You know what they say about old dogs? I don't think that applies to your uncle. He can still learn a thing or two as old as he is. And though it felt inconvenient for me at first it's better late than never. I am trying but I'm not perfect."

"I wish I could fix what happened, Ma, I do, if it would dilute all that pain and drama you went through with dad and grandpa," said Evan, frowning.

"It's in the past," said Diana, kissing her son's hand gently. Evan smiled and they leaned their heads against one another fondly, watching as a blue heron descended into the pond.

"What was dad like?" Evan asked, eyes still focused on the heron.

"He could play anything," his mother answered grinning. "Even play the strings of the human heart if you let him get close enough. The band never sounded sweeter than when he was around. Your Uncle Nate can attest to that."

"That's cool," said Evan.

"And he was respectful, a gentleman... and a dreamer," Diana continued. Then looking directly into her son's eyes she added, "Just like you."

Evan kissed his mom on the cheek and hugged her tightly. The residual feelings of betrayal and resentment were still fresh in his heart, but maybe learning more about his dad would loosen the cords. To hear his mother tell it, his dad, even by just talking about him, could have that effect.

"I don't want to leave anything unsaid, Evan, so I'll say this now. I'm proud of you. Deep down I don't have to dream about what you'll be because you work hard, just like him. And one day he'll be proud of you too."

A small tear formed in the corner of Evan's eye as they rose from the bench. It was nearing time for cutting the pastor's cake. But Evan had sampled a sweetness not found in dessert: his mother's pride and love.

"I'm proud of you too, mom. And Uncle Nate," said Evan as they walked back to the church arm in arm. "You never let me out of your sight, either one of you. I guess that's where I get my stubbornness from?"

A sharp but endearing swat on his hind parts was all the confirmation Evan needed from her. "Yes it is and that's why we keep having these little bouts. It's me trying to beat it out of you so you'll listen more and not be like me."

"Mom, I think that's exactly why I am so much like you," laughed Evan as they strolled into the church for some birthday cake.

"And you channel it into all that racket you make in your studio?" she asked.

"Exactly in fact brace yourself; the guys will be over this week. We got a new song we're writing," Evan cautioned with a chuckle.

"And just when I was getting used to the peace and quiet," his mother moaned.

Track 27:
Dry Run

The golf ball struck the surface of Evan's desk as it had a thousand times before while he sat in his home studio, Heaven's Gate. He needed guidance and direction. Once again the rhythms of the dribbling ball gave him a sense of comfort. His musings sent him pondering the way his life was unraveling and all who had tried to influence him culminating in three documents open before him. The first was the letter from his father to his uncle, second was his dad's old recording contract, and lastly a sheet of paper with the unfinished lyrics from Cory's song. Mouthing the lyrics to himself, Evan re-familiarized himself with the verse.

As I walk this road before me Lord
Searching to find my way
I get an empty, empty feeling Lord
You just might turn and walk away
But you must understand, I've not been here before
Will you walk with me Lord or am I going it alone?
Still you say...

There was a simple enough story within the words. Like Evan, the singer or character in the song needed guidance and a means to fight off isolation. As Evan looked back at his father's letter and contract, Cory's words came back to mind: *You tend to attack when the listener expects a rest – it brings out your unique sound.*

"He's in the studio, Cory" Evan heard his mother say.

"Well speak of the devil," muttered Evan.

Cory walked in toting his guitar, with Sam not far behind carrying his pouch of drumsticks and a snare drum. He and Cory had been assembling an elaborate drum set at the Spencer residence for rehearsals. Then, at home, Sam practiced on his little brother's drum set to keep up with the band and not have to rely on Evan's house to play.

"What up, Evan," Sam said, putting down the snare.

"Trying to figure out this chicken scratch that Faber's got us working with," Evan teased. He was used to working with Ryan to put down lyrics when The Mustangz first started out. That was before his friend moved and Evan hadn't had time to consider new avenues of songwriting.

"Guys, Jasmine and Camille are gonna be late so we can just play with this for a while," said Evan, dribbling his ball again.

"Oh no, see that's where it starts, Evan," Sam cautioned.

"Relax, Sam. They'll be here. Cut them some slack," said Cory, unzipping his guitar from its travel case. "Set up your drum, brother."

As the other two adjusted their instruments, Evan went back to Cory's lyrics.

"So did you write this?" he asked Cory.

"After Frankie, yes," Cory answered, tossing his guitar pick back into the pack.

"Well it's nice man. But I can't tell if this is a verse or a chorus or what," Evan said, scratching his braided head.

"Yeah, neither could I," Cory admitted with a sigh.

"Let's go back to that melody, Cory. Maybe you'll get some story ideas to pick up where your lyrics left off," Sam suggested. Evan retired his golf ball and took a seat at the keyboard. Following Cory's lead, the three of them launched into the melody. This routine went on as the days added up. The Mustangz sacrificed their lives and reconvened as often as they could to tackle Evan and Cory's newest labor of love which was playing another song from their upcoming EP, or sometimes just playing a rendition of a song by their favorite artists. Always in the furthest recesses of Evan's mind was his father's letter and contract. They factored in somehow to the story Cory was telling in his half of the song, but Evan still couldn't figure out how.

It finally came to him one night after Evan had finished playing at Club Soul-Light, his first time in a long time. The attendees had missed their favorite local DJ and gave Evan a standing ovation. He welcomed the adulation and dedicated the last song to the club.

"This song is dedicated to the one and only Club Soul-Light. You all stood strong and continued to endure even after the disruption and pain caused by others. Here's to your spirit and the healing power of music. You've allowed me and my band to be a part of the family. Thank you! We owe you so much. Together we will continue on!"

He'd learned so much at Soul-Light. Everyone was overjoyed and beamed with pride when he announced he was coming out with a small collection The Mustangz had put together. After passing out cards and expressing his gratitude, Evan packed up his gear and left.

He returned to the band's newest song with a renewed intensity. Sometime later, the band was back together in the studio reengineering the song. At first, the front women sang the words from Evan's letter, which he edited to protect his dad and his uncle's privacy. Evan also honed in on the few lines that jumped out to him musically.

In Heaven's Gate, Camille and Jasmine stood facing their band mates wearing jumbo headphones, lips kissing the microphones as everyone collectively attacked the song head on. The journey had paid off and the song was unlocked. Everyone was in sync, driven by Sam's fire on the drums, Cory's melodic acoustic guitar, and Evan's scales on the keyboard that were accented sparingly by his synthesizer. His actions, his movements were like those of a conductor bringing expression to the lyrics. The chords were the obvious part of the music but the mere movement of his hands to reach the chords seemed to introduce another dimension. Evan was in his world, at long last seeing a blend between his and Cory's finished lyrics. As the song faded out a collective cheer went up in the studio followed by hugs and high fives.

"Now that's what I'm talkin' about!" Sam said as he slammed his bass drum excitedly. Then more calm, yet just as seriously, he added, "Anybody else smell food?"

Everyone including Dorothy sat in the Spencer's dining room enjoying well-earned steaming hot pizza. The high from solidifying the groove on the newest track had not died down one iota and everyone was talking at once.

"Wow, Cory and the girls sounded great on that high note!"

"Pass me a plate, please."

"I know the synths add a little something to it."

"This is the only pizza left everyone, sorry."

"You guys yelled so loud I thought it was an emergency!"

"No, it sounds much better when we did it that way tonight for sure."

"You'd have been screaming, too. That song would not let up on us!"

"Next time, I'll make sure to go lower on the last 'ever alone' part okay?"

"Whoa guys, heads up!"

Everyone turned their attention to Sam who was answering a text message at the table.

"It's ready," he said looking around the table. *"The Mustangz EP* goes online next week!"

The table erupted with screams. Everyone was ecstatic. Their motley crew of friends and contacts (Evan and Sam loved the idea that they finally had musical contacts) made the EP a reality and the small marketing team had come through. Evan brought out one of his laptops and everyone gathered around to see that the online profile was set up counting down the days till download was available.

"This is real," gushed Camille, tightly holding Jasmine's hand.

"Camille, is that you cutting off my circulation or me?" Jasmine asked absentmindedly, never taking her eyes away from the screen.

"I don't know, maybe both," Camille answered dreamily.

"We need to get a listening party together," Cory offered. "For those who supported us of course, anyone we can think of."

"That's a great idea, Faber. We better get on it," Evan agreed, looking back with pride at the screen. The recording was comprised of seven tracks. The cover art featured a photo of all the band members that was taken at their show in Virginia Beach in front of King Neptune's statue. The king of the ocean couldn't be seen clearly; he was merely a dark silhouette in background brandishing his trident regally as the five friends sat hunched together beneath his imperial gaze. Evan kept staring at the screen. He'd never seen anything more beautiful than his friends and his music together, and by next week their music would be available to everyone. Cory's strong hand squeezed Evan's shoulder. This was their time.

Later that night after Diana had gone to bed, Evan and the rest of the band lazed around in the family room having come down from all of the excitement. As Camille lightly dozed in Evan's lap, he sat in the low light pondering again how his life had turned out. He had gotten his band off the ground and made his own destiny. But not alone, and Evan had to admit to himself that he had been influenced, sometimes even indirectly, to reaching this place of fulfillment. The good times continued but at the moment it was the near misses and close calls that stood out in his mind. How remarkable was it that his girlfriend lost one parent but regained another when she was at her lowest point in life? And on top of it all, his two best friends both cheated death and had helped the police arrest notorious criminals.

But then there were the sweeter victories. Not only had Cory taken Evan under his wing and later joined the band, but Evan had helped his friend find peace after losing someone that he cared about. And they had done the same for Camille when her mother returned. As much of a God-send as Ms. LaShea was, she and Camille had to work to put their family back together again.

Finally, Evan had come to see his mother in a new light. She wasn't the perfect, all-knowing, fearless woman he thought she was. In fact, Evan's perspective of Uncle Nate had changed as well. Neither one of them had it all together and they both turned out to be more than what they seemed. As ugly as things had gotten this year, Evan saw that his family and friends came out on the other side much stronger than when they went in.

Things could have gone so much worse, he thought. *I even walked out on my mom and she welcomed me back with open arms. I really have it good here.*

If only everyone could feel the way he did right now. If only people like Frankie and BeBe and the kids running the streets caught up in God-knows-what could find their power and security somewhere else. Somewhere that was less enticing than drugs and fast money, and also not as unpredictable as life on the streets. If only they could learn the lessons that Tony finally had. But he didn't know how and where?

This must be the number one question that all the greats have to deal with, Evan considered. Camille shifted in his lap snoring softly. Evan looked at her and smiled so brightly it would have illuminated the dimly lit room if it could.

What the world needs is sweet love, for real, delivered right to them just like a good meal. Looking around the room, Evan's eyes rested on the statue of the prophet standing dramatically with the Book of the Law displayed in his hands for all to see. Suddenly Evan sat up causing Camille to awaken.

"You ok?" she asked, sleepily. Cory and the others looked up from their cell phones or whatever had previously held their attention.

"What gives?" Cory said, holding out his arm.

Evan's gaze shifted from the statue to Cory, and then to his arm as the tattoo of the man balancing the planet of music on his shoulders peered at him.

Evan's slowly smiled as an idea unfolded.

"Not *what* gives Faber, but *who*?"

Track 28:
Da Capo al Coda

The party was jam-packed as guest after guest spilled into the LaShea house in support of Evan, Cory, Camille, Jasmine and Sam's first foray into full music production as The Mustangz. The band members' families were enjoying themselves and delighted to meet each member and catch up with their loved ones now that they were going to be stars. Family wouldn't be family without a little embellishment. Ms. LaShea and Diana were quarantined in the kitchen, helping the caterers prepare to walk food out to the guests. A mixture of R&B, Hip/Hop and Electro Funk styles played over the loudspeakers, accompanied by Camille and Jasmine's vocals.

As the party went on, familiar faces and friends came through to support Evan's music, including the managers from Club Soul-Light and other hotspots where not only Evan had performed, but the band as well. Sam's friends also stopped by, many who rapidly spread the word about the EP. Sam also noticed his name was being thrown around amongst the young girls of the community.

"Drink it in, Sam the Man," said Tony, slapping his friend on the back near the sound system.

Later, Evan and Cory were in the LaShea's family room talking when Uncle Nate walked in.

"There he is: Evan, the Man of the Hour!"

"Unc, you finally showed up! You remember Cory, right?"

"How could I forget?" replied Uncle Nate as he and Cory shook hands.

"Good to see you again too, sir," said Cory.

"I'm just glad you boys are ok, especially Tony after that fiasco with the police," said Uncle Nate earnestly. "He did a brave thing and you Cory?"

"I only lost my hair," joked Cory, his hair neatly coiffed to the side to compliment his casual wear for the evening's festivities.

"It's amazing how things have turned out for you two. It feels like it was years ago when we first met you at the pier, Cory." Uncle Nate shook his head in astonishment and smiled. "And look at you both now, musicians together and following the dream, working hard. It's awesome."

"They're a regular Dynamic Duo," they heard Diana say as she rounded the corner. "I thought I heard your voice back here, Nate." She and Nate hugged and he kissed her on the cheek.

"Speak for yourself," Evan happily added. His mom and her brother were united again. In Evan's eyes, they were the best of the Spencer crop and he felt lucky to have them here tonight to bask in this moment.

"Look at my handsome men. All three of you," Diana said smiling. She initiated a group hug and squeezed them tight. "Cory, can I steal you away for a moment?"

"Certainly Ms. Spencer, you let me barge into your home at all hours of the night, play music at a thousand decibels and eat your food. You can take me anywhere, looking as beautiful as you do tonight."

"Ooh, I like this one," laughed Diana, taking Cory by the arm. As they walked off she jokingly scolded him about addressing her by the term "Miss".

"This took a lot of heart on your end," said Uncle Nate, when they'd gone.

"From the whole team like you wouldn't believe," said Evan. "So much happened and I thought this day would never come because of what happened with Mr. LaShea, God rest him; and the incident with Tony right after that. I had forgotten about the music for a while there. So much more was important and at stake."

"You kids are tough and you do know what's important," nodded Uncle Nate. "This right here is what's really important. It's why we do what we do and become the people we grow to be."

Evan hugged his uncle who returned the embrace. Then, speaking softly into his nephew's ear, he said, "Stay ahead of the game, Evan. In your career, when you get married...no matter what, don't try to control everything. Just trust yourself and those around you."

Evan nodded, hanging on every word. He loved his uncle dearly and was thankful that he had a man like this in his life who was ready and willing to provide guidance should he ever need it.

"Yes sir," said Evan. "I'm glad you've got my back, Unc."

"Always Evan, I can see you've learned to let things flow organically. When you do that, you're able to see things more precisely instead of being blinded by grappling to control things. Take it from me, kiddo."

All of their friends were enjoying themselves. Music and laughter filled every room as Diana and Cory walked through the house.

"Dorothy is such a good friend to host this for you kids," Diana said, still arm in arm with Cory.

"Yes, this is great. It pays to be the lead singer's boyfriend, too. Thanks to Evan," laughed Cory.

"Sit down here with me. I'm a little tired," said Diana.

"I know you guys aren't my nuclear family," said Cory sitting next to her. "But you feel that way."

Diana squeezed his hand. "You three take up space and it's good. You have a strong presence. You're just what Evan needs and your bond looks like it runs deep." Cory smiled and nodded.

"Not too many people I know can fight and come back together again. I'm glad my son met you though. It's okay for friends and family to fight and disagree but everything else burns: the albums, this house, nice clothes, all of it. You two remember that when you get out on the road. Because it's all you ever really have."

"Trust me, Diana, if I didn't know it before, I sure know it now. I'm blessed to have met you all here. I'm so glad I came to Hampton Roads, it's become my new home."

"Welcome home, son," said Diana kissing him on the cheek. "Welcome home."

As the party drew to a close, two last pieces of business were in order. The first brought Evan, Cory, Camille, Jasmine and Sam to the rec room where Cory had taken up his guitar and Sam was sitting on his drum box.

"We hope you've enjoyed The Mustangz EP," said Camille to the crowd of friends, family and neighbors. "We put a lot of work into it, and right now we'd like you to have a taste of something we just put together; just a little taste."

The lights dimmed and, for the first time, they played part of their new song in a slower, acoustic version. All of them had learned to sing a pleasant sounding harmony. As they neared the chorus they resumed the start of the song and Camille and Jasmine ad libbed a few verses for this live and unplugged setting.

"It's not on the album. We just put it together recently," Camille said over the applause. "But maybe you'll hear it on something we do down the road. We just thought you'd like that surprise. The song is dear to our hearts. Now before we go, I'll turn it over to Evan. He's got a few things he'd like to say."

Evan stood up and looked out over the friendly faces as the lights brightened again. "You guys are great. Umm, I know Camille and Jasmine are the front women, but as the leader I figured that I should say something. From the bottom of my heart, and I speak on behalf of The Mustangz when I say, thank you so much for the love and support. And I especially want to thank Sam Molina, our drummer. He's networked so much better than the rest of us. Because of his hard work, this album has seen the light of day and our dream has been realized."

Cheers followed by a few sharp whistles sounded off as Sam waved to everyone and hugged Evan. Sam, the jack-of-all-trades, knew that the effort had to be a mutli-pronged approach. He and their rag-tag *street team* hit all the places that were familiar with Evan, Cory and the band's music. It was just the tip of the iceberg that revealed much more of the band's plans.

"We would like you all to know that on the 21st, we will be performing on the grounds of the Hampton Coliseum, thanks to the help of our friends, or rather Tony's friends, in City Hall. We invite you to join us as we raise awareness about gang violence and the kids that pay the price. Some of you may know someone who got hurt, or worse, due to drugs and gang warfare in this area, or anywhere for that matter. As you know, two of my closest friends didn't escape the carnage of gang wars unscathed, but here they stand tonight. And the father of a... of a friend of ours who wasn't so lucky... God rest him. But his surviving family is also lending their support in uniting the community. Enough is enough. So stand with us at the Coliseum for our children, for our friends - for each other."

The audience responded to Evan with raucous applause. People yelled in support of the music and the city they stood for. Evan shared that he and his planning team would reach out to their audiences through public service announcements to solicit donations to a scholarship fund, which would be given to a local, college-bound music or art student. The team set up an online account for people to contribute, and local businesses could kick in their support by matching donations of private contributors.

Evan had never felt so energized standing in front of people like this, spurred on by the cooperation and expertise of his friends and family who had done their part. And it felt good. It felt like he belonged there.

"Again, thank you. We hope you had an amazing time with us. Thank you to my lovely girlfriend Camille and her mother Ms. LaShea for opening their home up to us tonight. And also...thank you to our manager, Nate Spencer."

Nate looked on in awe, in total shock. But Evan just smiled at his uncle.

"Yes, that's right. Without this man's tutelage, we wouldn't know how important family really is or why we do what we do. Believe me, there's no other businessman in town that loves music like Uncle Nate does. There's no one else who can maneuver us through the traps of fame and fortune, who can show a bunch of crazy kids the way."

Track 29:
Finale

It was a momentous day for Hampton Roads. Men, women and children came to partake in festivities to celebrate community, justice and the young ones who would inherit the city one day. Tents dotted the grounds; some invited people to enjoy carnival snacks while others offered vaccinations or job opportunities. Security was tight, seeing as the theme was overwhelmingly against gang culture and organized crime. The city wasn't taking any chances with criminals itching to send an opposing message. The previous day, local news had reported that all active members of the small yet dangerous Epps Yard Crew had finally been caught. The streets, although not perfect, felt much safer and paranoia was put to rest for the time being. The city could thank its dedicated police and the justice system for this, including cooperative informants.

Tony and the ladies from his Bridge Club were out enjoying the rally and were ecstatic to hear about his involvement in making it all possible. He assured them it was nothing at all, just him doing his duty to protect and serve. But a look from Jasmine knocked his ego down a peg.

"The coppers love cotton candy, too," he said under his girlfriend's careful eye. "It's a shame for them to miss out. It's good to see you up and about, Ms. Goldstein. You look lovely today. And, I wanna thank you for your connections on the City Council."

Sadly, little Zarah had to miss out on the cotton candy but that didn't stop Ryan's wife, Rocky or her friend from enjoying the tasty treat. Evan and Sam played peak-a-boo with the little one while Camille chatted with Rocky.

"Ryan wishes he could be here but I've been taking videos all day for him. The new job is working him ragged and they really needed him today. He couldn't get out of it. But he did say thanks for the free CD."

"Free?" said Sam, whose lips were then plugged by baby Zarah's chubby fingers.

Cory, his parents, Ken Ellis and Leslie Senor were gathered nearby, laughing over old stories at a picnic table. Paris was cooling off in the shade under the table lying at Leslie's feet. Today, she was wearing the same bug-eyed sunglasses with an obnoxiously large new blue sun hat.

Everyone enjoyed themselves throughout the day. Soon all activities ceased and the crowd grew restless anticipating the highlight of the day: seeing Evan and The Mustangz perform. The warmth of the sun bathed the crowd as folks mingled with each other in front of the stage. The Mustangz took the stage as they were announced. Countless musicians from within the Hampton Roads area came to watch Evan, who was now a polished act. No longer a beginner at nightclubs or selling services online, he stood proudly on stage with his band, ready to introduce their music to Hampton. They assumed their places as the surroundings grew quiet. Cory began to pluck out a tune on the guitar to warm things up as Camille and Jasmine greeted the crowd.

"I just want to thank everyone for coming out, for all your support," Camille said taking the mic. "We are so honored to play for you like this. Some of you who have seen us play at local clubs or on the boardwalk; know you're in for a great time. And those of you meeting us for the first time...get ready!"

Speaking through her smile, Jasmine offered, "Yeah, not to sound like we're all that or whatever (because we are). But we love you guys!" A whistle from offstage got her attention and she waved liked a giddy schoolgirl at Tony. "That's my boo y'all."

"You know I wanna acknowledge someone special, too," Camille said, tightening her mic. "Without her, I wouldn't have known how to go on, if she hadn't come back into my life when she did. I love you mom." Dorothy LaShea, supported by her close friend Gloria, blew her daughter a kiss as tears formed in her eyes.

As Sam lightly tapped out a beat on the high hat and Jasmine hummed softly into her mic, Camille continued with the introductions. "I know you're not used to the band introducing their parents. It's usually someone introducing the band and showing off what instrument they play, but we'll get to that. We'd like to respectfully acknowledge a fallen member of our community. We'd like to send our love and prayers to his family, and welcome his stepdad who is here today on their behalf."

"YEAH!" was the collective response as the crowd applauded. From his place at the keys and synths, Evan could tell Camille was in the zone. She was feeling what he felt that night at the EP release party when he addressed the audience. He'd never seen her so fired up and her enthusiasm was contagious.

"That's the Hampton Roads passion I want to hear!" Camille gushed. "Well, before we get started, my handsome boyfriend on keys will have the final word." A few catcalls were hurled on stage and Camille threw a humorous warning glance.

"Thanks babe," said Evan, taking a microphone. "Yeah, that's my girl Camille on vocals everyone. And give it up for her partner in crime, Jasmine." The growing audience clapped and cheered and the leading ladies curtsied for the fans.

"Next, we've got Cory Lynn Faber on guitar, and Sam the Man on drums," Evan continued as their families joined in the cheering from backstage. Out in the audience, the teenaged guitarist from Diana's church pumped his fist when he heard Evan's voice. Mojo accidentally bumped a cage on the ground next to a young girl. The girl clutching her white-tipped cane adjusted the cage moving it closer to her.

"Oh, excuse me," he offered. "I got a little excited. Is that a bird in a cage?"

She smiled at him, adjusting her sunglasses and said, "Why, yes, I just got a new song bird."

"Really, and you brought him here?" Mojo asked.

She replied, "Yes, we're still getting used to one another. It'll take some time you know. But when he's comfortable he'll begin to sing. And when he sings, I can see the world better. Don't worry; I'm going to keep him safe near me."

Evan gripped the microphone, "Ah, and the really rowdy bunch back there are the Fabers, down from Portland, Oregon to see Cory play, followed by my own dear mother and Uncle, our manager. Go ahead, make some noise guys. You know you want to!" As they screamed and clapped, Evan turned his attention to the keys and joined his band mates in producing a sweet melody. Soon the crowd was clapping with the beat, including baby Zarah who was strapped to Rocky's chest backstage.

"Well," Evan stressed, "our hearts go out to these key people in our lives." And looking toward Cory he continued. "You know you might not always be in the same league as someone else or the same chord progression, but that doesn't matter. We're all different and when you think about it, that's not so terrible. Listen, this is a song that we just added to the EP that we released a while ago. It's a bonus track. All proceeds from sales will go to a new arts scholarship that we founded for promising students. It excites us to know that we can contribute to future generations and create a platform for others."

As the cheers grew in support of the fund, Evan nodded to Sam and he and Cory made the transition to their intended song. Camille and Jasmine caught the exchange and altered their key to match. The cymbals began to vibrate and slowly the high hat issued its purr. Onlookers froze in their places as the melody blanketed them.

From backstage, Diana and Nate watched Evan proudly as the music rose. Like his father before him, Evan had managed to manipulate the chords of his mother's heart and create a sensation so pure it brought her to tears.

This is the only chord progression that matters to me, Evan, Diana thought touching her chest tenderly.

Cory's Godfather Ken was near Diana and next to him were Mr. and Mrs. Faber. Cory caught the eyes of his parents and his Godfather. When he settled on Ken, he winked at Cory, casting an eye skyward. Cory got the reference and nodded his head as the rays of the sun kissed his face.

"The dream lives on, Frankie," he whispered.

Evan looked out over the crowd blissfully, feeling as if he were on top of the world. After one last remark, Camille and Jasmine initiated their song, their herald, their call, their story. It was the story that took both Evan and Cory and the whole band's lives to tell.

"My name is Evan Spencer and I bring you a message from The Mustangz. Don't ever forget this. And don't let anyone ever tell you different. As you walk the road before you, you are never ever alone."

As I walk this road before me Lord
Searching to find my way
I get an empty, empty feeling Lord
You just might turn, and walk away
As I walk silence it pounds my ears
Amongst the crowds the roaring bands
The closer you are, the further I appear
Is that the essence of your plan?

But you must understand, I've not been here before
Will you walk with me more, or am I going it alone
My mind fights with the plan but I'm going to understand
Still you say I'm never, never, never, ever alone

As I walk this road you're the compass that life gives
Some say it's only passing, some say it's deep within
As I walk feelings rise in my soul
Some were empty feelings; some were ones I used to know

But you must understand, I've not been here before
Will you walk with me more, or am I going it alone
My mind fights with the plan but I'm going to understand
Still you say I'm never, never, never, ever alone

Time and distance have not always been my friends
Misguiding me in what they say
As I walk this road before me Lord
I've learned the walk's beyond today

But you must understand, I've not been here before
Will you walk with me more, or am I going it alone
My mind fights with the plan but I'm going to understand
Still you say I'm never, never, never, ever alone

OUTRO

To say that The Mustangz had come a long way would be an understatement. As the band sat in the dimly lit room, familiar images began to grace the screen, images that each band member could call home. They were mesmerized by the sound of their own voices as their song played over the mini-movie. It began in Portland, Oregon. Images of the Arts District flashed from daytime to the brightly lit nightlife scene to rolling over snowcapped mountains, and back again to the city. A wall reading "Keep Portland Weird" bid them goodbye, and elicited a poke in Cory's side from someone, as they transitioned to another corner of the globe.

As the song grew stronger, the Philippines opened up over the Chocolate Hills, and passed the white sands of Boracay. They were dazzled by a vast landscape of green as the Banaue Rice Terraces came into view. The band's music played in time to each new vista as a silhouette of Sam nodding excitedly could be seen on the big screen.

A bright transition revealed the beautiful Camuy River Cave Park tucked away safely in Puerto Rico. Jasmine snapped her fingers happily in her seat as other exciting images floated by and her voice rang out strong over the speakers. The rustic and beautiful Castillo San Felipe del Morro rotated 180 degrees generating oohs and ahhs. Sweeping over Jobos Beach and ending on Ponce Cathedral, the images warped and changed as the final destination rose into view.

Hampton Coliseum, grand and imposing, appeared as the song reached its inevitable climax. Hampton University, Club Soul-Light and the imperial statue of King Neptune dissolved in and out as the song neared its end. The Virginia Beach Boardwalk melted into the friendly evening silhouette of Little Island Pier as the fishermen cast their rods. Finally the screen went black and transitioned to the familiar faces of Evan, Cory, Camille, Jasmine and Sam as they closed the song perfectly, nestled safely within the band's sanctuary at the Spencer residence of the studio Heaven's Gate.

Deliver me from the shackles that bind
Posing as dreams that were mine
Come on and set my soul free, to the journey
To the dreams I once knew, thoughts only of you
That's reality
Cause you're the journey
I love you with all my heart, and my strength
You're all I need
You, you set my feet straight you point me the way
You're the journey

Cheers and hollers erupted as the music video ended and the lights came on in the little home theater. The band hugged and kissed and shook the hands of all those who contributed to the music video for their single, *The Journey*. The video director walked over to congratulate Evan.

"What do you think? Came together well?" he asked, as Evan released him.

"It was amazing seeing all of our homes. It was a literal journey back to Hampton," Evan enthused, smiling brightly. "I think it's incredible. We made our first music video!"

"We'll meet up with you again, though," added the director. "Now that the footage of you and the band walking through those areas has been fixed we can do a quick re-edit and it will be perfect."

"It's awesome Mr. Harley, and if you need anything else for that let us know. This is a dream come true." Cory and the rest of the band surrounded Evan and Mr. Harley—everyone was laughing and celebrating.

"I can't wait for everyone to see this!" Cory said, slapping Evan on the back.

"You're amazing, Mr. Harley," said Camille, hugging the director. He smiled back and looked the group over proudly.

"It was my pleasure to work with you guys. In all my years of filmmaking, I'd never done a music video before. This was a new challenge."

"You nailed it, sir," Evan replied.

"Well thank you," Mr. Harley answered. "But please guys, call me Dennis. Everyone in Hollywood does."

FINE